Bolan smoothly ejected the spent round

Seconds later another grenade arced through the air and detonated against a truck at the end of the column, blowing it apart. A quick glimpse revealed that the vehicle's heavy tires had flattened two of the gunners who had crouched next to it as the burning circles of rubber had become airborne missiles.

The Executioner shucked the spent grenade, fed another into the launcher and punched a third HEDP grenade into one of the troop carriers. The angle wasn't good, but his goal was to create confusion and chaos. As the first group scattered, unaimed bursts of return fire began, and Bolan knew he had succeeded.

Unslinging his M-16, the Executioner stalked forward into battle.

Hell had come to Honduras.

D0912050

Don Pendleton's Mack
Bolan®
Savage Rule

A GOLD EAGLE BOOK FROM
WORLDWIDE®

TORONTO • NEW YORK • LONDON
AMSTERDAM • PARIS • SYDNEY • HAMBURG
STOCKHOLM • ATHENS • TOKYO • MILAN
MADRID • WARSAW • BUDAPEST • AUCKLAND

Recycling programs
for this product may
not exist in your area.

First edition January 2011

ISBN-13: 978-0-373-61542-1

Special thanks and acknowledgment to
Phil Elmore for his contribution to this work.

SAVAGE RULE

Printed in U.S.A.

Until the philosophy which holds one race superior
and another inferior is finally and permanently
discredited and abandoned, everywhere is war.
>   —Haile Selassie,
>   1892–1975

I don't see color when I see a man. What matters
to me is whether his intent is good or evil. If he's a
good man, then he is a good man, and that's it. If he's
a predator, I'm going to put him down.
>   —Mack Bolan

CHAPTER ONE

Mack Bolan, the soldier still known to a very few as the Executioner, crouched low and was perfectly still. His senses, attuned to the sounds of the jungle through long experience, picked out the telltale sounds of men and equipment some distance off. Some barely conscious part of his mind easily separated these from the ambient, natural noises of the beautiful—and deadly—terrain surrounding him.

The enemy wasn't far away.

He finished hiding the crumpled, night-black HALO chute, burying it quickly and quietly with a few shovel-fuls of moist earth and a handful of undergrowth. Then he silently folded the entrenching tool and replaced it on his small battle pack, next to his machete in its strapped-on scabbard. The pack had been specially prepared for him, at his request, by Stony Man Farm's armorer.

The Executioner paused at movement near the toe of his combat boot. A four-inch tarantula crawled quietly over his foot and continued on, oblivious to the hell that was about to be unleashed. It wasn't the largest specimen Bolan had seen, by a wide margin. He silently wished the creature a safe journey as he continued on in the opposite direction. An old joke echoed through his mind, a parody of a rallying cry: *Forward, toward the danger.*

Smiling grimly under the dark tiger stripes of black-and-green combat cosmetics smearing his face, Bolan made a mental inventory of his equipment. He was clad in his customary combat blacksuit, a close-fitting garment bearing multiple slit pockets. The web belt around his waist bore pouches for extra loaded magazines for his weapons. Grenades of varying types were clipped to the belt and to the web harness over his shoulders, to which his pack was also secured. Over this, in a ballistic nylon shoulder holster designed to withstand the humid climate, he carried a Beretta 93-R with a custom-made sound suppressor attached. The machine pistol, like the .44 Magnum Desert Eagle in a Kydex holster inside his waistband behind his right hip, had been specially action-tuned by John "Cowboy" Kissinger. Kissinger had served as the Stony Man Farm's armorer for so long that few of the weapons carried within the covert facility or taken into the field by the action teams hadn't felt his touch or undergone the scrutiny of his gunsmith's eye.

The rifle in Bolan's fists and secured by a single-point sling was a well-worn M-16 A-3. The 5.56-mm NATO weapon was capable of full-auto fire, and this one was equipped with an under-the-barrel 40-mm M-203 grenade launcher. Across the soldier's chest was a bandolier of 40-mm grenades, as varied and lethal as the handheld bombs strapped to his person.

Also attached to Bolan's web harness was a pair of truly lethal-looking blades, Japanese-style fighting tools manufactured by an American importer. The smaller blade had a single cutting edge over eight inches long, with a textured, guardless handle and a needle tip. The larger knife, a staggering weapon almost the size of a short sword, was also single edged, with a pronounced curve and a killing point, fully thirteen inches in the blade. Both wicked-looking knives were useful for only one purpose: killing people.

The Executioner was going to give them a workout.

He had been dropped here, in the dead of night, near the Guatemalan-Honduran border, for that purpose. The call from the secure phone in Hal Brognola's Justice Department office in Washington had been clear enough, reaching Bolan as he rested between missions at Stony Man Farm. The big Fed, director of the Sensitive Operations Group, had wasted no time telling Bolan that the request for SOG intervention had come straight from the President.

"The Man," Brognola had said, "wants us to stop an invasion of Guatemala."

That had gotten Bolan's attention.

Brognola had gone on to explain that in Honduras, a recent series of military coups had deposed two governments in six months. The beleaguered people of Honduras were no strangers to this type of governmental turbulence, but this time was worse than in the past. A new strong-arm dictator, "General" Ramon Orieza, had seized power, waging an ironfisted campaign of murder and intimidation to keep the terrified Honduran people under his control.

"It's bad, Striker," Brognola had said, using Bolan's Farm code name. "Orieza has turned Honduras into an armed camp. He's completely coopted the Honduran military, and he has a cadre of shock troops camped outside the capital. We've received reports of roaming death squads, political assassinations, even mass graves. Orieza makes Pol Pot look like an amateur."

"There's more to it than that, I'm guessing," Bolan said. He knew only too well that, as extensive as its resources could be, SOG couldn't pursue every injustice on foreign soil; it simply wasn't possible. For the President to involve Stony Man directly meant that something far worse was implied—something with international implications that also threatened the security of the United States.

"When the coup took place and toppled first one, then the second local government," Brognola explained, "I had Barbara put Aaron's team on alert." "Aaron" was Aaron "the Bear," Kurtzman, the Farm's wheelchair-bound cybernetics whiz and head of the team of computer experts at Stony Man. "Barbara" was Barbara Price, the Farm's mission controller. Bolan and the honey-blonde, model-beautiful Price had a romantic relationship based on respect and desire. That was as much as either could offer the other. And it was enough. These thoughts flashed through Bolan's mind unbidden as Brognola went on. "It turned out to be worse than just the usual military posturing, and it warned us of the threat to Guatemala. Bear's people intercepted several coded communiqués between Orieza and the president Gaspar Castillo of Mexico."

"He was just elected, wasn't he?"

"'Elected' is probably too kind a word for it," Brognola said. "While relations between the U.S. and Mexico have traditionally been hot and cold, depending on how the political winds of immigration reform were running, we could generally count on their government as a nominal ally. Castillo's coalition pushed the moderates out of power and immediately cut diplomatic ties with the United States. His election was marred by dozens of allegations of vote fixing, ballot tampering and voter intimidation. Our intelligence sources south of the border tell us that Castillo has seeded the Mexican military with hard-liners loyal to him, not to mention bribing anyone within reach of a handout."

"Hard-liners?" Bolan had asked.

"Castillo is a known entity to Interpol and various international antiterror groups. He has a file in our computers that goes way back, though he's slippery. He's never been tied, definitively, to the activities we know he supports."

"Which are?"

"Castillo is a racist, a Hispanic supremacist, if you want to call it that. Has a long history as a street criminal in Mexico City. You've heard of La Raza?"

"'The Race,'" Bolan said. "A term that applies to a pretty broad array of activist groups and even a radio network, if I'm not mistaken."

"Correct," Brognola had confirmed. "But the La Raza we're concerned with is a particularly effective and violent Chicano nationalist group, terrorists operating in Mexico and the Southwest United States. Starting in the 1970s, when the concept began to catch on, the group and other radical splinter cells like it have been pursuing the restoration of what they consider the 'Aztec homeland,' which they call Aztlán. Through a movement they call the Reconquista—the reconquering of land once possessed by their people, now unfairly held by the United States, as they see it—they want to reclaim those lands lost by Mexico in the Mexican-American War. When all the yelling and posturing is done, they'd basically like to secure as much of Southern California, Texas, New Mexico and Arizona that they can take and hold by force of arms."

"Understood," Bolan had said, nodding even though Brognola couldn't see him. "But what's that got to do with the coup in Honduras, and where do we come in?"

"Nobody took fringe groups like this radical version of La Raza seriously before," Brognola said. "And they weren't much of a threat, at the national level. They were violent, yes, and they managed to kill several people while pushing their racist views, but they weren't accomplishing much toward their goals. The sea change in Mexico's government, headed by a known Chicano nationalist who we think has no qualms about using terror tactics to get what he wants, changes that. Now the group has the force of Mexico's military behind it. Castillo's also using the military to crush dissent in Mexico."

"You're thinking invasion? It would be suicide."

"Not if it's done using guerrilla tactics rather than an outright declaration of war," Brognola retorted. "The Man knows he can't afford to make an overt enemy of Mexico, not unless he wants a full-scale battle on our southern border. Castillo knows it, too, and he's playing to that. We know, for example, that Castillo is using Tristan Zapata, a known La Raza terrorist wanted by the FBI and Interpol, to spearhead his operations on the Mexican border. Several border-patrol agents have been fired on, and last week three turned up dead wearing

Colombian neckties. Tensions have been rising since Castillo took office, and we've traced Zapata's movements thoroughly enough to know that he's met privately with Castillo on no less than three occasions."

"So why am I worrying about Orieza and Honduras when I should be dealing with Castillo and his La Raza forces?"

"Have you heard of O'Connor Petroleum Prospecting?"

"Can't say I have," Bolan said.

"They're an international firm that works with large oil companies, finding previously overlooked petroleum deposits. Under the former, stable government of Honduras, they had an agreement that allowed them to use deep-ranging imaging equipment to locate oil in Honduras. Just before Orieza took over, they found what they were looking for—a previously unknown find that is, as I understand it, quite extensive. When Orieza learned about it, he nationalized the equipment, and either took hostage or murdered the OPP employees operating in his country."

"The oil's worth a lot?"

"It could turn Honduras into a wealthy nation, if its government played its cards right."

"And what hand is Orieza holding?"

"That's just it," Brognola said, and Bolan could picture him frowning. "Orieza's ambitious and brutal. He knows a fellow traveler when he sees one. According to our intercepts, his government contacted Castillo's and cut a deal. They're building a pipeline from Honduras to Mexico."

"And Guatemala's in the way," Bolan said.

"Exactly. Orieza fights across Guatemala, building his pipeline as he goes. When he gets to Mexico, Castillo welcomes him with open arms, knowing that the results of that operation and the pipeline will enrich both nations—well, both *men*. This will solidify Orieza's hold on Honduras, and for all we know he's looking to annex some or all of Guatemala on a permanent basis. The oil wealth helps Castillo finance his personal vision of a recaptured Aztec homeland in the Southwest U.S., too. Orieza has made no secret of the fact that he despises the West. He's given plenty of speeches on state-controlled television, blaming America for Honduras's relative poverty. It would do his heart good to see our eye blackened, I'm sure. In the process, he makes a valuable ally, in his view, and strengthens his power at home."

"But Castillo can't think he can win a war against the United States," Bolan protested.

"He doesn't have to," Brognola said. "As I said, if he does it just right, he can make things difficult enough that portions of the country will effectively be under his control. He's counting on America's unwillingness to go to war with Mexico directly, probably because he thinks we'll hope to wait him out. The pipeline means he won't *have* to wait us out. Even if we apply international sanctions, he and Orieza will be able to find plenty of customers for the oil. They may be counting on the fact that, if they hold portions of territory for long enough—especially those parts of the Southwest United States that are predominantly Hispanic, thanks to largely uncontrolled illegal immigration—they'll effectively own it, and it will be too much trouble and cause too much unrest for us to get it back."

"Possession being nine-tenths of the law," Bolan had said.

"Exactly," Brognola confirmed. "The Man doesn't want to be put in that position, for obvious reasons. That's where you come in, and that's why our national security is tied to both nations. Striker, we've got to put a stop to this. Our analysts tell us that a sudden power vacuum in Mexico would allow the more moderate elements within the government to take control once more. Honduras is more turbulent, but removing Orieza would at least end the immediate crisis."

"So where do I start?"

"Our ties to Guatemala have always been close, give or take, and Orieza's troops have made several skirmishes over the border already. We've got satellite tracking of the invading force gathering on the border for yet another run. The Guatemalan military isn't up to the task of repelling a determined invasion. They're willing, but underfunded and disorganized. They're screaming for help, and Orieza's men have bloodied their noses already. Officially, we've told them there's nothing we can do. Unofficially, they're going to get some assistance as fast as we can get it to them."

"Me."

"You," Brognola said. "I don't have to tell you that this is delicate. The President isn't one for nation building, nor would Congress back him if he tried. We have to maintain plausible deniability in this, at least overtly. But we've got to stop both Orieza and Castillo, or all four nations will suffer—Honduras, Guatemala, Mexico and the United States. We've got to put an end to the crises on the Guatemalan border, and then deal with Castillo's forays across our own."

"How far are you willing for me to go?" Bolan asked.

"It was made very clear to me. Do what you do."

"He realizes the implications?" Bolan pressed. "We're talking about removing by force, however illegitimate, the leadership of two separate nations. I'm prepared to do that. Is he?"

"The President of the United States of course doesn't sanction any such action," Brognola said smoothly. "If those volatile regimes' leaders were suddenly to become…ineffectual, and perhaps fall from power, well, that would be fortuitous, wouldn't it? Yes, I believe *fortuitous* was the word they used at the State Department when I spoke to them."

"Understood," Bolan said. "Backup?"

"None, unfortunately," Brognola replied. "Able is tied up domestically, and Barbara's got Phoenix on assignment halfway around the world. You're it, Striker."

"Understood," Bolan repeated. "Let Cowboy know that I'll need a lot of equipment. I'll text Barb a list."

"Grimaldi is already on his way to you by chopper," Brognola said. "He'll get you to the nearest airport, where your flight will be waiting. A courier will be dispatched from the Farm and meet your plane with the supplies you specify."

"Then I'd better get to work."

"Striker?" Brognola said. "Good luck. I realize that every time we call you it's important. But I think we both know how much is riding on this now. More than ever."

"Thanks, Hal. And yeah. We do." He had terminated the call and immediately begun working out precisely what he would need, in order to fight a one-man war against the armies of two different dictators.

Now he was here, in Honduras, according the GPS coordinates provided by his secure satellite phone, and poised to strike a death blow to Orieza's troops. Intelligence and satellite imaging provided by the Farm had revealed that Orieza's pipeline was already under construction. To clear the way into and, thereafter, presumably through Guatemala, Orieza had an advance force preparing to move across the border. Bolan presumed it was this unit that had already carried out the initial attacks that had the Guatemalan government screaming. Apparently casualties on the Guatemalan side had been very high, as reported by Barbara Price. She had transmitted a detailed mission briefing to his secure satellite smartphone while he was in transit, with Stony Man pilot Jack Grimaldi at the controls of the long-range jet from which Mack had later jumped.

A black-clad ghost, he crept as close as he dared to where the enemy advance troops were massing. He checked his secure smartphone again; the screen brightness was turned down as low as it could go, and he cupped it with his hand to avoid giving away his position. The muted tones of the GPS grid told him his position relative to both the advance force, whose position the Farm had fixed using a "borrowed" NSA surveillance satellite, and to the semipermanent base camp from which the troops operated. That camp was a few miles down the "road"—a pair of ruts only recently cut through this densely forested area—that Orieza's advance team had used to move both men and equipment to the Guatemalan border. It was logical that it was from this same camp, detailed and enhanced satellite photos of which had been overlaid with tactical priorities in Bolan's mission briefing, that Orieza's troops had launched their previous raids across the border.

Silently, the Executioner peeled back the black ballistic nylon covering the luminous hands of the military field watch he wore. If he judged correctly, the enemy troops would be preparing for a predawn raid for maximum psychological benefit. They would cross the border, destroying anything in their path, using that most vulnerable period of early-morning darkness to their advantage. Bolan didn't know if they had a specific target in mind—if they planned to travel some distance once over the border, it would alter their departure time— but he judged that he still had at least a couple of hours before Orieza's military thugs were on the move. That would be plenty of time for him to bring the fight to the enemy, using their own anticipation of battle against them.

They would be preparing to strike the first blow, counting on having the momentum, the combat advantage. Bolan would strike before they were ready, and thus steal that most valuable of battlefield elements from them.

It was this advantage on which all his plans were built. For a single man to take on so many troops would be suicide. Bolan wasn't suicidal, nor was he insane. He understood only too well what it took for a small, motivated force to defeat a larger and largely unprepared opponent. In this case, he was a small, motivated force of one.

The enemy would never know that.

He unlimbered his compact but powerful field glasses, which were equipped with light-gathering night-vision circuitry. Through their green-tinged view he counted off the enemy column, resisting the urge to whistle as he gauged the strength of their force.

This forward raiding party would be composed of scouts and supporting infantry. They had come fully equipped. Bolan counted several Alvis Saladin six-wheeled light tanks, a couple of RBY Mk1 reconnaissance vehicles and a small fleet of two-and-a-half-ton trucks, whose canvas-covered cargo areas would be used to transport the infantry. Most of the soldiers Bolan saw milling about or gearing up carried M-16s, though a few had Galils and he saw at least one MP-5 submachine gun. He knew that the Honduran military fielded M-79 grenade launchers, though he saw none in evidence; the weapon dated to the Vietnam War and was functionally equivalent to the launcher slung under his rifle's barrel.

He brought up his own weapon. Pressing the latch, he shoved the barrel of the M-203 forward and flicked the launcher into the Safe position. A quick check with his finger showed him the barrel was clear. If he had picked up an obstruction at the other end during his silent crawl through the jungle, well, that was a risk he would have to take, as there was no way to be certain now. He removed from his bandolier an M-433 HEDP round. The High Explosive, Dual Purpose round could, if fired straight on, penetrate up to two inches of armor plate, and had an effective kill radius of five meters. For several meters beyond that death zone, it would still cause casualties. It was, therefore, the perfect weapon for attacking Orieza's column of invaders.

Bolan pulled the barrel of the launcher to the rear, locking it in place with an audible click. Then he aimed for the driver's-side front wheel of the lead deuce-and-a-half, flicked the safety to Fire and squeezed the launcher's trigger in one fluid movement.

The grenade exploded on impact. The heavy HEDP round tore apart the engine block and cab of the cargo truck, spraying deadly shrapnel in all directions. Men screamed, and for a moment the pitch-black of the night-time jungle was lit with an actinic yellow-white glare as the Honduran troops scattered.

Bolan smoothly ejected the spent round, loaded another HEDP grenade, aimed and fired. This time he took the truck at the rear of the column, blowing it apart between its cab and its cargo bed. He punched a third round into the vehicle next to it. He couldn't be sure, but he thought he caught, in the ensuing explosion, a glimpse of one of the vehicle's heavy tires flattening a pair of men who had been crouching next to it, as the burning circles of textured rubber became airborne missiles.

Bolan shucked the spent casing, fed another grenade into the launcher and punched the HEDP into one of the Saladins. The angle wasn't good, but his goal was to create confusion and chaos. As the first scattered, un-aimed bursts of return fire began—panic shooting, and nothing more—he knew he had succeeded. Flicking his M-16 A-3 to full-auto, he stalked forward into battle.

Hell had come to Honduras.

CHAPTER TWO

Spraying full-auto bursts on the run, the Executioner aimed in the general direction of the nearest invading troops. He wasn't concerned with hitting them; he wanted them to hear the gunfire and respond. Moving as quickly as he was, in a full sprint, he could have aimed precisely if he wished, but he could move faster by focusing on his destination: the nearest of the Saladins.

The six-wheeled light tank was an old British model equipped with a single 76-mm gun. Typically, such a vehicle also mounted coaxial and antiaircraft 7.62-mm machine guns, but Bolan saw no evidence of such weapons mounted externally on his target. There was no gun atop the turret, and the barrel of the machine gun that would otherwise poke from the turret parallel to the main gun was missing, the hole sealed and painted over.

The all-welded steel hull of the Saladin—more an armored car than a tank, really—had been painted a sloppy camouflage pattern more or less suitable to the jungle environment surrounding him. As he ran, his mind was already sorting through his extensive military knowledge, as if calling up an imaginary file. The Saladin, developed by the British in the 1950s, predated tracked light armor like the Scorpion combat reconnaissance vehicle, the Saladin's British successor. This specimen, from what little Bolan could see of it, was likely quite old, probably manufactured in the late sixties or early seventies. It would have a gas-guzzling 8-cylinder engine mounted at the rear—though this could have been upgraded to diesel, for all he knew— and a crew of two or three. The driver would be seated forward, behind a hinged hatch, and the gunner would be to the left of the center-mounted turret. If there was a third man, a loader for the gun, he would be seated to the right of that center position.

None of this mattered. Bolan had no time to waste, not if he didn't want to be bracketed and gunned down. He reached the tank, leaped onto the hull and pulled a pair of M-67 fragmentation grenades from his harness. Then he yanked the pin with his thumb and jammed the bombs down the barrel of the 76-mm gun.

He continued to run as gunfire erupted with much greater force around him. The muffled, staggered explosions came five seconds each after he'd pulled the grenades' pins, doing the men inside the Saladin no good and hopefully at least distracting and confusing them. It was doubtful the blasts would cause any serious damage, given that the gun was designed to contain the force of the shells it fired, but there was at least a chance that the grenades might cause a problem. At the very least, the explosions would add to the insanity Bolan was manufacturing for the enemy to experience.

He was just getting started. He jacked open the M-203 launcher and loaded an M-576 buckshot round. Then he crouched, blending into the dancing shadows, and paused.

The enemy fire became even more intense. They were

shooting in all directions, lit by the dancing fires of the burning vehicles. It was clear they thought they were being attacked from all sides, which was what Bolan wanted them to think.

The Executioner waited for the first knot of confused, frantic soldiers to close on his position, shouting to one another in Spanish. They were craning their necks at the tree line beyond their clearing, shooting sporadically into it, their fear-twisted features lit by the muzzle-flashes of their M-16 rifles. Bolan counted to three and, when they had come as close as they were likely to, he triggered the M-203.

The withering blast of buckshot from the giant bore of the 40-mm grenade launcher cut them down at waist level, leaving them broken and screaming, killing the nearest of the men who had taken the brunt of the wide-spread blast. Bolan was up then, squeezing precise bursts from his M-16 A-3, a veteran and virtuoso on the trigger of the familiar weapon. Soldiers, little more than thugs, fell before Bolan, who was himself the most lethal soldier they would ever encounter.

He paused, loaded another HEDP round in the M-203, and blasted yet another parked truck. The deafening sound of countless automatic weapons rolled over him in waves, much like the clouds of fitful, caustic smoke that poured from the burning vehicles. Two of the Saladins were mobile now, and one got its 76-mm gun working. It barked in Bolan's general direction, off by many meters, the shots themselves random.

Bolan was rapidly using the ordnance with which the Farm had equipped him, but he saw no reason to hold back now. He loaded yet another HEDP grenade and, moving in a half crouch through the smoke, avoiding clumps of wildly shooting Honduran soldiers, he angled around to the rear of the closer Saladin. Lining up on the other six-wheeled tank, he punched it hard with his grenade.

The battered vehicle shuddered, but through the haze and the strobe lights of the enemy guns Bolan couldn't tell how badly he had damaged it. Predictably, the turret traversed to bracket the Saladin next to which Bolan squatted. The soldier sprinted clear as the wounded tank fired again, this time hitting the closer vehicle.

Bolan stopped near the corpse of one of the fallen Honduran military men. He scooped up the boonie hat that many of the soldiers wore, and planted it on his own head. Then, trusting that his silhouette more closely resembled those of the invading troops, he started running urgently from group to group and shouting in Spanish, pointing at the next cluster of frenzied shooters.

Bolan hit the dirt as answering fire threatened to cut him down. The soldiers were soon eagerly, desperately shooting into their own numbers. The cry that infiltrators were among them was taken up by others. In the fusillades that ensued, Bolan was forced to roll close to one of the still-undamaged trucks to avoid the wild automatic gunfire. It wasn't long before those in charge began shouting in Spanish for the men to cease firing. At least one of these voices was cut short, screaming, when someone else trained a gun on the man and pulled the trigger.

Creeping along over the flattened undergrowth that had been crushed by the wheels of the enemy column's vehicles, Bolan held his rifle along his side, careful to keep it from dragging. He drew the Beretta 93-R machine pistol, flicked the weapon's fire selector switch to single shot and began peppering the enemy again. The sound suppressor threaded onto the pistol's barrel reduced the noise of his 9-mm rounds to a discreet cough—a sound drowned out by the automatic gunfire, terrified yelling and dying screams of the men all around him.

There was a rhythm to any combat operation, a palpable sense of motion and vibration that Bolan could feel, could pick out, thanks to so many years in the field. He rode that momentum now, felt that pulse, as he crept along in the darkness and placed his shots for maximum effect. Honduran troops fired their weapons into the trees beyond the clearing, and as they did so, several men at their left flank were felled, so it seemed, by the gunfire. When individuals there began to return fire, their shots were strangely, almost impossibly accurate, their wild blasts somehow becoming precisely aimed head shots. Bolan became the grim reaper among the disorganized, berserk gunmen, playing to their fears. By the time he was done firing covertly, the Honduran invaders seemed to be convinced, to a man, that a large group of enemy sappers had somehow penetrated their ranks.

Then the Executioner's knives came out.

The longer blade almost leaped into his right hand, the coarse weave of the handle wrap firm in his grip as if welded there. He drew the shorter blade, its textured handle stippled for traction, and spun the knife on his palm into a reverse grip, the edge oriented toward his own body. Moving silently, Bolan used the flickering shadows, the dancing flames and flashes of gunfire to his advantage, entering his enemies' midst, his blades flashing, stabbing and carving.

The first few soldiers went down silently, dead before they knew it. Bolan, implacable as he moved surgically forward, took no emotion from the act. There was no feeling of triumph; there was no sense of victory. He was simply performing a necessary function, grim purpose his only guide. The faces of the enemy invaders who fell before him were flash-burned onto his memory, joining the ranks of the countless others whose lives had ended as invisible notches on the grips of the Executioner's weapons. He remembered them all; he wasn't some unfeeling, unthinking mass murderer. The Executioner was a force for righteous redress, and as the agent of Justice, he would never shrink from acknowledging his lethal acts in that blindfolded figure's name.

The silent knifings did more damage than Bolan's clever shooting could have. As men began screaming, and then dying quietly, choking and gurgling in pain, a wave of renewed panic spread through the ranks of the already disorganized, terrified fighting men. Bolan narrowly avoided being shot by several Honduran soldiers who began firing at one another, screaming curses in Spanish. Rolling aside as one line of men advanced on the second, Bolan brought his large blade singing through the backs of their boots. The heavy knife chopped through the nylon and leather, slicing the left leg of the first man, both legs of the second and the right leg of a third, severing the Achilles tendons. The three folded, collapsing on limbs that could no longer bear their weight, and Bolan's knives were the last things the shooters felt in life.

From the perspective of the opposing gunners, it was as if a line of men simply disappeared into the flickering shadows and chaos, falling away in unison. They sprayed out their magazines, firing in all directions. Bolan flattened himself to the ground as bullets buzzed above him.

Crawling out of the immediate zone of crazed fire, he paused. Before him, in a small clearing where two dozen troops were arrayed, was a giant of a man. The sleeves of his fatigues had been ripped off and the muscles of his arms bulged impossibly, the result of what could only be steroid abuse. The big Honduran, who wore an officer's rank, was crushing the throat of one of his fellow soldiers in the thick fingers of one ham-size hand.

The men surrounding him were trying futilely to remove their comrade from the hulking officer's grip. Each time any of them moved in, shouting, the big man shoved them back. There was a sickening crack as the officer brought up his free hand, in which he clenched a wooden-handled entrenching tool. He wielded the shovel like a battle-ax, swinging the blade through the jaw of the closest soldier.

As Bolan watched, sheltered in the lee of one of the burning trucks, the massive Honduran made short work of his own soldiers. Like a wounded animal lashing out in pain and rage—Bolan saw blood trickling down the man's forehead, the crease in the side of his head an obvious bullet graze—he smashed them with his bloody, swollen fist, hacked at them with the shovel and stomped them under the heels of his heavy leather boots, which weren't the lightweight jungle footwear the rest of the troops wore. Bolan raised an eyebrow, amazed at the man's ferocity. The giant smashed the last two soldiers together and tossed them aside like broken dolls before fixing one bloodshot eye on the Executioner himself.

Something like recognition, perhaps realization, flitted across the bigger man's face. Bolan could see the wheels move in the big soldier's mind, even as the chaos of the miniature civil war Bolan had incited continued to swirl and rage around this temporary pocket of abrupt stillness. The officer was putting it together: Bolan wasn't one of his men, wasn't wearing a Honduran military uniform and wasn't supposed to be where he clearly was, a knife in either hand. The madness that had enveloped the raiding party had suddenly become, for the big man, the result of enemy action rather than bad luck or coincidence. His expression lost its mad, frenzied, berserker cast and hardened into something else. Bolan had seen the expression before and knew it only too well.

It was murderous determination.

Whatever firearms the officer had carried weren't with him. A flap holster on his belt was open and empty; he had lost his rifle, if he ever had one. If he hadn't simply lost it in the melee, he had probably fired it empty and discarded it. Bolan saw the behemoth of a man grope left-handed for the weapon, which would have looked like a toy in his fist if he'd had it. He stopped, remembering that the gun was gone, and instead clenched the wooden handle of the shovel.

Bolan could have dropped his knives and gone for one of his weapons, such as the assault rifle on its sling, but that would have defeated the purpose of his creep-and-shoot, crawl-and-stick campaign. He wanted these troops so terrified of their own shadows that they continued to fire at one another, doing his work for him. No one man could take on this many soldiers alone, not directly; to succeed, Bolan had to make them fight one another. He flexed his fingers around the grips of his knives, crouched low and, nodding once, waited for the big man to attack.

The giant Honduran took the nod as the challenge he was meant to see. He bellowed and charged, raising the entrenching tool above him for a killing blow. There was no way Bolan could meet that mad dash head-on; the man was a freight train of muscle powered by berserker rage. Bolan let him come.

At the last moment, just before the Honduran came within range with his shovel, Bolan feinted with his long blade. The soldier made as if to slip past the blade, barely altering his stride. Bolan, rather than completing the slash, fell onto his back in the blood-soaked loam.

Bolan's combat boots came up, and he shoved out with both legs. The waffle soles of his boots pressed some of the air out of the giant's stomach on contact, but not nearly enough. Feeling the muscles in his legs straining, Bolan continued to push, carrying the giant over his body. The big Honduran landed on his head in the dirt beyond. The Executioner thought he could feel the earth vibrating, ever so slightly, as the large man crashed to the ground.

The American swiveled and surged to his feet, closing the distance between him and his opponent. The big Japanese-style blade flashed downward—

The Honduran's hand snaked out and grabbed Bolan's wrist.

The shock hit Bolan like an electrical charge. Pain shot up his forearm as the big Honduran crushed it in his meaty palm, as if trying to grind the bones within his grasp.

Bolan brought the shorter knife over and down for a killing blow, but the giant blocked with the shovel. Metal struck metal with a sound like a cymbal's crash.

The noise was drawing attention.

The Honduran dropped his shovel and managed to get a grip on both of his adversary's forearms, squeezing for all he was worth. The pain was stunning in its sudden intensity. Some men might have passed out from that alone; Bolan could see spots swimming in his vision. Even as his mind raced to find a way out of this situation, he realized that the soldiers nearest them were falling back to brace the giant—and gasping in shock as they realized that the man held in the big man's grip was not one of their number, after all.

Bolan, with no other options, rotated his wrists. The blades of his knives came down, the reversed, smaller one doing a more thorough job than the other, but both edges slicing deeply into flesh. The giant Honduran screamed in agony and surprise as Bolan carved his way free from his grip.

Then the Executioner stepped in and drove his longer blade through the man's neck.

The big American didn't wait to see his enemy fall. He wrenched the big knife free, reversed it and slammed the bloody blade home in its Kydex sheath, also resheathing the smaller off-hand blade. Then his fingers curled around the grip of his M-16 A-3.

Weapons were coming up and seeking target acquisition as he blazed his way through the entire 30-round magazine on full-automatic, mowing down the first row of encroaching soldiers. He dropped the mag and inserted another, but not before triggering a buckshot round from his 40-mm grenade launcher, shredding more of the enemy.

It didn't take him long, working amid the Hondurans and in the fitful shadows of the burning night, to bring his manufactured chaos once more to a fever pitch. Again he shouted in Spanish as he ran, misleading one man, targeting another, misdirecting a third. He poured on the firepower as the answering guns of the dwindling raiding party increased their own pitch. The jungle came alive as staccato bursts of orange-white muzzle blasts mingled with the fires consuming the vehicles, and men screamed and died by the dozens.

As abruptly as this dance of death had opened, it drew to a close. The last pockets of resistance managed to wipe out one another, either through sheer determination or with Bolan's help. Finally, the night's darkness began to close in once again. The muzzle-flash blooms of illumination were few and far between, and the fires licking at the scorched hulks of the vehicles, though they showed no signs of truly dying, began to subside. Once more holding his rifle by his side on its single-point sling, Bolan drew the suppressed 93-R and began to administer mercy rounds to the dying.

Then, finally, nothing moved.

Bolan made two complete circuits of the raiding

party's camp, making certain. The Executioner had walked many a battlefield and ended the lives of countless gunmen...but it would never be a casual thing to him. He didn't dismiss them as he walked among them. He was careful to check those who might be shamming, too, using his small combat light. He would illuminate a body here, toe a corpse for reaction there, always moving lest the light make him a target.

When he was satisfied that only one other man remained alive among the raiding party, he reached down to his belt and clicked off the portable radio jammer he carried. The device, a powerful miniature electronic unit crafted by Able Team's Hermann "Gadgets" Schwarz at Stony Man Farm, was powerful enough to prevent radio transmissions for roughly one half mile. That had been more than enough range to prevent the raiding party from calling for help or alerting the advance camp where they had been based. Bolan unclipped the jammer from his belt and examined it. It had almost depleted its lithium battery pack; the device was very strong for its size, but exacted a heavy toll from its power cell. He replaced the unit on his belt and continued tracking the raiding party's sole survivor.

He had spotted the man during his second circuit of the devastated column. The soldier—who, like the giant Honduran Bolan had battled, wore the rank tabs of an officer—was badly wounded. He dragged himself through the muck of the clearing, among the bodies of his fallen comrades. Bolan closed in and then stopped, standing over him.

The officer turned over, painfully. The right side of his face was scorched black, and the eye on that side stared blindly. He fixed Bolan with his good eye and rattled off something in Spanish that the Executioner couldn't catch. Then he made to grab for a rifle still clutched in the hands of a dead man nearby.

"Don't," Bolan said. "Leave it there." He aimed the muzzle of the suppressed 93-R machine pistol at the wounded officer's face. The flickering light from the truck fires was the only illumination.

"American," the officer said, his accent heavy. "You are American."

Bolan didn't answer that. He stepped over and kicked the rifle out of the man's reach. "I can provide medical treatment," he said simply.

"Stay away," the officer spit. He started to get up, shaking on his lacerated legs.

"Stay down," Bolan countered.

The man didn't listen. Perhaps given strength by sudden adrenaline, he regained his footing long enough to draw an M-7 bayonet from his belt. He lunged with the blade in a clumsy overhand strike.

Still gripping his pistol, Bolan stepped in, meeting the raised arm and slapping it down and away. He folded the man's hand back on itself and drove the point of the bayonet toward the officer's stomach. The wounded man lost his footing and collapsed onto the blood-soaked soil once more. The knife had never touched him. It fell to the ground next to him.

"You…you are…a butcher." His voice had become a whisper. *"Los…campesinos…sufrirán para su insolencia."*

The Executioner's face hardened at that. "If I were a butcher," he said, jerking his chin toward the bayonet on

the ground, "that would be in your stomach right now."
He raised the 93-R for a mercy shot, but it was already
too late.

"You…you…" The man's good eye suddenly stared
at nothing. The tension went out of his body as death
finally took him.

Bolan shook his head. "The peasants will suffer for
your insolence," the man had said in Spanish. That was
what he was fighting. According to Brognola, some unknown number of Honduran citizens had already suffered under Orieza's ironfisted regime. Bolan didn't
intend to let that continue, or to let Orieza's thugs bring
their terror across the boarder to Honduras's neighbors.

Bolan surveyed the ruined column one last time.
Nothing and no one else moved.

The Executioner hurried off into the night, leaving
only guttering flames and dead men behind him.

CHAPTER THREE

Cupping his hand over its face, Mack Bolan checked his field watch once more before replacing the ballistic nylon cover that concealed it on his wrist. The first gray rays of predawn were perhaps an hour away, maybe less. That didn't leave him much time to operate; he would need the cover of darkness to execute his one-man assault on the Honduran base camp.

He surveyed the advance camp, taking special note of the pipeline that stood on prefabricated struts a few hundred yards to the west. Additional segments of pipe were piled nearby amid parked earthmoving and construction vehicles. The equipment and portions of the base camp itself were "protected" under camouflage netting that had proved insufficient to hide the operation from NSA's satellite surveillance.

Bolan, crouched in the dense undergrowth bordering the cleared no-man's-land surrounding the camp, took a moment to check the briefing on his smartphone. He had memorized the basic layout in transit, but now compared his intel to the reality of the camp before him. He saw no glaring contradictions. In the field, knowledge—real-time intelligence verified through direct experience—was invaluable. The more he knew, the more flexible he could be, tailoring his strategies and tactics to the fluid and ever-changing conditions of the modern battlefield.

That was at least the theory; from long practice, the Executioner knew that a great deal was driven by sheer will, by determination and ferocity.

The camp's layout was basic, but sound. Any trees and scrub had been slashed and burned, clear-cut around the base perimeter to deny an enemy cover or concealment. The camp itself was ringed by sandbagged machine-gun emplacements, not all of which were manned at any one time, from what he could see. The guns were FN Minimis most likely chambered in 5.56-mm NATO, Bolan suspected. Guards moved casually among the widely spaced pits, occasionally conferring with sentries stationed at other posts.

The last line of defense around the camp itself was a rough palisade apparently built from the materials cleared for the base, and topped by razor wire. Four small watchtowers, made of prefabricated metal struts, with what looked like metal-bucket crow's nests at their tops, were placed at the corners of the square perimeter.

Even at this distance, Bolan could hear screams.

The faint sounds of human torment carried to him on the night breeze, which would have been refreshing in the Honduran undergrowth if not for those chilling noises. Bolan could just make out, through his field glasses, the blue epaulets on the uniforms of the men guarding a prefabricated metal hut near the center of the advance camp. These would be, according to the Farm's briefing, Orieza's shock troops. They formed the vanguard of Orieza's campaign of terror within Honduras, according to the information in Bolan's files.

It stood to reason; that was a common enough tactic

among strong-arm dictators and their ilk. Creating a cadre of loyalists whose powers exceeded those of the regular military fostered a sense of fear among the lower echelons of a dictator's power base, while shoring up—through preferential treatment and a sense of elite status—the core of men willing to fight and die for their leader. This had been, after all, the theory and concept behind Iraq's Republican Guard, essentially a special-forces unit tasked with protecting Saddam Hussein's regime as well as with the dictator's most critical military operations. Republican Guard recruits were volunteers on whom many material perks were lavished. They'd enjoyed their often cruel jobs and were well rewarded for them. There was every reason to believe that Orieza's shock troops were every bit as brutal and every bit as highly motivated.

Out here on the border, it was unlikely the prisoners were Honduran citizens. They could be Guatemalan troops lost in the previous forays made by Orieza's raiders. They might even be Honduran soldiers accused of disloyalty, real or imagined. Hard-line regimes like Orieza's were notorious for their paranoia, Bolan knew. It didn't matter. The advance camp had to be destroyed, and completely, for the Executioner's daring one-man blitz through Honduras to succeed. It was merely the second step in a chain of raids that would take him, before he was done, to the heart of Orieza's government… But first things first. Whoever the prisoners were, Bolan would make sure they were freed. And before he was done, their torturers would answer in full for what had been inflicted upon those captives screaming in the night.

Bolan crept along the brush line until he found a suitable target: a sentry who had ranged just a little too far from his sandbag nest, smoking a truly gigantic, cheap cigar that was producing large volumes of blue smoke. From the banter being exchanged in stage whispers between the sentry and his compadre still in the machine-gun emplacement, it was clear that the fumes were objectionable to the second man; hence the smoker's distance from his post. Bolan listened to them trade vulgar insults in Spanish. There were at least a few threats. Both men, if Bolan heard them correctly, were vowing to stab each other. Shaking his head and questioning his fellow soldier's parentage, the sentry with the cigar grudgingly moved a few paces farther.

Perfect.

Bolan removed a simple fork of carbon fiber from a ballistic nylon pouch on his belt. He unsnapped the wrist brace and attached a heavy, synthetic rubber band to the two posts of the fork. Then he produced a small ball bearing from the belt pouch, placed it in the wrist-brace slingshot he held and stretched the band taut.

The sentry turned away, sucking in a deep mouthful of smoke. When the tip of the cigar flared orange-red, Bolan let fly.

The ball bearing snapped the man in the neck, hard. The sentry swore and slapped at the spot. His cigar fell down the front of his uniform, spraying dull orange sparks, and he slapped at them, as well, cursing quietly. He was reasonably discreet nonetheless. No doubt he would be disciplined, perhaps harshly, for drifting from his post to enjoy a late-night smoke.

"Come here!" Bolan whispered in Spanish, beckoning

from the cover of the brush and hoping the man could see his arm despite the damage the burning cigar would had done to the sentry's night vision. "You have to take a look at this. Hurry!"

"What?" the man whispered, confused. "Tomas?" He stepped forward hesitantly.

"Hurry up!" Bolan urged.

The sentry's curiosity, and perhaps some overconfidence characteristic of Orieza's raiders—who, after all, had met little resistance from the disorganized Guatemalan troops—got the better of him. He groped for his cigar, picked it up and hurried forward, firing a series of whispered questions in Spanish. Bolan couldn't catch it all, but he gathered the sentry thought this was some practical joke played by a friend in his unit, the "Tomas" he kept naming.

Up close, Bolan could see this man wore the blue epaulets of the shock troops. The joke was on the sentry, all right.

Once he was in range, Bolan struck. He reached for the man as fast as a rattler uncoiling, and grabbed him by the shoulder and the face, his fingers jabbing up and under the sentry's jawline. The sudden move brought a gasp of surprise from Bolan's target as the man hit the ground like a sack of wet cement. The big American lifted his hand from the man's jaw and slashed down savagely with the smaller of his two fighting knives, silencing the sentry forever.

Wiping the gory blade on the dead man's uniform, Bolan searched him and found what he wanted: the sentry's radio. Then he drew the suppressed Beretta 93-R, crouched to brace his elbow against his knee, and waited for the sentry's cigar-hating fellow trooper to pop his head up over the sandbags. The fact that an alarm hadn't already been raised was proof that nobody had seen the Executioner grab the man in the shadows. Now, when the cigar-smoking soldier was nowhere to be found, it shouldn't take long for the other soldier to wonder where he went.

It didn't. The curse in Spanish was another loud stage whisper, and when the Honduran soldier propped himself up above the sandbags to call to his wayward comrade, Bolan put a silenced 147-grain 9-mm hollowpoint through the man's brain.

Working his way in the darkness across the cleared perimeter as far as he dared, he found Claymore mines placed at intervals to cover the dead soldiers' position at the southwest. No doubt there were more mines similarly spaced all around the advance camp. He kept an eye on the crow's nest of the tower on that corner of the base as he crawled back the way he'd come. The guard appeared to be slumped in his metal enclosure, possibly napping.

The combat clock was ticking, now. The Executioner had no idea on what schedule the perimeter guards called in, or if they did at all, but it was standard military procedure to do so. He worked his way around the perimeter of the camp as stealthily as he could. When he faced the north side of the camp, he was ready. He picked up his stolen radio, keyed it twice, then started groaning into it.

Answering chatter in Spanish came immediately. Bolan keyed the mike a few more times, as if having trouble with it, and then muttered something about

dying. He managed to dredge up the appropriate ter-
minology, again in Spanish, and hissed into the radio as
if with his dying breath, urging his brave comrades to
activate the mines guarding the southwest machine-gun
emplacement.

The camp came alive. Searchlights on the towers
buzzed to life and began sweeping the no-man's-land
around the base, while somewhere inside, a hand-
cranked siren slowly worked its way to a gravelly, mechanical wail. Bolan could hear the shouts of alarmed
soldiers grow in intensity. He pictured them finding the
dead soldier behind his sandbags, next to his machine
gun. Their fears confirmed, they would reach for the
Claymore detonator nearby, if not clutched in the dead
man's hand….

The thumps of the Claymores detonating were followed by screams even more horrifying than those that
had stopped coming from the interrogation building in
the midst of the camp. They would be from the Honduran soldiers responding to the alert—where Bolan
had reversed the Claymore mines he had found, the
shaped charges directing their deadly ball-bearing payload inward over the machine-gun emplacements rather
than outward from the palisade.

Blind reaction fire erupted from several locations
outside the camp and from within the perimeter. The
noise was deafening. Several other Honduran soldiers
triggered their own Claymores, apparently fearing an
unseen enemy was advancing on their positions. Bolan,
well clear of the mines from his location beyond the
no-man's-land, was in no danger. This was the moment

of frenetic panic he required—and the moment he had engineered.

He methodically loaded and fired the M-203. It was a difficult shot, but his first 40-mm fragmentation grenades struck true, blowing apart the crow's nest of the watchtower closest to his position. He worked his way out, dropping a grenade into the midst of the camp, then annihilating another of the guard towers.

Bolan fired a grenade into the middle of the no-man's-land. He was rewarded with the thumps of Claymores again. He sent another 40-mm payload downrange, but there were no more explosions; the Claymores had been fired, and now the way was clear. He moved easily through the darkness, avoiding the wild firing of the machine guns as he slipped through. As he had expected, Third World soldiers who were brave when facing outgunned opponents were quick to break discipline and give in to fear when faced with a determined aggressor. Gaining and keeping the battlefield momentum, the initiative in an engagement, was Bolan's stock in trade. He was very good at what he did.

He leveled his rifle and sprayed bursts of 5.56-mm fire into the guards manning the nearest machine gun. They didn't appear even to notice him, until it was too late. Their attention was focused inward, on the base itself. Bolan loaded his grenade launcher once more and blew a hole in the palisade large enough for him to enter the camp.

The explosion drew fire, but the Executioner ignored it, throwing himself through the splintered gap and rolling with the impact. He came up firing, stitching the confused, surprised shock troopers he encountered. As he ran, he yanked smoke grenades from his harness and threw them. The plumes of dense, green-yellow smoke added to the confusion and helped further cover his movements.

Working his way through the camp, he exhausted his supply of 40-mm grenades, blowing apart as many pieces of equipment and protective structures as he could, while always avoiding the roughly centered pre-fab hut he had dubbed the holding cell. He finished destroying the watchtowers and punched several holes in the protective palisade. There was nothing to be gained by destroying the wooden walls themselves, but no harm in allowing it to happen, either.

Resistance was ineffectual, as he had expected it to be. Most of the troops from the advance camp had, as was only logical, been assigned to the raiding column massing at the border. This base was, after all, the staging area that permitted the raiders to do what they had come to do. A token force had been left behind to guard it, but it was clear they had expected nothing serious by way of retaliation.

If they had been alerted by their loss of radio contact with the raiding party, nothing about their reaction to Bolan's assault indicated so. It took him a little while, nonetheless, to work his way through the camp and eliminate any stragglers. He took down several men wearing the blue epaulets of the shock troopers, some of them in the act of fleeing, while others stood their ground in the smoke and flames and tried to take him. It didn't matter, either way. These men might be the elite of Orieza's killers and the best the dictator could field, but they weren't in the same class as the Executioner.

Thinking of radio contact reminded him to check the radio room, which he recognized by the small, portable transmitting array jerry-rigged to the top of a corrugated metal shack in the northwest corner of the palisade's interior. Inside, Bolan expected to find a man or men desperately screaming for help, but the shack was empty. The radio equipment was undamaged, so the big American emptied the last of his rifle's ammo into it. He dropped the magazine, slapped home a spare, then picked his way through the wreckage of the base interior once more. As he moved he was mindful of the dangers, for there still could be men hidden between him and the holding cell.

Nevertheless, the man who threw himself from concealment next to a burning military-style jeep almost managed to take Bolan by surprise. He was incredibly fast, with a sinewy build that translated into a painful blow as the tall man drove a bony elbow into Bolan's chest. The Executioner allowed himself to fall back, absorbing the hit as he let his rifle fall, and moved to draw one of his knives….

The man surprised Bolan by leaping over him and continuing to flee. The Executioner rolled over and regained his footing, snapping up the rifle and trying to line up the shot. He caught a glimpse of the thin, hatchet-faced man as the evidently terrified Honduran soldier bolted through the smoke, running as if the devil himself were close behind. Bolan didn't bother to try for the shot; the angle was bad, and too much cover stood between him and the rapidly fleeing trooper. Just as he had been unconcerned with a radio distress call, the Executioner wasn't worried about a soldier or two running for help. By the time Orieza's forces could muster a relief effort, Bolan would be long gone.

A bit chagrined despite himself, he was even more vigilant as he advanced on the holding cell. A heavy wooden bar set in steel staples secured the door. He lifted the bar and tossed it aside. The door couldn't be opened from the inside, which meant there would be no guards within—unless their own people had locked them inside with the prisoners.

"Step away from the door!" he ordered in Spanish, careful to stand well aside. He let his rifle fall to the end of its sling, and drew both his Beretta and his portable combat light, holding the machine pistol over his off-hand wrist. There were no answering shots from within, so he chanced it and planted one combat boot against the barrier. The heavy door opened, and Bolan swept the dimly lit interior.

What he saw hardened his expression and brought a righteously furious gleam to his eyes. There were half a dozen men and women, ranging from their late teens to quite old, hanging by their wrists from chains mounted in the ceiling. They had been repeatedly flogged. A leather whip was hanging in the center of the room, from a nail set in a post that helped support the corrugated metal ceiling.

"*Señor,*" an older man called, his eyes bright. He fired off a sentence in Spanish so rapid that Bolan couldn't catch it.

Bolan went to him. "Easy," he said. "I'm going to let you down. It's over. *Ha terminado.*"

"You are American?" the man asked in English.

Bolan looked at him, pulling the pin that secured

the chains. The old man fell briefly to his knees before Bolan helped him up. "I'm a friend," he said.

"You are sent from God." The old man smiled. "And you are an American."

Bolan didn't answer that. Instead, he said, "Can you walk?"

"I can walk." The man nodded. His lightweight clothes were bloody and ragged, stained a uniform dirty brown, and clearly, he had suffered badly at the hands of Orieza's men. But he stood tall and defiant under Bolan's gaze. "What is your name?"

"Just call me 'friend.'"

"I am Jairo," the old man said. He grinned. *"Amigo."*

Bolan gestured to the others, who were watching with an almost eerily uniform silence. "Help me with them," he said simply.

"Of course," Jairo said. "Do not worry about them, amigo. They were strong. They will be all right."

"Does anyone need medical attention?"

"I will make sure they get it," Jairo said. "Our village is not far."

"Village? Where?" Bolan asked.

He pointed. "Over the border."

"You're from Guatemala?"

"Sí. The soldiers raided our village and took us prisoner two days ago. It has been a very long two days." Jairo worked his way among the others with Bolan, freeing the captured villagers from their chains. From what Bolan could see, the victims had indeed been cruelly tortured.

"You were fed? Given water?" he asked.

"Sí." Jairo nodded.

That was interesting. Bolan completed his survey of the villagers. Many had bad wounds on their backs, and a couple, including Jairo, sported cigar and cigarette burns, but the damage was largely superficial. There had been no intent to kill these people.

"Jairo, did your captors say anything? Did they explain why they took you, or what they wanted from you?"

"No," Jairo replied, shaking his head. "Nothing. Only that we would do well to tell others, if we lived, just what General Orieza will do to us if his men are resisted."

So that was it, Bolan mused. Orieza and his people were pursuing an explicit strategy. It wasn't atrocities for the sake of atrocities; Orieza's shock troopers were softening up the resistance, both within Honduras and across the border, by instilling fear in the populations of both nations. Combined with the military raids, it was a very good strategy, from Orieza's perspective. It would enable him to continue rolling over the Guatemalans and probably guarantee at least some cooperation, if not simply a lack of interference from the frightened locals.

"Did he say he might release some or all of you?" Bolan asked.

"No," Jairo shook his head again. "But I think he would have. His heart, it did not seem to be in it. El Alto had a cruel look to him. He was not so soft as to let us live unless he meant to."

"Who? 'The Tall One'?"

"*Sí,*" Jairo said. "It was El Alto who did the whipping, and the talking. Always him. Never the other soldiers. I think he liked it. He looked, in his eyes, as if he enjoyed it." Jairo shook his head yet again and spit on the ground in disgust. "He left not long before you found us. Had he wished, he could have cut our throats."

A tall, cruel-looking man. It was very likely that El Alto, this torturer, was the same Honduran soldier Bolan had seen fleeing the camp. He made a mental note of that. If luck and the mercurial gods of combat were with him, he would encounter The Tall One again.

"Come on," Bolan said to the old man. "Let's get your people gathered together, treat their wounds and move them out. Can any of you handle a weapon?"

There were a few murmurs of assent. Jairo grinned. "We are not so helpless. We can see ourselves safely home. We will take what we need from the soldiers," he said. "The ones who are outside." He nodded to the door. "The ones you killed."

"How do you know that?"

"Because you, too, have a look in your eyes, amigo."

"Oh yeah?"

"*Sí.*" Jairo nodded solemnly. "*Su mirada es muerte.* Your look is one of death."

CHAPTER FOUR

The blue-tagged shock-troop guards outside General Orieza's office snapped to attention as Roderigo del Valle stalked down the corridor. Dawn had broken, yellow and inviting, the sun's rays streaming through the floor-to-ceiling windows on either side of the corridor. This had no effect on Del Valle, who carried with him a darkness that no light could penetrate. At least, this was how he preferred to be seen. Better to be feared than loved when one of the two must be lacking, as the old saying went….

He swept past the guards as if he barely saw them, and in truth, he didn't. It had been a very long, very frustrating night, and he hadn't yet even begun to catalog the damage dealt to their operation on the Guatemalan border. He snarled in reply as one of the guards greeted him respectfully and managed to get the door open before Del Valle rammed it, for the tall, hatchet-faced man didn't break his stride as he made his way into the anteroom of General Orieza's private lair.

Orieza's secretary glanced up, her face as pretty but as stupid as ever. She pursed her lips and greeted him quietly. Her eyes were full of fear, and that pleased him, for she was only too aware of what he could do to her if he chose. Orieza wouldn't object, at least not too loudly, if Del Valle decided to use the woman and throw her away. Another just like her, even prettier, would be sitting in her chair come the next dawn.

It wasn't that Del Valle didn't have his own needs, where women were concerned. He had them on occasion, and when he did, the union was brief and brutal. He had little use for a woman clinging to his arm and making demands of his time; what man would put up with such impositions, truly? And he had no respect for the empty-headed trollops who invariably did serve his purposes. How any man chose to saddle himself with a woman's constant whining and complaining, he didn't know. Orieza himself had been married, not so very long ago, and the woman had grated on Del Valle's nerves. She was forever bitching to Orieza about whatever whims came to her head, demanding his time and diminishing his focus. It had been a relief when Orieza had finally confided to his chief adviser that the general found his wife somewhat of a nuisance. Del Valle had jumped at the chance to arrange an "accident" for the miserable harpy. And Orieza, while he suspected that Mrs. Orieza's car didn't perhaps roll over of its own accord that fateful morning, hadn't asked many questions. The old man was content to spend his time with the slatterns Del Valle's lieutenants dug up for him. He tired of them quickly, and more than once Del Valle had made use of these castoffs before leaving their broken bodies on the floor for his men to clean up…. But such were the privileges of power.

He paused to survey himself in the full-length mirror that dominated one wall of the opulently appointed anteroom, while the woman fidgeted nervously. He ignored her. His angular, lined face looked back at him as he tried to smooth the creases in his uniform. He wore the same fatigues as did his shock troops, with no insignia of rank whatever. This was an affectation, but a deliberate one. No strutting peacock to dress himself in worthless ribbons and medals, or gold braids and colorful cloth, Del Valle preferred instead to let what he could do speak for itself. His shock troops were loyal to him, and him first, for he had proved time and again that he would deal violently with any challenge to his authority. When the time came, even General Orieza would learn that the blue epaulets on the shoulders of those armed guards surrounding him bespoke devotion to Roderigo del Valle, and not to their "general," but by then… Well, by then, it would be too late for poor Ramon.

Del Valle frowned at the widow's peak of stubble prominent on his forehead; it was time to shave his head once more. This was, however, the least of his concerns. His eyes were bloodshot, his uniform stained and torn. He hadn't paused to change or truly to right himself after making the trip here, using the SUV he had hidden near the advance camp for just that purpose. There had been no time. By now, Castillo's spies within the ranks of Orieza's people—and Del Valle knew the Mexican president had them, for he permitted them to remain— would know that the general's troops had suffered a serious setback on the Guatemalan border. Orieza would have to speak with Castillo, and that meant El Presidente himself would be phoning. Orieza couldn't be permitted to take the call alone. He would need Del Valle on hand, lest the simpering old fool lose his nerve and back out of the plan.

Del Valle would give his general the courage he

needed in dealing with the Mexican. That would be simple enough. Explaining to the general what had happened in the simplest, most casual terms would require a more delicate balancing act. Orieza had to know; it couldn't be kept from him, lest the fact of Del Valle's power behind the old man's throne become too apparent to those with whom the General dealt regularly. There was no benefit to pulling a puppet's strings if your audience focused on the puppeteer.

Del Valle knew that others considered him paranoid; he had been told as much, by many fools who this day didn't draw breath. He dismissed them. To hold power, true power, required that one not be the constant target of assassins. Doing what was necessary carried with it many dangers and made many enemies. His shock troops were now camped about the general's residence, a standing army devoted simply to keeping the old man safe. Let Orieza be a prisoner in his own home, content to play with his women and believing he was commanding legions. Del Valle would be there to reap the true benefits, forever in control, never far from the shadows.

Roderigo had risen through the ranks of the Honduran military, always unofficial, always an "adviser" or a consultant to men of power. Attaching himself to Orieza's coattails had been simple enough, becoming known and respected as his adviser easy. The old man was handsome and well liked, a silver fox who, in his younger days, had shown much brilliance and inspired much loyalty. But Orieza was no saint. He knew and valued the services a ruthless agent could provide, and Del Valle shrewdly and masterfully played to the old man's ego while bolstering his failing courage. Creating the shock troops, training them and assigning them their missions had been Del Valle's brilliant move, and it had served them both well. Orieza liked believing he was protected by a private army within the Honduran military. The shock troops, meanwhile, were fiercely loyal to the man who had elevated them to elite status, to wealth, to almost unlimited license within the world permitted to them. Special privileges, women, weapons, money... the shock troops knew that they benefited greatly from the arrangement. They also knew that these things were conferred on them not by Orieza, but by Roderigo Del Valle.

After orchestrating Orieza's coup, his rise to true power in Honduras, and after seeing to it that the old man's claim to governing was shored up by blood and terror through his shock troops and his command of the Honduran military at large, Del Valle wasn't satisfied. It was he, therefore, who had seen the potential of the oil pipeline. Nationalizing the country's remaining private concerns had simply been a matter of course, but knowing what to *do* with those resources...well, that had been Del Valle's brilliance at work, as well. It was Roderigo del Valle who had concocted the daring scheme to build the pipeline to Mexico, and it was Roderigo del Valle who recognized that a man like President Castillo would be receptive to the power play that Del Valle offered. Of course, Castillo thought all this was Orieza's doing, and that was as it should be. If it went wrong, Orieza would take the blame. If somehow Del Valle's hold on power was broken and the regime crumbled, it would be General Orieza's back against the wall before a revolutionary firing squad.

When you were the power behind the throne, you could hide behind it, too.

But he was drifting. Back to the problem at hand. Castillo would call, would want assurances that the plan was to continue. Del Valle, through Orieza, would provide those assurances. President Castillo would be easily enough placated; he was many miles away, and understood the military might that General Orieza could yet bring to bear. Castillo also had a weakness that Del Valle was happy to exploit: the new Mexican president was a believer. His faith in this La Raza business, this Chicano nationalism, burned deeply in him. His hatred for the United States and his desire to take what he could from the Yankees north of his border would be the carrot that continued to lead him down Del Valle's garden path. Only Roderigo del Valle would know that it was he who held the stick....

In offering these assurances to Castillo, of course, it was critical that Del Valle shield his general from the shock of the attacks near the Guatemalan border. Above all, Orieza couldn't be allowed to know the true extent of the damage done.

Del Valle had seen the man. He had seen the big soldier and known him instantly for what he was, this Caucasian with dark hair. There was no way to be sure, but something about him—the way he moved, the equipment he carried, just something indefinable about his bearing—had made Del Valle place him as a an American. Certainly his willingness to invade, to kill, to cut a bloody swath across a foreign nation's sovereign borders, was typical of his kind. Del Valle had seen U.S. Special Forces soldiers in action, and this man was very likely one of them.

His head still reeled with the knowledge of what the soldier had done. It was clear that the invader couldn't be working alone, not given the extent of the carnage. He would likely be a leader, however. He had that look. Even in his brief contact with the big foreigner, Del Valle had felt something like fear tickling his guts. He had brushed against death and escaped, this man whose clothes were stained with blood, who smelled of smoke and of gunfire. This man with the two large knives mounted on his combat harness.

It was only after escaping the ruins of the base camp that Del Valle had learned of the true fury of the invading onslaught. His raiding party, massing on the border for another strike into Guatemalan territory, had been wiped out utterly. No doubt the American soldiers, if that was what they were, had brought a sizable team into the country. They were perhaps Marines, or SEALs…. It didn't matter. He would have to make inquiries, once he returned to his own offices, in order to perform damage control.

The lesson they hoped to impart was clear enough: leave Guatemala alone. In truth, Del Valle hadn't credited them with the courage to make a minor show of force, much less this. They were fools if they thought a bloody nose would be enough to dissuade him. He would find their forces, if they hadn't already fled, and he would make lessons of them. But first there was Orieza….

Del Valle finished his useless attempts to clean

himself up and turned to the door. He gestured to the
woman, who pressed the buzzer beneath her desk. The
door opened automatically, the locks releasing. That
door was bulletproof, of course, the walls of Orieza's
office reinforced against explosives. The general himself
sat within, looking far older and more tired than his
troops would ever be permitted to see him.

"Roderigo," he said weakly in Spanish, looking up
from his ornate chair behind his equally ornate desk. "I
am glad you are here." He looked pale and sallow, his
white hair flat against his skull. The elaborately gilded
white uniform he wore hung limply on his frame, as if a
size too large. He was staring at the phone on his desk,
with its faux-antique receiver and engraved casing. It
was ringing.

"Is that…?"

"Castillo." Orieza nodded. "He has been calling all
morning. I thought it best you be here before I spoke
with him."

Thank heavens, Del Valle thought, that the old fool
can be trusted to follow my instructions at least that
far.

"Of course, General," he said, bowing smartly at the
waist. "Forgive me for keeping you waiting. I will be
honored to assist you."

Orieza looked relieved. Del Valle took up a position
perched on Orieza's desk, where he would be able to
listen to the call and quietly offer suggestions to the
general out of range of the telephone.

After Orieza's secretary and the operator on the other
end traded formalities, the leaden voice of Mexico's

president blared from the device. "General Orieza," Castillo said. "I have heard disturbing things."

Del Valle whispered, and Orieza repeated his words verbatim. "I know full well what you have heard," he said, the steel in his voice an act, but the role one he was quite accustomed to playing. It was as if the simple fact that Del Valle was there to think for him liberated him from whatever had turned him into such a shriveled shell of himself. He was free to be the powerful general, the macho hero of the new Honduran regime, as long as Del Valle did the heavy lifting—in this case, by telling him what to say.

"Then you know that I've learned your forces have been dealt a defeat on the Guatemalan border," Castillo stated smoothly. "I don't know how bad it is, but it worries me. Tell me, my friend, how bad *is* it?"

Worse than I will permit your spies to learn, useful idiot, Del Valle thought. Through Orieza, he said, "A small matter only. We believe the Guatemalans have called on their allies for assistance. It may have been the American directly, or some international force, which amounts to roughly the same thing."

"And?" Castillo demanded.

"And they obviously seek to send us a message," Del Valle said through the general. "One that, clearly, will have no effect. You know the Americans. They are gutless."

"This I agree with," the Mexican said. "But you are guessing. You do not know that it was the United States."

"No," Orieza repeated obediently. "But then, I do not know that it wasn't, and in either case, it does not matter.

Only a few men were killed. The operation will not be significantly slowed. The pipeline will be completed on schedule."

"I have my doubts," Castillo murmured. "Though, in truth, I owe you a debt of gratitude."

"In what way?" Orieza asked, sounding genuinely as curious as Del Valle was.

"When you first came to me," the Mexican president said, "telling me of your…shall we call it newfound wealth, and suggested the pipeline, I thought the plan insane. Waging war through your neighbors and mine in order to bring us the oil directly… Why, yes, the resulting wealth is most welcome, and with wealth comes power. But I got to thinking. You were dreaming big. I should do no less, I thought, and so I started to dream bigger."

"We discussed this," Orieza said, his cautious tone mirroring Del Valle's. "You will use your money, your power, to accomplish your own goals in your upcoming battle with the Americans. We provided you significant material assistance in exchange for your cooperation with this plan, which is very detailed and has a specific schedule."

"Assistance? You speak, no doubt, of your fine little helicopter. Yes, well," Castillo said, "do not fear. We shall be putting it and the missiles to good use."

"The time for your incursions is soon to be reached in that schedule—"

"That's just it," Castillo interrupted. "There is no 'soon to be.' My operatives are already in position. The first moves are already being made. Soon I shall bring those weaklings north of the border to their very knees, and we, the proud people of Mexico, will take what belongs to us."

"But this is not what we agreed," Orieza repeated for Del Valle.

"I do not give a damn for schedules any longer," Castillo said. "I will take what I wish from the Americans, with or without your oil money. I will gladly take that, of course. Do not count it against me. But you have inspired me, General. I am taking what I want with or without your help. I shall gladly use the toy you have sent us to do it, too."

"Is that wise?" Orieza asked, and this time he spoke before being prompted. Del Valle let it go, for he was about to ask the very same thing. He whispered, and Orieza repeated his next words: "If you alert the forces of the West too early, they may respond with greater force than they have already done."

"Ramon, Ramon, Ramon." Castillo tsked into the phone, setting Del Valle's nerves on edge. "You refuse to acknowledge with whom you are dealing. These Americans are a fundamentally inferior race. We have discussed this."

"Please do not ply me with your racial theories," Orieza said, unbidden, and Del Valle had to admit that he felt much the same. "I am aware of your notions, and we agree that the territory you will seize rightfully belongs to you. But if you move too far too fast, before we have filled our coffers and purchased more weapons and equipment, they will crush you."

"We have been eating them alive for years now, from within," Castillo said with a sneer. "But perhaps

I misunderstand. I am informed that you have suffered material damages. That someone has interfered with your operation on the border."

"And I," Orieza said, his tone mirroring the venom in Del Valle's, "would very much like to know how you are aware of this."

"We are all friends," Castillo said. "Friends talk among themselves."

"Indeed," Orieza dutifully repeated. "We will not discuss that for now. As we—" He stopped abruptly as Del Valle shot him a look. "As I said, everything is under control. Pipeline construction continues on schedule. The Guatemalans cannot stop us. They do not have the means, nor the strength of will. Our own people can be counted on to do as we order them. It is a good plan and we shall stick to it."

"Then I have nothing to worry about, do I?" Castillo said. "So I'm moving my people into position earlier than we discussed. It means little, provided the pipeline does go through. And, frankly, if you fail, Ramon, I will not be held back by your weakness. The Race demands more. It *deserves* more."

"Just tread carefully," Orieza said. "Remember what I have said." He looked up at Del Valle as his adviser snatched the receiver and slammed it down on the cradle.

"That miserable pig!" Del Valle hissed. "He could ruin everything!"

"Roderigo…" Orieza said hesitantly, gazing directly at him for the first time since he'd entered the room. "You look terrible. Are you all right?"

"I am fine," Del Valle said sharply. He softened his tone, catching himself. "Please, General, think nothing of it. All is well. There are simply many things to monitor, many things I must keep a watchful eye on."

"Yes, I suppose that would be so," Orieza said, sounding unconvinced. "But who is it that attacks us? Have they done us much harm?"

"No, no, General." Del Valle spread his hands, smiling broadly. "You know that a man like Castillo must always try to impress others with his great power. If he makes us believe he thinks us weak, he gains an advantage. We are in no danger, and our plans progress according to schedule. Our dream for our great nation progresses accordingly. There is no need to worry."

"But, Roderigo, I have doubts. I have heard from some of the men that the people are angry."

"Angry? Who told you that?"

Orieza shrugged. "One hears things from the staff. Is it true that the elite guard are interrogating our own people?"

"My men? Your bodyguards? That is absurd," Del Valle lied. "Really, General, you must give this no thought. These are the kinds of rumors spread by the bored, the idle and the envious. You must know that your great power and popularity will bring unfair criticism."

"I suppose," Orieza said, his forehead knotting. "I simply do not understand—"

The intercom buzzed. Del Valle, grateful for the distraction, pressed the button before he could continue, and made a mental note of the fact that some people had been far too free in their conversation with Orieza. Roderigo would determine who the general had been listening to, and would make sure those persons disappeared permanently. Orieza was asking far too many inconvenient questions.

"Yes?" he said, leaning over the intercom.

Orieza's secretary spouted a stream of apologies for interrupting, and then begged their pardons, but could Commander Del Valle take an urgent call from the field? One of his men had been trying to reach him for some time, she said, and she had delayed connecting the call for as long as she thought prudent.

"Yes, yes," Del Valle said testily. "Put it through." He picked up the large receiver. "Yes?" he said again in Spanish.

"Commander," stated one of his field lieutenants, whose name escaped him at the moment. The soldier was out of breath, or frantic in some way, as if he was frightened or had run to reach the phone. "Sir, I must sound the alarm urgently, sir! There is great trouble here at the terminal!"

"The pipeline terminal?" Del Valle demanded.

"Yes, Commander, yes!"

"Well?"

"Sir...it..."

"What, damn you?" Del Valle roared. "Spit it out, or I will wring your neck!"

"Sir, the terminal burns."

"What?" Del Valle shouted. "What are you talking about?"

"Sir—" The voice was cut short by a loud clap of sound, a noise Del Valle couldn't escape.

"Report!" he yelled. "Report, damn you!"

The muffled click of the receiver being replaced in its cradle was the only reply.

CHAPTER FIVE

Thick undergrowth between closely packed trees gave way to the blade of Mack Bolan's machete, ending abruptly at a large clearing that was dominated by the pipeline terminal. This, too, was concealed beneath camouflage netting, but the NSA's satellite surveillance had easily picked out the facility with thermal imaging. Bolan was no expert on the technology used for oil drilling, but he gathered that this nationalized plant had been an innovative one before it was essentially stolen from its owners by Orieza's regime.

Intelligence operatives posing as interested parties from the United States government's international trade commission had interviewed key employees of O'Connor Petroleum Prospecting, according to the files sent to Bolan by the Farm. They had provided blueprints of the proposed plant layout, which Bolan consulted on his phone's muted screen. There were supposed to be changes made to these preliminary plans, alterations that would be filed on-site only. If there had been any major departures, he couldn't see them as he surveyed the terminal.

Of particular interest to him were the office buildings, a collection of interconnected, prefabricated sheds south of the pipeline cluster. The cluster—it was designated as such on the plans—was a complicated mass of piping, tributaries of some sort that came together at a junction of the oil line. That pipeline, constructed by Orieza's people after the takeover, stretched off into the distance, the way Bolan had come. It ended, he knew, at the advance camp he had just destroyed.

There had been no point in targeting the pipeline itself, for it was far longer than Bolan could deal with. Destroying portions of the line would slow the progress of Orieza's invading teams, but Bolan didn't believe in chopping off tentacles when he could attack the head of the monster. The OPP terminal had to be destroyed, if the pipeline project was to be ended effectively. Destroying the equipment would deny Orieza's regime access to the oil, which, in Bolan's relatively limited understanding of petroleum prospecting, wasn't accessible without the new technology OPP had brought to the project. Once the terminal was eliminated, there would be no point in continuing to invade Guatemala in order to bring the pipeline through to Mexico.

That was the plan, anyway.

Brognola had told Bolan that the employees present when the facility was nationalized had been killed or taken hostage. The Orieza regime had said nothing about them publicly, nor had the communications between the two nations intercepted by the Farm's intelligence sources included any mention of them. This was likely because the human beings caught in the power play cooked up by Orieza and Castillo meant very little to the two leaders. It was Bolan's hope that those OPP employees were still alive. If they were, the most likely location to hold them would be those offices, if the hostages were still on-site. The cyber team at the Farm had analyzed the available data and come to the same conclusion.

Bolan consulted another file on the phone, this one the instructions provided by OPP management for shutting down the drill house and its pump valves. The deep-ranging equipment was connected to a series of turbines heated with geothermal energy, the briefing explained. Tapping this power helped make a project on the scope of the OPP operation possible, and it was the reason the company had managed to find oil where none had previously been detected. Bolan skipped over the technojargon elaborating on that. The gist was that if he shut down the pumps and valves in the order specified by the company's technicians, then reversed the turbines, overrode the safety circuits and instructed the drill equipment to perform a self-cleaning procedure with the pump power at maximum, a mechanical disaster would occur.

The OPP technicians had been very clear on that point. A self-cleaning operation reversed the drills and drew full power from the pumping network. If the safeties were disengaged and the procedure implemented with the turbines also at full reverse, the harmonic vibrations created by the drills would shake the casings apart. The turbines, disconnected from the shafts and overdriving the pumps, would then overheat and explode, shattering the pumps. What was left of the terminal would be torn to pieces by the shrapnel. Any of the equipment still functioning would be so much scrap metal, useless to anyone without the associated high-tech equipment. With the valves shut beforehand, any environmental damage would be minimized; there would be no spewing geysers or burning plumes of oil smoke.

Bolan snapped his phone shut and stowed it. The immediate problem was how to penetrate the facility. It was heavily guarded by Honduran troops who, he could see through his field glasses, wore the blue epaulets of Orieza's shock forces. They patrolled the fenced perimeter of the terminal, a chain-link affair to which strands of razor wire had been added. He could tell the wire was new because it hadn't yet begun to discolor or corrode in the tropical climate, while the chain-link fence itself already looked much older than it could possibly be. No doubt Orieza's thugs had beefed up security once they'd seized the terminal.

The men walking sentry duty in twos carried M-16 rifles. Bolan observed the guards for half an hour, timing them and judging the gap between patrols. It wasn't a large one, but it was there. Orieza's gunmen had become complacent. They would regret that—but not for long.

Bolan gathered himself for his charge. He didn't have the advantage of darkness now. Once he began to fire on the shock troops, the element of surprise would be lost and full-scale combat would commence. There was no room for error.

He counted down the numbers. When he hit zero, he ran.

Bolan's sprint across the clearing to the fenced perimeter carried him between the two closest pairs of sentries. He knelt, brought his rifle to his shoulder and waited, aiming in the direction from which the next team would come. The two men rounded the corner at the far end of the perimeter.

They saw Bolan and froze.

It was all the Executioner needed. In the fraction of a moment that the gunmen's brains failed to process what their eyes saw, he fired a single round through the face of the man on the left. Bolan rode out the mild recoil of the 5.56-mm NATO round, acquiring his second target smoothly without delay. He squeezed the trigger, completely at ease, completely relaxed. The second shot was echoing as both bodies hit the ground.

Bolan let go of the rifle, trusting to his sling to keep it with him. He plucked a grenade from his combat harness, pulled the pin and let the spoon spring through the air. He threw the bomb underhand at the chain-link fence, just beyond what he judged to be a safe distance. Then he hit the dirt and covered his head with his arms.

The explosion did more damage to the ground than to the barrier, pelting Bolan with clods of moist earth. He drew himself into a crouch, bringing the rifle up again, and wasn't disappointed. Armed men were running for him, firing as they went, spraying their weapons blindly.

The Executioner added his own weapon to the cacophony. While his enemies' shots went wide and wild, his own precise bursts were true. First one, then another, then a third of the Honduran shock troopers went down. Bolan pushed to his feet and made for the opening torn in the fence.

He squeezed through with just enough room to spare, despite all the equipment he carried. Once on the other side of the fence he quickly dropped and rolled aside. Lines of automatic gunfire ripped into the dirt where he had stood, again spraying him with debris.

At the awkward angle he now lay, Bolan couldn't bring his rifle to bear. Instead, he let it rest beside him, tethered to its sling, and drew the Beretta and Desert Eagle from their holsters. With a weapon in each hand, he waited, and when gunmen moved into view, he started shooting.

The .44 Magnum Desert Eagle bucked in his hand. The Beretta machine pistol chugged 3-round bursts with each press of the trigger. Like cattle driven to slaughter, the shock troopers kept coming—and kept dying.

There was a pause and Bolan took advantage of it, moving deeper into the pipeline terminal, stepping over bodies as he went. He swapped magazines in his pistols and then holstered the guns once more, bringing his rifle back into play.

He could hear shouting in Spanish and even hear a few bursts of rifle fire, but whatever the men were shooting at, it wasn't Mack Bolan. Most likely it was more panic fire. The urge to do something, anything, when death was at a man's doorstep was a powerful impulse not easily ignored. Bolan had the benefit of many years as a guerrilla fighter, many years on the front lines of a private war that was if not of his choosing, then of his making. Orieza's shock troops were no doubt feared by the citizens of Honduras, but they had proved to be little threat to the Executioner.

There were three battered military-style jeeps parked near the entrance to the small complex. He took note of these and ducked under a large, steel-gray pipe that was mottled with rust spots. Everywhere around him he could see, as he passed by machinery that dwarfed him, that the climate was having an effect on the largely untended OPP equipment. It was possible that in time, without the technical expertise to run the facility, Orieza's regime wouldn't be able to pump the oil at all. The people of Guatemala, however, didn't have the luxury of waiting out the Honduran hard-liners. Nor was it acceptable to let an emboldened Castillo, drunk with the thought of coming oil riches, continue to terrorize the Southwest United States by proxy.

In truth, that worried Bolan more, and he could tell it worried Brognola just as much. The new regimes in both Honduras and Mexico posed threats to United States security, or Bolan wouldn't be making this daring raid on first one, then another national government. But Castillo was the more direct threat, and only the Farm's understanding of the Orieza-Castillo operational timeline had made the Guatemalan border Bolan's first strike.

Then, too, there was the fact that just because Orieza was struggling to maintain the nationalized equipment so recently stolen didn't mean that would always be the case. Technicians capable of understanding what OPP had built here could be hired, for a price. There were plenty of former Soviet Bloc scientists currently on the market in any of several fields related to mining and oil drilling, selling their knowledge to whoever had the cash. Bolan supposed that someday the fallout from the end of the Cold War would finally stop affecting the world counterterrorism landscape, but he really could not begin to imagine when.

He followed a memorized route through the maze of

machinery: a right here, a left there, straight through a tunnel of sorts, formed by arching tubes of heavy steel. As Bolan moved deeper into this man-made maze, the sound of the pumping, chugging, churning equipment grew louder. Soon, it was so loud that he wouldn't be able to hear an enemy coming. The advantage he had, he knew, was that no enemy would be able to hear him, either.

He reached the office complex, some distance from the drill house. From his vantage point behind a large piece of equipment whose purpose he couldn't guess, he watched the flurry of activity around the small building. Armed men rushed here and there in what appeared to be complete confusion. A Klaxon began to sound from somewhere in the complex, belatedly, but that didn't alter the disorganized rushing. It seemed the men within were too late to do anything effective about what they probably thought was a full-scale invasion. That was good. That was how a one-man raid of this type was supposed to go.

Bolan let his rifle fall to the end of its sling, drew his Beretta and made sure the suppressor was securely affixed. He braced the weapon with his other hand, curling his fingers around the folding metal foregrip, and flicked the selector to single shot. Then he waited.

It didn't take more than a couple of seconds for several frantic soldiers to run past his field of fire. He took each of them in turn, his honed, veteran sniper's reflexes serving him well. Each muffled shot, no louder than hands clapping, was lost in the din of the poorly attended machinery cranking and churning all around him. The soldiers fell like dominoes, one after another, each a clean head shot. A single 147-grain 9-mm hollowpoint bullet sent each man to the beyond before he even knew his life was threatened.

Scratch four more of Orieza's blue-tagged bullyboys, Bolan thought.

There was no way to know how long to wait, or if there would be more guards, so Bolan simply stepped out across the opening in the piping fields, moving toward the metal door of the office enclosure. He could see as he approached that the door was barred, crudely, with a section of steel strut. It was wedged into elbows of piping that had been equally crudely welded to metal supports on either side of the door. All of it looked as if it had been sectioned from the machinery of the terminal, burned through inexpertly with whatever torch had been used.

The jerry-rigged barrier, lockable only from the outside, gave the Executioner hope that the OPP employees lost in the takeover of the plant might still be alive. After all, if there were no prisoners, there would be no need to lock the offices to keep them inside it. Bolan reached out with his free hand and pulled the spar—a piece of sharp-edged pipe four inches in diameter, he saw once he hefted it—away from the door. He let it fall to the paving slab on which the office building had been set. Verdant plumes of weeds were already pushing up through cracks in the cement.

A guard with an M-16 appeared from the far corner of the building. Pressed against the wall as Bolan was, the angle was bad, and there was no time for a proper sight picture. Bolan extended his arm and triggered the Beretta, almost not looking at the man. It was a reflex, a point shot performed from long familiarity. The hollowpoint bullet took the gunman in the throat. He fell to his knees, gurgling. Bolan stepped back, turned and extended his machine pistol, firing off a suppressed mercy shot that plowed a furrow through the dying man's brain.

Bolan turned his attention back to the door to the offices, planting the sole of his combat boot against it and kicking it in. He followed the Beretta in, crouched low, moving his gun this way and that, covering each angle.

The hallway leading into the offices was empty, except for quite a bit of litter. He stepped through this, kicking in a flimsy, hollow-core connecting door. This took him into a waiting area with a desk counter that could have been for a receptionist, though it was more likely some sort of coordination area. A large schedule grid on a whiteboard against the wall behind the counter was half-smeared and hopelessly out-of-date.

There was a dead man slumped over the desk.

Judging from the smell and the state of the body, the man had been dead a long time. A pool of dried blood soaked the counter space beneath him and the floor below that. Empty casings littered the floor, and bullet holes pocked the walls. A computer, dead several times over, sat silently in the corner, its monitor and casing full of holes small enough to be made by 5.56-mm NATO, the same rounds Orieza's men used. Well, that figured.

Bolan's nose told him further what he didn't want to know, but he wouldn't give up without making certain. He found the connecting door, the one leading to the main suite of office cubicles, and tested the knob. It was frozen shut, perhaps simply by rust. The handle itself was of steel and mottled with oxidation. Another kick made short work of the barrier.

The charnel stench of death, only too familiar, made Bolan flare his nostrils. The room was a slaughterhouse.

He realized, then, that the bar outside the door hadn't been to keep prisoners in. It had simply been a way to seal off the offices, an unwritten warning to any of Orieza's men stationed at the terminal that there was nothing good within. The office enclosure had been turned into a mausoleum, the OPP employees left to rot where they'd been shot down. Bolan counted them silently, checking the adjoining cubicles and another little storeroom beyond. With the one at the counter, the number was exactly right. He had just accounted for all the potential hostages.

His jaw set in righteous anger, he backtracked. He stopped at the outer door, waiting and listening, but the roar of the pumping operation was far too loud for him to learn anything of use. He did hear gunfire in the distance, cutting through the white noise of the machinery. It was sporadic and seemed to be coming from all directions. It was likely that Orieza's men were shooting into the trees beyond the terminal. Sooner or later, they would realize they had no targets. A reasonable field commander would then dictate an internal search, to find whoever had penetrated the plant. While Bolan hadn't been very impressed with the caliber of Orieza's people so far, it would be prudent to assume they could figure out that much. He would have to hurry.

He consulted the digital plans on his phone one last time, then stowed the device before holstering his pistol and shouldering his rifle once more. Then he threw open the door, ducked out quickly and hit the cracked paving slab hard.

He had anticipated trouble and he wasn't disappointed. Gunmen, probably noticing the bar removed from the office door, had been waiting for him to show himself. Their automatic fire raked the air above him and pounded the door and wall beyond.

Bolan fired from the prone position. The soldiers were exposed, no doubt counting on the element of surprise. The Executioner gave them credit for understanding what the missing bar meant, and responding to the threat in a methodical, patient manner without really knowing what that threat entailed. But that wasn't enough.

Bolan fired, tracked left, fired again, tracked right and fired once more. He squeezed measured bursts from the rifle, not rushing, taking quick but precise aim each time. The soldiers collapsed before him, their weapons falling from their hands.

On his feet once more, the Executioner broke into a jog, his eyes scanning left and right. Twice an enemy presented himself, and twice he snapped up the rifle on the run and triggered a short burst into the soldier. As before, he could hear the sounds of unaimed, misdirected panic fire from several points around the terminal. What the Honduran guards thought they were accomplishing, he couldn't say.

He found the drill house. Logically, the building should have been heavily guarded, but if men were stationed here, they had left their posts in reaction to Bolan's attack on the facility. He paused just inside the door, found a rusting metal desk not far away that had been inexplicably pushed into the corridor and shoved the desk in front of the door. It wasn't much of a barrier, but it would have to do.

He followed the directions he'd been given and made his way to the control center. There was dried blood on the floor, and some bullet holes in the walls, but no bodies. Apparently any OPP employees murdered here had been dragged into the offices. It made sense, and was the lazy man's escape. Why dig graves when you can throw the bodies into a room and bar the door?

The control panel was as it had been described. Bolan set to work. He began throwing levers and turning dials to shut down the pumps and close the valves, all done according to the order specified by OPP management. Next, he reversed the turbine controls. Red warning lights began to flash—he noticed that at least two of the lamps were burned or shorted out—and he pushed the safety overrides all the way up. Another Klaxon began to squawk. He set all the turbines to maximum power.

Bolan found the controls for the drill equipment and began the self-cleaning procedure, again moving the override lever down and back again. Several sirens began to howl, and the vibrations from deep below him and in the machines surrounding him suddenly increased. Metal shuddered against metal. He could feel the pulse traveling up through the floor, through his boots, all the way up to his teeth. The harmonics were starting.

Bolan finished his work. Then he stepped back as far as he could, drew the Desert Eagle and emptied the hand cannon's magazine into the control panel, which sparked and smoked as the heavy .44 Magnum slugs pounded it. The damage should prove enough to prevent any last-minute heroics from the terminal guards, should any of them happen along to try to reverse the procedure Bolan had implemented. He thought that unlikely, though. Even if there was someone on hand who knew how to undo what had been put into motion, there wouldn't be enough time.

As he left the drill house, his rifle once again in his hands, Bolan heard a recorded announcement playing over speakers throughout the terminal. It was in both English and Spanish. It warned of critical danger, of an imminent explosion.

Bolan had reached the outer periphery of the equipment maze when the first eruptions began to rip through the terminal. He could feel the heat and vibrations. The blasts echoed off the canyons of metal piping around him, as if some giant hand were striking countless tuning forks. He picked up his pace.

He found the jeeps again. Pausing, he fired several 5.56-mm rounds into the tires of two of them. Then he jumped into the third, found the keys still in the ignition and started the engine. He was rolling for the main gate, which now stood open and unguarded, when he spotted a single uniformed figure huddling in a small guard shack just inside.

Bolan stopped the vehicle. He got out, drawing the suppressed Beretta with his left hand with little difficulty. The guard, obviously terrified as flames began to consume the terminal from the inside out, took no notice of the Executioner. He was speaking to someone on the phone.

"Sir, the terminal," he was saying. "It burns." Bolan couldn't hear the response. The guard noticed him at last, his eyes going wide as his head whipped around.

"Sir—" he had time to say, as he clawed for a pistol in a flap holster on his belt.

Bolan put a 9-mm bullet between the guard's eyes.

He reached out and quietly replaced the phone in its cradle.

CHAPTER SIX

"Striker to G-force. Striker to G-force."

Jack Grimaldi, ace Stony Man pilot and a seasoned veteran in his own right, was no stranger to combat, but he jumped slightly when the radio came to life. He shook his head and, mildly chagrined, checked the cut-down, fully automatic M-16 next to his seat in the cockpit. The dramatically shortened barrel jutted from a Vietnam-style triangular foregrip that had likewise been chopped, producing an inelegant, bastardized submachine gun that fired the same 5.56-mm NATO ammunition Grimaldi carried in the helicopter. He had an entire duffel bag full of loaded magazines, explosives and other vital elements of resupply, all of it waiting for the Executioner's return.

Grimaldi picked up the radio microphone and keyed it. "G-force," he said. "I got you, Sarge. Go ahead."

"I'm inbound, Jack."

Grimaldi checked the portable GPS receiver he carried. The dot indicating Bolan's position was indeed moving toward the second blinking dot, which indicated the chopper. The soldier would be using his secure satellite phone's GPS application to track Grimaldi's position. This signals were relayed through a borrowed NSA satellite, so there was no chance either man's position could be monitored by someone other than Bolan, Grimaldi or the cyberteam at Stony Man.

Their radios were another matter. Bolan's voice was clear over the encrypted channel. The radio equipment he and Grimaldi were using, however, wasn't exactly the NSA's latest. It was, Grimaldi admitted to himself, little better than what the Honduran military could field, if they bothered with coded communications at all. On a plausibly deniable operation like this one, high-tech field hardware was kept to the bare essentials. It was bad enough that what little equipment Bolan might leave behind, were he caught or killed, would raise certain questions. It wouldn't do to clutter the landscape with high-tech electronic devices that would invariably point a finger of blame at the United States. Although, Grimaldi thought cynically, it wasn't as though these little Third World dictators ever needed much prodding to blame the United States for all their problems, regardless of whether the U.S. actually was involved.

"Message received, Sarge. The welcome mat is out."

Grimaldi replaced the radio microphone in its slot. He wasn't worried about their code-garbled signal being picked up by the Hondurans. Unless enemy forces were practically on top of Grimaldi and his chopper, they were unlikely to receive a signal. Still, he paused to glance down at the 30-round magazine jutting from the well of his chopped M-16, to which a second, inverted magazine had been fabric-taped for a fast reload.

With the big guy on his way back, Grimaldi began running through his preflight checklist. The HH-1H Iroquois helicopter was a solid old girl, a machine provided for Stony Man locally by covert elements within the Guatemalan military. Its camouflage had been hastily repainted to more closely resemble the pattern used by the Hondurans, who used the same workhorse Hueys.

Grimaldi checked the auxiliary fuel tanks that had likewise been added at the last minute. The flight from Zacapa, Guatemala, to put Bolan within striking distance of the pipeline terminal and advance camp had barely made a dent in the Huey's fuel supply, but he and Bolan had miles to go before they slept. Grimaldi next had to put Bolan down within range of the Honduran capital, then get them back both across the border to safety. The round trip was going to strain the old girl's range before they were done.

He was confident the chopper would serve them well. He couldn't remember exactly how many hours he had logged in similar birds, but even an experienced commercial pilot would think it a staggering number. Grimaldi knew the Huey inside and out. His skin still crawled at the thought of taking fire from the ground, as any pilot's did, but he'd long ago learned to ignore that. When you flew with Mack Bolan, you got shot at. It was one of those facts of life.

Inserting the Executioner into Honduras after the relatively fast flight over the border had been easier than one might think. The Honduran air force could put some reasonably dangerous equipment in the air, and they had spotty security coverage of the country's airspace, but there were plenty of holes. By staying fairly low and blending in, Grimaldi was confident they could bluff their way into and out of the country without difficulty. The airspace close to the capital would be more dicey.

He was glad of their camouflage, which would let him impersonate a Honduran military craft unless someone looked too close. He wouldn't be able to drop Bolan on the lawn of the presidential palace, or whatever it was they called the government building here, but he would get the Sarge as near as possible and then lie low until it was time to extract again.

He began flipping switches and watching his gauges, prepping the bird for takeoff. The Lycoming turboshaft engine growled to life. The Huey had a ceiling of 15,000 feet, about 4,500 meters to the locals. Its top speed was well over a hundred knots, which meant it topped out around 130 miles per hour. That was more than enough to get this job done.

Given the circumstances, Grimaldi would still have preferred a Cobra gunship, a dated but nevertheless solid, serviceable attack craft he had flown countless times in support of both Mack Bolan and the commando teams of Stony Man Farm. Unfortunately, the Hondurans were unlikely to ignore a hostile gunship prowling their skies. Besides, if he did his job correctly and if luck was with him, he wouldn't take the kind of enemy fire he might draw in a gunship, and that idea appealed to the cautious side of his nature.

Not that he listened to that part of himself often.

As if some part of the universe were listening to his private thoughts, the staccato sound of distant gunfire reached him over the thrumming of the Huey's rotors. Grimaldi's eyes narrowed. He checked the GPS tracking unit, fixed Bolan's position against his own and strapped himself in.

"Hold on, Sarge," he said to himself. "Support's on the way."

Grimaldi lifted the chopper's collective lever and the Huey cleared the ground, its rotor wash whipping the trees surrounding the little clearing in which the Stony Man pilot had been waiting. He nudged the cyclic and made a minute adjustment to the throttle, bringing the nose down slightly as the Huey rattled forward on a heading that would take it to Bolan. A person didn't really pilot a helicopter, the old saying went; the pilot just prevented it from crashing from minute to minute. To Grimaldi, handling the controls of the chopper was second nature, the act of flying as familiar, nearly as automatic, as breathing. He could fly just about anything with wings and an engine, or with just one or the other… but nothing made him feel as alive as when he sat in the pilot's seat of a chopper.

Now, the trick was to stay that way.

Far in the distance, he could see the plume of smoke rising from what could only be the pipeline terminal. That was the Sarge, Grimaldi thought, and he grinned broadly. There was something philosophical, or funny, or both about the fact that countless times, Jack Grimaldi had dropped Mack Bolan in some part of the world, and shortly after that, that part of the world had blown up, fallen down, caught fire or otherwise exploded. Bolan was a one-man wrecking crew, an individual death squad. He could infiltrate, demolish or remove any target. He was twelve feet tall and bulletproof, and shot fire and lightning from his eyes…or at least, that was how his enemies had to have seen him, after one of Bolan's patented blitzes through their midst. The Stony

Man pilot shook his head, marveling at just how much smoke there was, visible for miles.

That plume of smoke was a good reason to get Bolan gone as fast as he could, too. The Hondurans might be slow to organize and respond to this attack, but they *would* respond. Grimaldi had no desire to be on scene when the jungle started swarming with soldiers. That was, however, part of the plan. Hitting the terminal ended the immediate run by the Hondurans into Guatemala, and would take the pressure off the United States' allies in the Guatemalan government—not to mention giving affected citizens some relief from their neighbors' aggression. But it was also going to make a lot of noise. Burning in the middle of the jungle, the terminal would collect Honduran military like flies to a bug zapper, drawing heat off the capital. The Farm—and the ace pilot—were counting on this to make it easier to fly an unregistered helicopter into the airspace surrounding the city. There was no doubt in Grimaldi's mind that there, too, Bolan would work his destructive magic, leaving a wake behind him that Godzilla would envy.

The dense jungle beneath the aircraft blurred as he poured on the speed. The thick, mottled green carpet was cut here and there by small clearings, most of them offering insufficient clearance for his rotors. He was approaching one of these holes in the verdant landscape below when he saw the muzzle-flashes.

He brought the chopper in low and slow, surveying the firefight. The shooting increased in intensity as he approached, but none of the fire came his way. He guided his Huey about, gauging the enemy numbers and their position.

A lone shooter, who could only be Mack Bolan, was concealed in the trees at the edge of the clearing closest to Grimaldi's position. He checked his GPS locator and was pleased to see he hadn't gone senile; the blip on his screen was right where he figured Bolan had to be. He inched the bird closer.

The enemy shooters were clustered at the edge of the clearing opposite Bolan. They had spread out, but from his position above them Grimaldi could easily index their locations.

He was low enough that he could see several of the enemy shooters waving and signaling to him. They thought he was air support for them, dispatched by some providential force. If they were trying to make radio contact, he didn't have their frequency set. That wasn't important. From what the Farm knew of the state of Orieza's co-opted Honduran military, loyalty to Orieza was emphasized, but functional discipline and tech training weren't. The ground troops would simply assume the chopper's pilot was too busy doing something else to respond, if they were trying to call at all.

He brought the chopper down in a neighboring hole in the tree canopy close to the Hondurans. He didn't like leaving the helicopter unattended, but there was no other option. He gave the old Huey an affectionate pat as he grabbed his gear and put his jungle boots in the dirt.

Over his flight suit he slung a canvas bandolier of short 20-round magazines. He checked the cut-down M-16 one last time, verifying that a round was chambered, then set the safety and made a run for it.

He moved quickly but quietly, his pace more a fast trot than a true run, allowing him to weave through the thick undergrowth. There was no danger that he could get lost, though he carried the GPS tracking unit just in case. Ahead of him, the sharp popping and cracking of 5.56-mm gunfire grew louder and louder, a clear beacon.

He paused, crouching at the base of a particularly gnarled tree, to verify that Bolan was still where Grimaldi had originally clocked him. The blip on the screen hadn't moved significantly; the big guy was right where he should be. Grimaldi crept closer and, as he got within range of the enemy guns, lowered himself to one knee.

There was not a lot of cover, but the Honduran shooters were hunkered down behind the larger tree trunks and scrub they could find. Once or twice, a soldier would turn and look back in Grimaldi's direction, probably wondering where the cavalry might be. With any luck, the gunners would assume their backup was even now working its way around to flank their opposition.

Grimaldi could hear the chatter of Bolan's rifle over the louder crackle of enemy gunfire. The Executioner seemed to have them convinced they were firing at more than one man. The Hondurans were shooting across a broad arc that couldn't possibly constitute only Bolan's position; they either had no idea where he really was or, more likely, he was cycling back and forth across several positions in order to make them believe they were shooting it out with at least a small squad of men.

Grimaldi found a good spot with plenty of over-hanging cover. His muzzle-blast—the short-barreled weapon spit a gout of flame that would be visible for what seemed like miles, he knew—would give him away, but hopefully he could move quickly enough to prevent that from being a problem.

The short barrel of his weapon was doing him no favors, but at this range and from his position Grimaldi would have to work hard to miss. He leveled the assault rifle, flicked the selector switch and started squeezing bursts from the M-16.

He tagged the first enemy soldier in the back of the head. The man never knew what hit him. One second he was there; the next, he wasn't. Grimaldi reflected that there might have once been a time, long ago, when he thought it a bit unsporting, a little unfair, to shoot a man from the back that way. If he had learned anything from Mack Bolan over the years, however, it was that in combat your enemy was your enemy; you didn't offer him politically correct considerations. There were things one didn't do, atrocities one didn't commit, and Grimaldi knew that Bolan was a man of strict moral codes and convictions. But when engaged in a firefight, there was no such thing as notions of "fair" or "sporting." You removed the enemy as efficiently as you could with as little risk to yourself as possible, to better move on and continue doing your job. That was simply the fact of battle in modern warfare.

Grimaldi sprayed out the last of his magazine and managed to take down another Honduran soldier before his weapon went dry. Still crouching, he started to move, putting distance between himself and his last position. Sporadic return gunfire pulped small trees and undergrowth where the Stony Man pilot had been.

Grimaldi switched magazines, then yanked the plunger and gave the weapon a hard slap for luck.

Bolan was pouring on the fire from his own location, and unless Grimaldi's ears betrayed him, the soldier was moving closer to the remaining Hondurans, pressing the advantage of the ace pilot's surprise attack.

Grimaldi hit the ground, flat, at the unmistakable sound of men pushing through the jungle, heedless of the noise they made. A second later, two soldiers rushed into view. The two blue-tagged shock troopers were running for their lives, the weapons in their hands all but forgotten.

Grimaldi popped up to one knee. "Drop 'em!" he shouted, even as he cursed himself for taking the risk. He wasn't about to blast a pair of men actively running from a fight.

One of the soldiers actually shrieked and dropped his weapon, either from fear or because he understood Grimaldi's English command. The other turned his weapon toward the pilot. A short burst punched the gunner to the ground.

Grimaldi registered the sound of the shot only after the soldier hit the dirt.

Bolan stood behind the dead man, his M-16 at his shoulder. He let the barrel dip to low ready when he saw his friend.

"Hi, Jack," he said.

"Hi, yourself, Sarge," Grimaldi answered. He went to secure his prisoner, while Bolan checked the immediate area to make sure they were in no danger. When the Executioner had satisfied himself, he rejoined Grimaldi, who had the Honduran shock trooper on the ground and was searching him. He found a few spare magazines, a couple of the usual pocket items and personal effects, but nothing of interest.

"He's clean, Sarge," Grimaldi reported. "I'll truss him up for you."

"Much obliged," Bolan deadpanned.

Grimaldi used heavy-duty zip ties to secure the soldier, who was looking up at Bolan as if the big man were death incarnate. That wasn't so very far from the truth, the Stony Man pilot admitted to himself.

"Who are these guys, anyway?" Grimaldi asked.

"Apart from the obvious?" Bolan nodded toward the shock trooper. "They're leftovers from the terminal. It took them a few minutes to regroup, but once they did, the troops I didn't take down came after me. I led them on as far as I could, until they got so close I had to turn and deal with them. Thanks for the assist, anyway."

"De nada," Grimaldi said, grinning again. "What do you want me to do with him? If he doesn't die of fear, I mean."

Bolan made the faintest of shrugs. "Leave him here. He'll work his way free soon enough."

"He's seen you up close. Heard you speak English."

"Unless he's packing a digital camera we should be okay."

"I didn't figure you'd plug him," Grimaldi said, grinning. He became more serious. "We had better move out, Sarge. We've got a long way to go before it's over, and the heat's going to be on us fast. We better 'get to da choppah,' as they say."

"Understood." Bolan nodded. Still without cracking

a smile, he added, "And I'm going to pretend I didn't hear you say that."

Grimaldi led the way, with Bolan covering their withdrawal. The pilot glanced back once or twice. The bewildered Honduran shock trooper made no attempt to follow. He looked stunned.

"They all that hard-worn, Sarge?"

"I make it a habit," Bolan said as they trotted for the helicopter, "not to underestimate them. But apart from bad attitudes and the willingness to lean on civilians, they don't seem to have much going for them. These dictatorial regimes always field that type. It goes with the territory."

Grimaldi could only nod. They reached the Huey and Grimaldi became all business, running through his checklist and again firing up the helicopter's power plant. As he worked, Bolan unzipped the duffel bag and began refilling his pouches and pockets with fresh magazines. He had retained a few empties and dropped them back in the bag. Then he started going through the explosives. There was no real need; he had checked the gear on their flight out, and knew as well as Grimaldi that the detonators and plastic explosive charges had been handpicked and set up by Stony Man Farm's armorer. John "Cowboy" Kissinger would hardly let a faulty piece of equipment slip through, especially on a critical mission like this one. But Bolan was both meticulous and methodical. He had been away from the gear while hitting the terminal; he would therefore check it again before trusting his life to it.

"Do you have the hat?"

"And the coat," Grimaldi said. "In the locker under your seat."

"Got it."

"Here we go," Grimaldi said as they lifted off. "I'm going to be trimming the tips of some of these trees, Sarge. I'll get you as close as I can to Tegucigalpa, but there's going to be a point beyond which they'll patrol the airspace too tightly for me to slip by. You'll have to take it on foot from there."

"Understood, Jack." Bolan nodded. "These boots were made for walking."

It took Grimaldi a moment to realize that Mack Bolan was, in fact, cracking a joke.

"Now that," he said, without looking back at Bolan, "hurt. I mean, seriously, Sarge."

Bolan said nothing.

The helicopter flew onward, toward the Executioner's next battleground.

CHAPTER SEVEN

Tegucigalpa, the capital of Honduras, sprawled in every direction as Mack Bolan walked briskly through its streets. He wore a tropical-weight overcoat and white Panama hat over his blacksuit and combat gear, his head low, his gait that of a man in a hurry. His was the walk of someone who had somewhere to be and would brook no interruptions.

His outfit, a concession to concealment, was a bit warm, but not terribly uncomfortable. Despite its tropical climate, Tegucigalpa's high elevation, roughly three thousand feet, kept it reasonably cool. As for the look itself, it wasn't nearly as nondescript as Bolan would have liked, but it was haute couture for drug dealers and street criminals, of which Tegucigalpa had plenty.

The city, home to over a million people, was located in southern Honduras's Francisco Morazán province. It was a curious mixture of old and new, at once vibrant and busy while very worn around the edges. A remarkable number of American fast-food restaurant chains had set up shop in Tegucigalpa. Familiar, brightly lit signs stared at him from every direction, boasting fare found as readily in an American shopping mall. Bolan had few political opinions on the nature of commerce, but he wondered if perhaps something of the character of

Tegucigalpa was lost as the city was swamped by cynical corporate purveyors of chain pizza and hamburgers.

Tegucigalpa was divided into two classes of neighborhood—the inner city barrios and the more upscale *colonias.* The latter were residential suburbs, invariably enjoyed by those who dominated Honduras's seemingly ever-changing political landscape. The nation was, after all, no stranger to abrupt transitions of government, not to mention military coups like the one that had put Orieza and his enforcers in charge.

Still, as Bolan navigated the streets of the capital, working his way toward the presidential residence, he was struck by the upbeat nature of the people of this city. Like many oppressed citizens of various Third World nations, they walked with their heads up and were generally cheerful. They had suffered much and would suffer more; they obviously saw no reason to dwell on it.

There was something very admirable in that attitude.

Tegucigalpa's former presidential palace was now a museum, a tourist attraction of some repute. Bolan, however, was headed for Liberty Square, which neighbored the Casa Presidencial and had become, according to his briefing, part of the sprawling armed camp with which Orieza now surrounded himself.

In his left hand Bolan carried the duffel bag Grimaldi had brought him. It now contained only explosives, and these had been specially prepared with some supplies the pilot had been instructed to transport. Now, it was simply a matter of distributing them properly and setting this leg of Bolan's bold, one-man plan into action.

The grounds of Orieza's residence had been delineated by a chain-link fence. Plenty of guards were in

position, not to mention the Saladin armored vehicles
that Bolan was seeing sporadically patrolling the streets
of Tegucigalpa itself. As well, Orieza's shock troops
were camped en masse in and around the square. They
had appropriated several blocks of the city surrounding the presidential residency. Signs in Spanish forbade
citizen interference beyond this border.

Bolan was about to break some rules.

He took his time. There was a lot of ground to cover,
and he didn't wish to draw attention. There was also the
fact that he was hiding significant weaponry, including
his rifle, under his flowing, lightweight overcoat. He
couldn't afford to move so quickly that he revealed the
extent of his hardware.

The key to his success here in Honduras was simply
to look as if he belonged. Years earlier he had learned
the principles of "role camouflage," the psychological
warfare of blending in by programming one's movements and demeanor to fit in to the surroundings. People,
from civilians to security personnel, often didn't notice
those who looked as if they were completely comfortable in their settings. If Bolan was just another man on
the street, no one would consider him a threat. It was
his long experience in this vein that he now employed,
walking casually along the far sides of the improvised
fortifications, barricades and antivehicle barriers erected
around General Orieza's residence. Whether the man or
his regime ever went about establishing something like a
presidency, perhaps for more diplomatic legitimacy—or
the perception of the same—didn't matter. Orieza
and his power structure weren't destined to survive
this day.

Once the big American was in position in what was, for all intents and purposes, the "rear" of the governmental perimeter—farthest from the front entrance of the Casa Presidencial—he looked around to make sure he wasn't being watched. There were few men at these outer stations of the barricades; the armed soldiers were farther in, guarding the inner perimeter, and stationed in canvas temporary barracks erected in Liberty Square. At the center of the compound sat the tiered, column-fronted building that housed Orieza's offices. Bolan could just see the roof from here, past the trees surrounding the building. He would get there soon enough. First he had to lay the groundwork.

From the duffel bag he produced the first of his explosives. Each bundle was roughly cylindrical, and each had been inserted into a rumpled paper bag. On each bag, a number had been scrawled in black permanent marker. The handwriting was Grimaldi's. The bags had been the pilot's contribution; he had helped out by preparing the bombs and numbering them as he waited during Bolan's strike on the pipeline terminal. Each bomb now resembled a discarded bottle, and was dropped in numerical order, the numbers corresponding to receiving circuits in the bombs.

Moving quickly but casually, careful to raise no alarms were he observed by unseen eyes, Bolan quietly pulled charge after charge from the duffel bag. These he let fall whenever he got close enough to a barricade for the concrete and steel to shield his body. He counted off his paces as he went, spacing the explosives for maximum effect.

Methodically, he worked back around the outer

perimeter to the front. From here, he could see past the barricades to the barracks set up on the paved plaza fronting Orieza's residence. The guards here were greater in number. With an amateur's nearsighted tactical thinking, whoever had planned the troop placement had concentrated their numbers for a frontal attack. It left the flanks and rear of the compound, and thus the government building, vulnerable.

In this case, however, the placement of men, machines and fortifications was likely as much a product of arrogance as naïveté. Dictators like Orieza, and the men who followed him, didn't expect much in the way of opposition. Yes, resistance movements were formed, and yes, such movements had succeeded in fomenting revolution in nations like this one, but Orieza and his loyalists held the Honduran military. There was no chance a ragtag group of discontented citizens could overthrow the nation's ruler, not unless elements within the military were persuaded to change sides. That was why, no doubt, the core of Orieza's defense was made up by his shock troopers. That was also why, according to the Farm's briefing, he was reportedly using his special force to ride herd on the military, seeding each segment with men who could be counted on to enforce his will.

What Bolan intended to do now was a more localized version of the plan he had already executed. On the flight to the capital city, the Executioner had conferred briefly with the Farm. Barb Price, Stony Man Farm's mission controller, had confirmed that U.S. intelligence satellite imagery was tracking a large volume of outbound military traffic from the capital. That meant that

Orieza's forces were responding to the destruction of the pipeline—too late. The diversion would draw them off just long enough to make possible Bolan's assault on the seat of government.

Which didn't mean the odds still weren't against him.

Bolan didn't care about odds. Hundreds of men could fall to a single individual if that individual had the will, the preparation, the training necessary to be more capable than his opponents. Preparation before battle was what made the difference in it, combined with adaptability, initiative and an iron-hard will.

Bolan had will to spare.

Affecting a drunken stagger for any shock troopers who might be close enough to notice, Bolan crouched behind one of the concrete barricades fronting the street leading to the paved plaza off Liberty Square. He removed from his blacksuit the keypad detonator. The small electronic device had been approved by Cowboy Kissinger, but it, like so many of the advanced electronics equipment he used in the field, had been designed by "Gadgets Schwarz," a member of Stony Man Farm's Able Team. The technical wizard had been an ally for many years and had never failed him yet.

Bolan was roughly aligned with the front of the square and with the imposing, columned facade of the Casa Presidencial. Many troops moved in formation or milled about the barracks in the square, and guards paced to and fro in sentry patterns. If the plan was to work at all, now was as good a time as any to begin it.

Bolan tapped out a key sequence on the detonator: 001.

An explosion from the rear of the compound tore

the night apart. Pieces of concrete and steel ripped through the air and, while none came close to reaching Bolan at the opposite end of the perimeter, he could hear fragments pelting the pavement. The effect on the rear of the government building would be much more pronounced.

Bolan gave it a five-count and then tapped out the next number in sequence. Waiting a few seconds between each, he set off half a dozen of his charges. The explosions reverberated off the buildings and raised shouts and even screams in exponential waves. As the compound became a roiling, confused mass of running, yelling shock troopers, Bolan unleathered his suppressed 93-R machine pistol. With the detonator in his left hand, the straps of the duffel bag over his left wrist, Bolan counted to sixty before he stood.

The paved plaza and the front of the armed camp were rapidly emptying as armed men, calling commands frantically in Spanish, picked up M-16 rifles and raced toward the rear of the compound. As Bolan rose to his feet, he shucked his hat and coat and strode boldly toward the closed gates of the inner perimeter— the fence bordering the lawn of the residence, which was an incongruous, lush green. The color contrasted sharply with the urban grays of the neighborhood.

A man with a rifle spotted Bolan and called a challenge above the din of the shouting, the crackle of random, pointless gunfire and the roar of Saladin and jeep engines. Bolan raised his suppressed Beretta and fired a single 9-mm round through the man's head. He fell, his expression registering surprise as he passed into the beyond.

Bolan walked calmly toward the fence. As long as he kept his cool, he could and would survive this maneuver. Orieza's defensive measures were designed to keep out an invading army or, more realistically, an armed rebel force. They had never been designed to keep out a single individual. One man also wouldn't be seen as a threat, at least not instantly. Despite the M-16 hanging from its single-point sling harness, despite the bag of explosives Bolan carried, despite the other weapons in evidence and the deadly knives strapped to his chest harness, he wouldn't register as opposition in the minds of many of these men.

They were brutal, yes, and more than a few of them would be considered tough in a bar fight on a Saturday night. But very few of them, if Bolan was any judge, had spent real time in combat. Most were too young, and the ones old enough to have seen time on the battlefield surely wouldn't have made a career of it in the Honduran military. Local coups and military exchanges were usually brief, sometimes bloody and sometimes not, but the few true conflicts in which the nation's armed forces had engaged wouldn't encompass any experience of note for Orieza and his loyalists.

Those that survived this day might be able to say differently.

A Saladin armored vehicle started to roll in his direction, its turret swiveling toward him. That, Bolan thought, was like using a howitzer to swat a mosquito, but the danger was real enough. He paused, lowered the duffel bag to the pavement, holstered his machine pistol and reached into the bag.

As the Saladin's gunner prepared to fire, Bolan

withdrew a single M-72 LAW rocket. The Light An-
titank Weapon snapped open under his experienced
hands. He had used such weapons to destroy all manner
of targets, but the Saladin was one of those vehicles for
which the LAW had been designed.

Perhaps because he saw what Bolan was doing, one
of the men within the Saladin began to crawl from its
hatch. Why the vehicle hadn't simply withdrawn, Bolan
didn't know; it was possible that panic had robbed the
crew of its common sense.

The Executioner followed, by rote the textbook
arming and firing procedure for the LAW, aiming
through the gaps in the vertical bars of the front gate.
Then he punched the Saladin with a fiery, godlike
fist.

The shock wave tore through the gate and knocked
one side off its hinges. The man who had been attempting to escape was turned into a screaming, burning
monster. Bolan dropped the now-useless LAW tube
and whipped up his M-16 with one hand. He aimed
from the hip and fired once, putting a single 5.56-mm
round through the burning man's head. The mercy shot
dropped him instantly.

Bolan sprinted through the gate, avoiding the metal
framework as the broken half hit the pavement and rang
loudly. He again let his rifle fall to the end of its sling,
using his Beretta for its suppressor's effect. Each man
who braced him, singly or in small groups, he shot down
with either a single round or a well-placed burst. As he
ran, he would periodically stop, reach into his duffel
bag and throw a bomb. He had diverse targets, from
the entrances to the canvas barracks, to under vehicles,

to inside temporarily abandoned, sandbag-protected machine-gun nests. The bulk of the shock troops were responding to his diversion, and this meant Bolan could deal easily with the disorganized men left behind.

When he had exhausted his supply of explosives except one last, small bomb, he pocketed the device and dropped the duffel. Turning on his heel, he jogged back the way he'd come, once more changing out magazines in his Beretta. The machine pistol had gotten quite a workout, and he could feel heat radiating from the barrel as he replaced it in its holster. With one hand on his rifle and the other on the detonator, he made the inner perimeter gate and the other side before the first blast of automatic fire chased him.

The bullets stitched a ragged trail up the paving to the side of the barrier behind which he took cover. By now the main force of defending shock troops had figured out what was going on and were responding, returning to their posts and firing at the first moving figure they identified. They were closing in on him as one single, clotted mob, a mass of enraged humanity now clustered in the center of the government compound. This was what Bolan had hoped for. Within seconds, he would be overrun. In only a few moments, he would be surrounded by an army and cut down.

Bolan quickly slipped into his ears a pair of electronic earbuds taken from his pocket. The digital plugs were designed to protect his hearing.

The Executioner pressed the key sequence 666 on his detonator, and the world erupted in fire.

The explosives detonated simultaneously. There was just enough lag in the signal travel that Bolan could feel the chain reaction roll over him, its touch coming as wave after concussive wave of heat and noise. He turned away.

The blasts ripped through the barracks, erasing them. It blew over armored vehicles, scattering machine-gun emplacements to the four directions of the compass. It sandblasted the front of the Casa Presidencial, blowing out windows and scorching the building's facade. Those guards still standing were blown over and eliminated by the pockets of hellfire that washed across the face of their world. Liberty Square was decimated. The blasts echoed across the buildings on the streets surrounding the compound. Had Bolan not been wearing his digital hearing protection, he was quite sure he would have been temporarily deafened.

A pall of smoke, like a palpable, living force, was suddenly everywhere, the choking black fumes reeking of charred bodies, fuel, plastic explosives and hot metal. It took several minutes for the oily smoke to dissipate enough for Bolan to make out anything, during which time he breathed through a black bandanna he took from his pocket. Tying the cloth around the back of his head like a mask, the Executioner stalked forward into the devastated square, his combat boots crushing debris underfoot.

He removed the earplugs with one hand and pocketed them, holding his rifle braced against his hip in the other. Then the soldier advanced, moving briskly in a combat crouch.

An eerie silence filled the air. He could hear the crackle of small fires burning, but the explosions had spread so hot and so fast that there wasn't much incendiary effect. The compound looked as if some giant, white-hot threshing machine had been dropped on the shock troops' tents and fortifications, churning them to pieces and scattering them at whim.

Bolan breathed shallow breaths through his bandanna mask, like a black-clad outlaw from another era.

Somewhere in the distance, a siren began to wail. It was joined by another, the offset howls of distress combining with the artificial darkness of the smoke pall to create what surely had to have seemed to be the end of the world to those men still alive. Bolan passed several of these as he neared the Casa Presidencial. Some of them called out for help, while others could only groan. He left them there, no longer any threat to the citizens of Honduras or to the civilians of Guatemala. If someone were to hasten them on their way, it wouldn't be the Executioner. He had done what he needed to do to remove them from the play, and while he would fire a mercy round into any man who was clearly suffering and could only die, he wasn't a butcher.

A shock trooper with a bloody right arm was waiting for him on the steps to the main entrance of the presidential residency. Bolan slipped past the crude slash the man made with his combat knife. The shock trooper's arm hung limply, as if it was no longer attached but for the sleeve of his uniform. Clearly fighting past the excruciating pain of the dislocated shoulder and whatever other injuries he had sustained, he gathered himself and lunged again. Bolan slapped the clumsy thrust away and slammed the butt of his rifle into the side of the trooper's head. The man's eyes rolled up and he hit the steps with a sickening crunch.

Bolan entered the building and found himself in a foyer of some sort. A spiral staircase led to the second level, and he could see another entrance, to an interior courtyard, across the corridor. He scanned the signs posted there and turned left, his goal the offices of the president. He assumed that General Orieza would have established himself in whatever suite or office the president of Honduras normally called his own. Dictators loved the appearance of legitimacy, and whenever possible usurped the trappings of the leaders they had supplanted.

He was almost surprised when several gunmen appeared, to fire from the cover of the doorway opposite the foyer. He had, however, been expecting resistance. He took a fragmentation grenade from his harness, pulled the pin, counted off as the spoon popped free and tossed the bomb through the doorway.

Someone shouted in Spanish, but Bolan had left the enemy no time to deal with the threat. The hollow kettledrum boom of the grenade sprayed the soldiers across the wall surfaces on the other side of the doorway, blowing the open wooden door off its hinges and into kindling.

Instead of ducking immediately down the corridor, the Executioner waited again. The shock troopers around the corner doubtless thought themselves very crafty, waiting while Bolan dealt with their comrades. They had, no doubt, thought to take him as he was lulled into a sense of complacency by his initial victory. This might have been successful with an amateur operator. But Bolan was no amateur, and he was never complacent. He was also capable of being much more quiet than were the troopers hiding down the hallway. He had been able to hear them moving, whispering to one another and scuffling about, even after the grenade explosion had temporarily affected his hearing.

Suddenly annoyed at the amateur-night antics of these would-be hardmen, Bolan let his rifle fall and drew his Desert Eagle. When one of the shock troopers became impatient or found his courage, he poked just one eye around the corner at the end of the hallway.

Bolan put a .44 Magnum bullet through that eye.

The thunder of the Desert Eagle echoed down the corridor. Spurred to action by the death of their team member, the shock troopers ran forward, probably hoping to overwhelm their enemy before he could target them. It was a bad play even under better circumstances, but the soldier gave his enemies credit. They tried.

The triangular snout of the Desert Eagle blossomed into orange fire again and again. The heavy hollowpoint slugs dropped each shock trooper in a bloody mess to the floor of the hallway.

Then all was quiet, for the moment.

Bolan marched forward. He held his pistol in two hands, ready to engage.

The Executioner was on a roll.

CHAPTER EIGHT

Mack Bolan was surprised by just how little resistance he met in the blast- and fire-damaged interior of the government building. He could hear emergency vehicles outside in the courtyard, and the shouts of those responding mingled with the hoarse cries of the survivors in a way that told him all was chaos beyond the walls. This was integral to his plan, for if he was to extract himself and make his way back through the streets of the capital to where Grimaldi would pick him up, he would need that chaos.

With his weapons and his nondescript combat clothing, he could pass for a special operator attached to the Honduran military, especially if he shouted commands loudly in Spanish as he went. He would retrieve his coat and hat outside the perimeter and then simply melt away. The walk would feel like a long one, after the exercise he'd gotten over the past several hours, but the end of any leg of a combat mission always felt that way.

Several times he encountered blue-tagged shock troops, and each time he engaged them they were easy to gun down. Given how little real resistance Orieza's bullyboys had been able to field, Bolan had to wonder at how poorly trained these men were.

He was about to take the stairs to the second level, mindful of booby traps, when he spotted the open door to a makeshift building off the inner courtyard. Something about the enclosure looked incongruous. It took him a moment to realize what it was, but he was used to trusting his instincts on the battlefield. He realized that the enclosure was a prefabricated, corrugated metal building that had been painted to match the interior of the presidential residence.

The Executioner checked his watch. He would be pushing it, time wise, because he had to move quickly if he was to leave the grounds of the compound before the Hondurans managed to reestablish control. Still, something had snagged his attention and he had to check it out.

He entered the room and knew immediately what it was that had caught his eye. A set of blueprints was pinned to the wall. Workbenches and carts with machine parts dotted the floor space. There were tools and some oil stains. Equipment of some kind had been staged, stored or maintained here.

Movement in a corner of the room caused him to bring his gun up. A man in a white lab coat, obviously a technician of some sort, held a laptop clutched to his chest. In his right hand, he held a Browning Hi-Power pistol. He shouted something in rapid-fire Spanish.

"Drop the gun," Bolan ordered, covering the man with his Desert Eagle. The technician shouted something back. He was sweating and glancing down at the pistol he held.

"Don't do it," Bolan warned.

The technician tried to shoot him.

Bolan punched a .44 round through the man's face, just as the technician brought up the laptop as if to shield himself. The bullet blew a crater through the laptop and bored out the back of the man's head, leaving whatever else he might have said on the wall behind man and machine. The body slumped to the floor and the now-useless laptop landed with a clatter.

There was no point in checking him; he was dead before he stopped falling. Bolan hoped nothing of critical significance to the mission had been held on that computer. He picked it up and looked it over, but the hard drive had been blown to pieces. Not even the cyberteam and its miracle equipment would have been able to recover the data on that device. Bolan let it drop.

He turned back to the wall. There was still no resistance being offered, but that couldn't last, and he was very aware of the numbers falling. He had to hurry.

The picture on the blueprints was of a helicopter, but something about the aircraft didn't look right. Bolan checked to his rear, then took a closer scan of the plans. The image of the armed chopper seemed out of proportion because the craft had no cockpit.

The chopper bore stubby "wings" that were fixed points for missiles. On its landing skids were mounted a pair of what appeared to be machine guns, though of a type Bolan hadn't seen before.

He removed his secure satellite phone and used its built-in camera to snap shots of the prints. Then he lifted the pages and took pictures of the blueprints below. When he was done he sent the images to the Farm, waited precious seconds for the upload to complete, then dialed the number for Stony Man Farm's operations center.

"Price," Barbara Price acknowledged. "Go, Striker."

"I am sending images of a set of plans I've found on the grounds of the Honduran government building," Bolan said. "It looks like an advanced UAV. I need an analysis. If this thing is somewhere on the grounds, I don't want to run into it by surprise."

"I am switching you over to Akira," Price said. Akira Tokaido, one of the Farm's ace computer hackers, was already scanning through the images and running a recognition program at his workstation. He donned a wireless headset and spoke into its microphone.

"Striker," Tokaido said, "Akira here. I have your images. I'm running…ah, here it comes now. Oh. This is not good."

"Analysis?" Bolan prompted.

"Striker, what you're looking at is basically a copy of the RQ-8, the forerunner of the U.S. military's MQ-9 Reaper. The Army, the Navy and some special-ops units use it. It's an unmanned, remote-controlled rotorcraft, armored against small-arms fire, agile enough to avoid many types of rockets. According to the scales on your plans, this one's about seven by three meters, with an eight-meter rotor span."

"Range? Limits?"

"Not specified here, but it's powered by a Rolls-Royce 250-C20 turbine engine running on nonvolatile jet fuel. Four-blade rotor, payload up to 700 pounds for short-range missions. Based on the Fire Scout specifications, I think you're looking at a ceiling of six-thousand-plus meters and a cruising speed upward of 125 miles per hour. I can run conversions for you if you—"

"What's it armed with?"

"These plans show it fitted with six antipersonnel

missiles, probably similar to the Hellfire. That makes each missile about a hundred pounds in weight, probably bearing shaped-charge blast fragmentation warheads."

"Meaning it will shred people on the ground."

"Exactly, Striker. Your model also has twin machine guns, one to a side, with high-capacity helical-feed magazines. The caliber isn't specified but it looks like something small, maybe a 9 mm, or even a .22 if the drawing isn't very precise. The guns would give the UAV the ability to harass and eliminate targets at ranges that would cause its own destruction were it to use its rockets. Without the rocket specs I can't really tell you what the effective range is, but given the range of the Hellfire—"

"I get the picture," Bolan said. "Now what are the chances this thing will be waiting for me on the roof?"

"I'd say—" Bolan could hear Tokaido tapping keys "—that you're in the clear. We've been running enhanced satellite imagery over our Honduran targets since the start of your operation and well before it for premission recon. I see no sign that this machine is in your vicinity. The Hondurans haven't been using it for anything up to now, anyway, if it is there. You said the hangar is empty?"

"No sign of it, no," Bolan said. He reloaded his weapons and checked his M-16. "I've got a man to talk to about government policy. Keep an eye out for me, will you?"

"Will do, Striker."

"Striker out."

After grabbing the plans off the wall, folding them

and shoving them into one of the cargo pockets of his blacksuit, Bolan took the nearest stairwell. No traps or other problems were evident...until he hit the next floor. Then he heard footfalls farther down the corridor and wondered if he had lingered too long.

He need not have worried. As he approached, his rifle in his fists, he was met and passed by fleeing household staff. Three cleaning ladies and at least one man in the white jacket of a steward ran past. Bolan let them go. It was possible that any of them could be a person of military importance in disguise, but none was General Orieza. Bolan wasn't here to capture the entire regime; he was here to chop the head from the snake.

He met true resistance at last in the corridor leading to the suite of offices once held by Honduras's last legitimate leader. Several shock troops blazed away in the anteroom with assault rifles. They didn't hit Bolan, who took cover at the opposite end of the hall, around the corner, but they did considerable damage to the opulent furnishings of this portion of the building.

The next duly elected president of Honduras, Bolan considered, was going to have a lot of renovations to make at this rate. He'd need a good groundskeeper, too, if the exterior of the compound was ever to be presentable again.

Bolan leaned out and took a few shots with the Desert Eagle, not really expecting to hit anything. As long as he had plenty of ammunition, there was no reason not to try, and the Executioner hit anything he aimed at. With no clear target, however, he was limited simply to suppressing fire. In this way he felt out the shock troopers' defenses, obliterating several pieces of desktop equipment in the process.

As he had suspected, he wouldn't be able to do much more unless he could draw the guards out. The men were well dug in, using for protection solid-looking wooden desks that were a far cry from the flimsy items so common in commercial office spaces. These were heavy antiques, and while they wouldn't hold up forever, they provided plenty of short-term cover.

Chipping away at them would take far too long. Bolan thought there might be another way. He reached out, grabbed a phone from the small, square stand in his corner of the corridor and looked it over. The ornate model was heavy enough that it just might work.

"Hey!" he called. "I want to talk!" He repeated the request in Spanish. "Any of you guys speak English?"

"I speak," one of the shock troopers shouted. "No talk! You leave and we no kill you!"

"Yeah," Bolan said, "I'll go, but I want to take my demands to the general first."

"Nobody sees the general!"

"Fine, fine," Bolan said. "Nobody sees the general. But will you take him this phone?"

He heard the men whispering to one another. It was possible they didn't realize he could understand Spanish, but the more likely case was they thought he couldn't hear. Regardless, it was obvious they were, in fact, plotting to kill him as soon as they were confident he was distracted by his phone call. That was fine; they wouldn't get the opportunity.

While the guards were occupied, Bolan finished preparing the phone, cutting the cord connecting it to the wall. He was careful to snip it close to the unit so there was no telltale nub. He only hoped the guards were too keyed up to notice that the phone he was offering them wasn't connected to anything. Unless General Orieza planned to talk to ghosts like the little girl in that old movie about poltergeists, the phone would be useless disconnected. But then, come to that, it *would* help him talk to the spirit world….

He held the phone out with one arm, wagging it a little. "Just take this phone to him. I need to talk to him, and then I'll leave. Nobody else needs to die."

They didn't like it, but one of the troopers agreed to take the phone. He got as far as the anteroom door with the device. When he shouted for someone to open up, Bolan could hear the angry response from within. The gist of it was that the trooper was a fool, and there was no way that door was going to open. Bolan could see, as he peered cautiously around the corner, that those doors were reinforced. There would be no shooting through them.

He removed his pocket detonator and keyed in a four-digit sequence.

The small, square block of plastic explosive, wired to a detonator receiver, exploded.

Bolan waited. He drew the Desert Eagle once more, checked it and strode down the blackened hallway through the shattered remains of the Honduran dictator's fortifications.

The bomb had done its work. The two guards had been eliminated, and there was almost no sign of them. The explosion had caused part of the ceiling to fall in, as well, but not so badly that the anteroom was impassable.

Bolan stepped through the debris, the big hand cannon ready, and surveyed the damage inside what had to be the office of the president of Honduras.

There were more shock troops here, lying dead or stunned amid the wreckage. The heavy reinforced doors had been blown free of their hinges, crushing at least one guard underneath. The walls themselves had sustained very little damage. Whoever had designed the safe room that was the presidential office space hadn't counted on concussion damage, nor had the hinges for the doors themselves been up to the task. Bolan didn't have to look long to satisfy himself that the men standing guard were out of the fight. Some of them were obviously dead, though probably not all. It didn't matter. He would leave them behind, for they offered no threat, and they could stand witness to the fact that General Orieza was no longer in power.

The precise nature of the general's removal from power remained to be seen. As Bolan stepped through the doorway, he found Orieza alert and waiting for him. His face was bloodied by a cut in his forehead that was oozing badly. Apparently he'd caught a flying piece of shrapnel, perhaps even a chunk of one of the door hinges.

In his grip he held a pearl-handled, gold-plated automatic pistol.

Bolan approached with his weapon rock-steady. Orieza held the small pistol, an ornate Walther PPK, under his own chin, pointed toward his brain. Mack Bolan pulled the bandanna from his face, letting it fall around his neck.

"General Orieza?" he asked.

"The same." The general nodded slowly and carefully. "I am Ramon Orieza. I am…I was…the leader of the Honduran people."

"You know why I'm here?"

"You are an assassin," Orieza said with contempt. "You are here to murder me."

"I'm here to put a stop to your reign of terror."

Orieza waved a dismissing hand. "You… No matter. You are an American? I do not suppose you could tell me if you were. Well, tell your CIA masters that you have succeeded. You may take credit for my work. I have done enough taking of credit from others. Why not you?"

"I don't understand," Bolan said truthfully.

"No," Orieza said. "I do not suppose you do. I am an old man, assassin. Old men do things. Things that are perhaps not so smart. Things they might not do in their youth. Things on which they look back with regret. Now leave an old man be. I wish a moment's peace."

"I can't do that," Bolan said. "Put the gun down. Come with me. Your rule is over, Orieza, but it doesn't mean your life has to be."

"Come with you for what?" Orieza spit. "To spend the rest of my days moldering away in some American prison? Perhaps you will send me to your Guantanamo Bay, hmm? Or exile me to some convenient island? No. It is here and now, or not at all."

"Have it your way," Bolan said. The triangular muzzle of the Desert Eagle never wavered. Orieza ignored it.

"Mark my words," the general said. "When old age comes for you at last, you will remember me, and you will know the horror that it is to grow weak and feeble with years."

"If I live that long," Bolan said, "I'll count it a blessing."

"To hell with you," Orieza said, and shot himself.

The body slumped to the desk. The little Walther had made almost no noise, muffled as it was by Orieza's jaw. The Executioner checked the man's pulse to be sure, but the general was indeed dead. Bolan took out his secure satellite phone and took several pictures. He got shots of Orieza's corpse, the men in the room and the destroyed anteroom. He also made sure that Orieza was clearly identifiable, and clearly dead. The man's brains on the wall behind him left little doubt of that.

The pictures would be of use to the Farm, both for verification and also for public-relations purposes if it became necessary to prove to the world that Orieza truly was dead. Once Bolan had slipped away, the whole thing could be filed under the heading of yet another military coup, staged by elements from within Orieza's own shock troops. After all, wiring the compound with explosives would surely look like an inside job. Disillusioned over the betrayal of his troops and perhaps unwilling to live as a prisoner or a figurehead, Orieza had chosen suicide as his way of escaping capture. That would be how the Farm and its contacts within the intelligence community would present the story to the world. Bolan had little doubt it would be accepted, plausible as it was.

His photos had just been sent when the device vibrated in his hand. He put it to his ear. "Striker."

"Striker, this is Barb," Price said quickly. "Listen very carefully."

"Go ahead," Bolan said.

"We've just received reports from Tucson, Arizona. They've experienced a rapid-fire series of what we're pushing the media to call terrorist attacks. These are, in fact, incursions across the Mexican border, staged by a large force of men using military weapons and support equipment. The United States government has deployed elements of the National Guard to bolster the Border Patrol and the locals down there. We've scrambled a blacksuit field team from the Farm to handle spin and to provide a firm leadership presence."

"Tucson?" Bolan asked. "Barb, are you telling me Mexico has invaded the United States?"

"Nobody's calling it that," Price warned, "but that's basically what's going on. The Man is screaming and Hal says we've got to do something, now, before things go so far that it can't be effectively cloaked as an isolated terrorist event. The only result could be full-scale war with Mexico, unless we can get a lid on this fast. Striker, it's bad. Nobody's saying it out loud, but there's talk of a massive retaliation among the highest levels of U.S. intelligence."

"Is there any doubt that Castillo is doing something related to the scheme he was working with Orieza?"

"None," Price said. "That would be a little too… coincidental."

"Yeah," Bolan said. He shook his head. "I'll meet up with Jack for extract. Just exactly how quickly can you get me back there?"

"We're sending him coordinates and details," Price

confirmed. "I'll arrange for a fast jet to get you to Arizona, and we'll have another vehicle waiting so Jack can get you on scene without delay. The blacksuit field commander is a Jason Platt. His team has already been deployed. I'll transmit you his dossier while you're in the air. He'll have satellite communications and field operations control set up there by the time you arrive."

"I'll need support for an operation like this. Can you give me anybody I know?"

"No," Price told him. "Able Team is occupied elsewhere, and Phoenix Force is in Europe. The blacksuit contingent we're sending you is made of some of our best support field personnel, however. They'll handle whatever you can throw at them. You can depend on Platt."

"All right," Bolan said. He looked down at the corpse of Orieza. "You got my photos?"

"Filing them as we speak," Price said. "Good work on this part of the operation, Striker. Hal will be relieved that we can play this off as a suicide."

"It was Orieza's idea, not mine," Bolan said. "He went out with some dignity, though. I'll give him that."

"Go fast, Striker. Base out."

CHAPTER NINE

Through the pain in every part of his body, through the pounding agony in his head, through the ringing in his ears, Roderigo del Valle thought he was dreaming. When the big, dark-haired man entered the room, he thought he truly had gone mad. A man with a mask over his face stood there. When he pulled the cloth down around his neck, Del Valle could see it was the man from the advance camp, one of the American soldiers. What sort of nightmare was this?

The big man, who spoke English with an American accent, exchanged words with Orieza. Del Valle couldn't understand what was being said; the ringing in his ears was too great. He struggled to find a weapon, any weapon, but his arms wouldn't move. He tried to cry out, and he couldn't. It was as if he hovered over his own body, able to observe but not to act. Was he dying? Was this what it was like, to feel one's soul slowly lifting from one's prone form?

No. No, this couldn't be death, for surely death brought peace and not pain of this kind—

Roderigo del Valle gasped and sat up.

He immediately regretted the sudden movement, for it brought fresh, shooting pains spiking through his skull. A deep wound over his eyes had half blinded him. He was sticky with dried blood from the top of his head to his deeply stained chest, and was covered in fine white plaster dust.

Del Valle had lost his weapons. He looked around and, spotting the dead Orieza, he gasped.

"No!" he shouted. He struggled to get to his feet, finally dragging himself to the desk. The blotter was stained with Orieza's blood. Del Valle pried the gaudy little Walther from the dead man's grip and stared into his lifeless eyes.

This was intolerable! Everything he had worked for, everything he had struggled to achieve…ruined! Del Valle was the power behind the throne, and his shock troops were loyal to him, but this would destabilize everything. With the Casa Presidencial in ruins, the pipeline terminal burning, the invasion of Guatemala forestalled and his deal with Castillo likely off the table now, there was no leverage. Certainly he couldn't hope to transition power to himself, not under these circumstances. Even his shock troops would be uncomfortable with it, and the people would revolt, no matter how strongly he stood on their necks. Another coup would come, regardless. With Orieza he could have found some plausible explanation, some way to blame the United States specifically or the West in general for what had happened. Common enemies were convenient that way, and scapegoats even more so. He could have used Orieza to rally the people. With the man dead, Del Valle would lose the faith of the masses. After all, it was his shock troops who had supposedly protected the life of the general!

As he moved, Del Valle felt his body screaming in protest. He probed at his head gingerly, then delicately at his ribs, and lower, at his abdomen. Something wasn't quite right, most likely cracked ribs. He was in much pain, but he didn't think anything was permanent. His knowledge of internal organ damage was rudimentary, and much of it had been gleaned through interrogations, but he thought he knew enough to judge himself intact.

He checked the Walther's action, found it fouled and cleared it. Then he put it in his waistband. He found one of the guards' M-16 rifles, but it had been badly damaged when the heavy reinforced doors had fallen. In the anteroom, he found another, this one bloodstained but apparently functional. He tested it, firing a couple rounds into the already damaged wall, and was satisfied with its performance.

The radio on his belt was smashed. Del Valle checked one of the desks in the anteroom. It was bullet-scarred, and he feared the worst, but the backup radio he kept in the drawer was there, and it worked. As he turned it on, it immediately came to life with the voice of his lieutenant, Manuel Giarelli. The man was frantic, desperate to find him.

"This is Del Valle," he acknowledged. "I am with the general. Meet me here. I require your assistance," he said as he returned to the general's side.

Those words, "I require your assistance," were code. They indicated that Del Valle was in severe distress and that Giarelli should be prepared for the worst.

Even with the coded warning, Giarelli looked shocked when he arrived and found Del Valle in the company of a dead General Orieza.

"The general," he said. "He is…?"

"What do you think, you fool?" Del Valle snapped. "We must make haste."

Giarelli winced at the rebuke but nodded obediently. The team of men with him were Del Valle's loyal personal guard, his most experienced fighters. He was confident they could be trusted.

"Get me a medic," Del Valle said. "I require attention before I will be able to travel." One of the guards hurried to obey.

"Commander, what shall we do?"

"I will call President Castillo," Del Valle said thoughtfully. "He can help us. He may be an obnoxious, uncooperative, arrogant fool, but he thinks we have helped him in the past, and he believes Orieza is to blame for any friction between us and him. If I contact him, tell him that Orieza has fallen victim to his own arrogance, and that I, an experienced military man commanding a loyal force of soldiers who could be swayed to lend their guns to his, he will be pleased. He will help me at least to enter Mexico and then the United States, if I wish it. I will promise him the use of our men, and he will believe me. He has no reason not to…unless one of you is a spy for Castillo."

"Of course not, sir." Giarelli shook his head.

"It does not matter," Del Valle said. He gritted his teeth against a scream as his lieutenant helped him from the demolished office. Once in the anteroom, he sat on a bullet-scarred desk, doing his best not to jostle his ribs. "Give me a report, Manuel. Can our people be trusted?"

"My team is loyal to you, sir," Giarelli said, wide-eyed. "Unfortunately, we have lost a great deal of men.

The destruction wrought by our enemies has left dozens, perhaps hundreds unaccounted for. While I waited for your call, I did my best to direct recovery efforts, but we are losing control, sir. The people are in a mad panic, and General Orieza's political enemies are already starting to shout loudly that he has lost his grip on the capital. The rumors of attacks on our military are starting to spread beyond our ability to suppress them, no matter who we threaten, beat or kill. There is even talk that the press will cover this in today's papers, regardless of the rules General Orieza set in place."

"I see," Del Valle said. He had feared as much. To maintain control required fear, and to maintain fear demanded one show no weakness, ever. A few military losses were one thing. Wholesale destruction of the military infrastructure he had built under Orieza, combined with this high-profile attack on the seat of government that so fully annihilated the symbols of Orieza's might, couldn't be concealed. Nor could it be absorbed by an already malcontented citizenry chafing under Orieza's rule. Showing weakness emboldened the myriad forces who would only too gladly depose Orieza, and with him Del Valle's enforcement arm.

For some time, Del Valle had fought to suppress the workings of a resistance movement in Honduras. This had taken a great deal of time and effort. Many men and women had disappeared into his secret prisons. The potential for armed resistance was there, of course, but more fundamentally, there was a seething, lurking sentiment in the people that was only barely kept in check. Given any hope of breaking free of the yoke Del Valle and Orieza had put on them, the people would jump at the chance the moment they thought they might succeed.

There was precedent for this behavior. Del Valle was a student of such politics. He was reminded, for example, of the student protests in theocratic Iran. The regime there kept very tight control of its people, and those who dared speak out were punished harshly. Yet periodically, when emboldened by what they saw as any hint of weakness in their masters, those young enough to be brave and bold enough to commit their lives to a cause would take to the streets despite the dangers of imprisonment and execution. No doubt Iran, too, had its secret prisons, and no doubt someday the people would storm their walls as the French had the Bastille.

He suddenly had a premonition.

"Manuel," he said. "The prison here. What is its status?"

Giarelli swallowed. "I was coming to that, sir. We have lost contact with the warden."

There was only one prison to which Del Valle could be referring. It had no name; it was a secret facility here in the capital, where those who opposed Orieza's regime were dropped until they died of torture or were forgotten. Despite Del Valle's best attempts to keep it hidden from public knowledge, these things had a way of coming out, and he had suspected for some months now that its location and its purpose were known to at least some who had rebel tendencies.

Del Valle turned pale. "It is worse than I thought," he said.

"Sir?"

"We are losing control, Manuel," he said. "We will

be fortunate if we are not ourselves caught and hanged before this is over."

"Sir, the people would never—"

"Please, Manuel—" Del Valle waved a weary hand "—spare me any naive proclamations. The people most certainly would. And you know it as well as I."

A medic was finally found and brought to him. Del Valle suffered the man's ministrations in silence. The doctor taped his ribs, checked him over as best he could, and cleaned and bandaged his head wound.

"Sir," the medic said with a trembling voice, "if that will be all, I must see to the other wounded."

"You seem very nervous, Doctor, for someone so eager to tend to the suffering of others."

"Sir?"

Del Valle felt a cold fury rising inside him. These worms, these cowards, had served him when he paid them, when it was clear he held power. He could set a stopwatch by their loyalties the moment things started to go wrong, however. How dare this miserable wretch—

"Sir!" Manuel yelled.

"Wh-what?" Del Valle broke from his reverie. He realized he was standing. The little gold-plated Walther was in his hand, its slide locked half-open by a stovepipe jam. The medic lay dead at Del Valle's feet, leaking blood from four bullet holes in his chest.

"Sir, did he do something wrong?"

Del Valle shook himself. He forced himself to clear the Walther but, realizing he had no spare magazines, he threw the weapon aside. "I need a pistol," he said absently.

"Take mine, sir." Manuel handed the weapon butt-first to Del Valle. It was a Browning Hi-Power, common enough among Orieza's forces. He slipped it into his holster without thinking.

"We must make preparations to leave, Manuel," he said finally. "It is neither safe nor prudent to remain. What happened in the street outside?"

"There was much damage, sir," Giarelli admitted. "We do not have enough men to secure the Casa Presidencial. Several times now, the few guards I have posted outside have been fired on."

"Fired on? By whom?"

"Armed insurrectionists, sir. Rebels."

So. It had started already. Del Valle, looking at his wristwatch—somehow it had survived the blast that had injured him so badly—realized that he had to have been fading in and out of consciousness for quite some time. Long enough for news of the devastation here in the capital to spread like wildfire, as Del Valle knew it would. Long enough for emboldened revolutionary elements to screw up their courage and take up arms against what remained of the power structure he had put in place.

"Bring me a satellite phone," Del Valle demanded.

"Here, sir," Giarelli said, handing his commander an ungainly Iridium unit.

"Come with me," Del Valle said. "Bring the men. We are leaving. We are leaving *now*."

Surrounded by his contingent of shock troops, Del Valle mustered all the dignity he could. Already, his sense of self was returning. His injury had left him vulnerable, had caused him to lose control. But he saw now that this was a weakness, an indulgence, that he couldn't afford. He was Roderigo del Valle, and if these peasants couldn't see how Orieza's leadership—as helmed by Del Valle, of course—had benefited them, then to hell with them. He would find a place within Castillo's regime and prove his worth, working his way up once again into a position of power.

It was to this end that he established the call, finally, with one of Castillo's underlings. It took some doing, but eventually he was able to get the president himself on the line. Castillo, as he always seemed to, knew more than he had let on.

"Well, well," Castillo said mockingly. "If it isn't the power behind the throne."

"You know of me?" Del Valle asked.

"Of course I know you, Roderigo," Castillo said. "Your work behind President Orieza was not so secret, you know. I had many spies within the ranks of your shock troops, at the height of your power and our working relationship. They were easily enough purchased. I make it my business to know with whom I am dealing. With whom I am *really* dealing."

"Then you know why I am calling."

"I can guess. News from Honduras is not good. I saw a report on CNN just now. Your domestic woes have made the Western press. It will only get worse."

"A coup has taken place," Del Valle lied smoothly. "General Orieza, unfortunately, did not survive."

"And your own plans?"

"I seek employment elsewhere," Del Valle said. "A man of my talents can be very useful."

"In what way can you be useful to me?" Castillo pressed.

Del Valle had to think quickly. It was time to put Castillo off his footing by showing him that he wasn't the only one with inside information of the other's activities. "President Castillo, unless you do not wish to see your operation in Tucson, Arizona, devastated as was Orieza's regime, I suggest you make use of what I know."

"What do you know?" he asked. Del Valle could picture the man's eyes narrowing.

"I know that the Americans were behind this 'coup,'" Del Valle said, though he was certain of very little. "I know that they are aware of what you are doing in Tucson, and they have dispatched the very commando team used to assault my nation. They are coming for you this time, *Mr. President*."

There was real concern in Castillo's voice when he spoke again. "You have knowledge of these men?"

"I have seen them," he said, and that was only partly a lie. "I know how they operate. And I have a force of experienced fighters, dedicated enforcers loyal to me, who will come with me and hunt them."

Castillo wasn't stupid. He had little to lose from accepting Del Valle's offer, and much to gain. "Very well," he said. "If you can reach Mexican airspace, I will see to it you are not molested."

"You can arrange from there to get me and my men across the border into the United States?"

"We have methods for this," Castillo said. "It can be done."

"I will need knowledge of the specifics of your operation."

"I will have a briefing prepared for you. I am sure you'll know what to do with it."

No doubt this briefing would be heavily redacted; Del Valle had no illusions that Castillo trusted him, nor would the Mexican president share any information about his machinations than weren't absolutely necessary to Del Valle's search-and-destroy mission.

"We will need weapons and ammunition."

"They can be provided," Castillo said. "If you manage to do this, you will secure a place for yourself in my administration, Roderigo."

"So it shall be," Del Valle said. He swallowed his distaste. Now wasn't the time for pride, no matter how much he might be picturing ramming Castillo's teeth down the arrogant man's throat. The call was ended without another word from Castillo's end.

Del Valle swore as he handed the phone back to Giarelli.

"Sir?" The lieutenant looked concerned.

"We have a home, if we can earn it," Del Valle said.

"Where are we going, sir? Mexico?"

"Yes." Del Valle nodded. "And from there to Tucson, Arizona."

"Sir?" Giarelli now looked confused. "Why do we wish to go there?"

"Unfinished business," Del Valle said hotly. "We follow the smell of smoke and the flicker of flames until we find these destroyers of men who have so ruined us.

The Americans who did this must pay for their crimes. I want revenge, Manuel, and I shall have it."

"Yes, sir. We will follow you, of course." Giarelli asked no questions. He didn't wonder how his leader could simply label the attackers Americans without evidence. He didn't question the wisdom of Del Valle's course of action. He did not express his wish to stay safe in Castillo's Mexico, or to travel somewhere else. He obeyed, quickly and completely, and that was what made him valuable.

"I expect nothing less," Del Valle said.

As they emerged from the fire-blackened, bomb-scarred presidential residence, small-arms fire rang out. Del Valle was pleased to see his contingent of elite guardsmen spread out to protect him, their weapons ready. They returned fire from their M-16s, but the attack wasn't in force. They were being sniped at from behind the perimeter barriers by the first and boldest would-be rebels.

In this way empires were dashed to pieces.

The heliport, miraculously, was undamaged. The Bell 412 utility chopper Del Valle kept fueled and ready was still waiting under its camouflage netting. Nearby, a Saladin armored vehicle smoked, its hull blackened by fire. Perhaps he had this vehicle to thank for the work of providence; the six-wheeled armored car had taken the brunt of the blasts that had dealt such terrible destruction to his elite troops' encampment.

Giarelli would act as pilot, and he readied the air-craft as two other guards removed the netting, and the remaining men guarded their position. Several times they fired their weapons. It was no longer the sporadic small-arms fire that worried Del Valle, however. He now feared something more.

The people were coming.

He could hear the crowds massing, filling the streets and spilling over the barricades surrounding what was left of Liberty Square. The crowd produced a unique murmur, an undercurrent of speaking, shouting, interwoven with the rallying cries of agitators. It was the sound of major discontent. Orieza had asked him if it was true that the people were angry. That sound told Del Valle that, yes, the people *were* angry, and he had better flee.

That sound was the sound of a mob.

Del Valle had no desire to end his life kicking at the end of a rope thrown over a lamppost. As he climbed into the chopper with his men, he felt a sense of relief. Manuel would fly them to Toncontin International Airport. There, in a closed hangar known to very few, he kept a jet prepared for immediate departure. Its range was far more than necessary to take him to Mexico. He could still escape.

As the Bell 412 took to the sky, the shouts from the mob entering the grounds of Casa Presidencial rose to a fever pitch. A few brave souls fired on the chopper, but they didn't have the weapons necessary to do much damage. One of Del Valle's men shoved the sliding door aside and poked the muzzle of his M-16 out the opening, firing back. It would be next to impossible to spot any snipers on the ground, and even more unlikely that the trooper would hit them, but at least the man showed initiative.

Suddenly, Del Valle had an uncontrollable urge.

"Give me your weapon," he demanded. He held out his hand and snapped his fingers impatiently. The trooper handed over the weapon and proffered a fresh 30-round magazine, which Del Valle snatched eagerly.

Depose his regime, would they? March in the streets demanding his blood, dared they? He would show them. He was Roderigo del Valle, and the penalty for disloyalty was death!

"Manuel," he called over the noise of the helicopter's rotors, "take us in low and across that crowd. Keep my side pointed toward them."

Giarelli looked back. He understood what Del Valle intended, and he obeyed. He nodded and piloted the helicopter as instructed.

Del Valle fastened his harness and leaned as far out the open sliding door as he deemed safe. Then he braced the assault rifle in his arms, took careful aim and squeezed the trigger. He fired repeatedly, milking bursts from the weapon until the partially spent magazine was empty. Then he dropped it, replaced it with the 30-rounder his shock trooper had given him, and bent once again to his bloody work.

He couldn't hear the screams. As he swept the crowd of Honduran civilians with pitiless bursts of 5.56-mm fire, killing women, men and even children indiscriminately, he could hear only one thing.

The sound of his own hysterical laughter.

CHAPTER TEN

Darkness had fallen again when Bolan reached Tucson, Arizona. Wearing his 9-mm Beretta in a shoulder holster and the .44 Desert Eagle on his hip, his rifle on its single-point sling at his side, he stepped out of the Boeing AH-6 light attack and reconnaissance helicopter. Other weapons of war hung from his combat harness. He jerked his chin at Grimaldi—waving wasn't the best idea when standing under a chopper's spinning rotor blades—and made for the barricades, where several armored police vehicles, countless local squad cars, SUVs belonging to the Border Patrol and a large black panel van bearing roof-mounted satellite equipment were parked.

Based on the Little Bird scout choppers originally designed for the U.S. Army for service in Vietnam, Grimaldi's loaner AH-6 bore an M-134 7.62-mm six-barrel minigun and an M2-60 7-shot, 70-mm rocket pod loaded with remote-fusing Hydra 70 rockets. It was an impressive little machine, and Grimaldi was obviously happy to transport Bolan in something that could bite back. He lifted off now, giving the Executioner the thumbs-up. The Farm was coordinating activities through the field communications van and giving Grimaldi his orders. He was, Bolan knew, tasked with providing air support and reconnaissance while the soldier assessed the situation. The Stony Man pilot wore night-vision gear and flew with his running lights off, the black chopper blending into the night sky with surprising ease.

Bolan made a beeline to the communications van. Barbara Price had told him to look for Jason Platt, the Stony Man Farm field commander for the blacksuit contingent. If he was anywhere, he would be with that van, or nearby. The blacksuits were Stony Man Farm's collateral-support commando teams. They assisted Able Team, Phoenix Force and Bolan when necessary. Every one of those men and women was a highly trained operative. In situations like this one, where a large perimeter needed to be secured under semicovert circumstances, a blacksuit team was ideally suited to the task.

PLATT, EITHER BY BRIEFING or simply intuition, picked Bolan out of the crowd the moment the big soldier came into view. He motioned for the Executioner to join him at the side of the van. The sliding door was open, and one of the blacksuits who reported to Platt operated a field communications rig that looked like the cockpit of a spacecraft. Surrounded by screens and wearing a microphone headset with a monocular feed over one eye, the operator was typing on two different keyboards set at angles facing his chair.

"Striker?" Platt asked, using one of the cover identities the Farm had assigned to Bolan. He almost did a double take as his eyes traveled over the reversed hilts of the knives strapped to Bolan's combat harness, but to his credit he didn't miss a beat. He extended his hand.

Bolan nodded and accepted the handshake. "You'd be Jason Platt?"

"I would, sir." His grip was firm. In his early forties, Platt kept his head shaved to just the barest whisper of a receding hairline. He was as tall as Bolan, but leaner, tending toward a wiry build Bolan associated with tunnel rats and scouts. He was, as the commando's namesake implied, wearing a combat blacksuit, the formfitting battle-dress utilities bulging with pockets and pouches. A .45-caliber pistol was strapped to his chest in an almost antique leather tanker holster.

"Here, sir," he said, and held out his other hand. In it was a plastic case, and inside that, Bolan found, was an earbud transceiver of the type the Farm's commandos regularly used for short-range local communication. He fitted the device in his left ear.

"Check, check," he said.

"Five by five," Platt answered, and Bolan nodded to indicate that he could hear the man's words in his transceiver, as well.

Bolan looked around. The squad cars had their LED light bars running, but the night was quiet except for the engines of heavy armored vehicles moving. Somewhere in the distance he could hear the thrumming of Grimaldi's helicopter. He thought he heard distant shouts, too, but that might have been his imagination.

"Why is it so quiet?" he asked.

"Calm before the storm, sir," Platt said, grimacing. "You got here too late to see us turning away family members."

"What do you mean?"

"Family and friends of the hostages. You know how

people are, sir. When something like this happens, they show up out of the woodwork, usually because the cell-phone calls have already started from inside the target zone. It's very common when active shooters hit schools and other public places. We had to broom at least thirty people out of here."

"How many hostages are inside? Do we have an estimate?"

"Upward of twenty or thirty, at least," Platt said. "The hit started during the tail end of the working day. There were a lot of government employees still inside when it went down, and there have been some threats to start shooting them. The invaders haven't made any coherent demands yet, though. My guess is they're testing us. They want to see if we'll use force to dislodge them, and so far we've got them thinking we won't. With luck that will buy the hostages some time. If they think there's no hurry they won't be so fast to take this to the next level."

"Agreed." Bolan nodded.

"We've got the local media corralled at a bottleneck at the end of South Randolph Way. It will keep them far enough from the action that none of them gets hurt. We've put together a package—" Platt nodded to the blacksuit at the communications station "—that will blame the whole thing on fringe domestic terrorists, a homegrown racist outfit. That will explain away the broadcasts they've made."

"Broadcasts?"

"As soon as they arrived on site, the invaders set up a portable transmitter and started broadcasting a video signal," Platt explained. "They were doing the standard hostage dog-and-pony show for a while, forcing the public employees they've captured to beg for cooperation from authorities, that sort of thing. Then the leader started raving about the Reconquista, saying they were going to restore to Mexico what was rightfully hers, drive the Anglos back into the sea. That's what flagged the operations team at the Farm. We scrambled shortly thereafter. As soon as we set up our perimeter, we fired up full-spectrum jamming equipment." He pointed up at the dishes and other equipment on the roof of the van. "They're cut off now, no RF or wireless phones in or out. Only our commo gear will work inside the sphere of our range. That means Zapata can't make any more speeches."

"*Tristan* Zapata?"

"Yes, and that's confirmed by the Farm, sir." Platt nodded. He showed Bolan a printed screen shot. The blurry image of Tristan Zapata, recognizable from Bolan's briefing at the mission's outset, was staring wild-eyed at the camera. Zapata was a lanky, gaunt man with a tangled shock of curly brown hair. In the photo he was wearing what appeared to be an old green flight suit, over which he wore belts and bandoliers containing ammunition and equipment. An old wooden-stocked Uzi submachine gun was gripped in his fist, and his finger was on the trigger.

"So Castillo is probably the man in charge, given his file," Bolan stated.

"Exactly. Unless he's an unknowing figurehead for other interests," Platt said darkly. "I'd swear that we're dealing with elements of the Mexican military, sir."

"What makes you think that?"

"The weapons and uniforms they're carrying and wearing are off-the-rack for Mexican army," Platt said. "From what we've seen in our surveillance and reconnaissance, anyway. My men and the locals heard them shouting commands in Spanish, too."

"That's not much to call evidence."

"Call it a gut feeling then, sir." There was a hard edge to Platt's voice.

Bolan nodded. "I do. Give me the layout. What are we up against, specifically?"

Platt produced a printed color map, most likely produced within the operations van. It was an enhanced satellite image of the terrain on which they stood. It showed the government facilities at 900 South Randolph Way, next to a park and several paved lots full of cars. On the other side of the road, buildings fronted a large golf course. Several notations had been overlaid on the map in high-contrast print.

"We haven't been able to verify their numbers," he said, "but the invading force is large enough that they've been able to take and hold the government complex with undisputed authority. Local police and fire responded to the first reports of an incident, and were cut down the moment they arrived. It was a real slaughter. Our initial satellite imaging shows them camped throughout the golf course, through here, and here—" he pointed at the map "—not to mention throughout the park on this side. They hold the buildings and have been digging in since we arrived and erected our perimeter. We've been able to keep them contained, but they've taken shots at us. Right now, anything from south of East Twenty-Second street is a no-go zone. The rest of the perimeter extends here, here and here." He pointed again, defining a roughly rectangular area on the map.

"Armament?" Bolan asked.

"Automatic weapons, explosives and rockets, at the very least. It's a full-scale military operation, sir. Before we got on scene they were giving the locals a really hard time. They blew up a couple of squad cars and one SWAT van. Casualties have been light so far among the locals, but we're tracking some disturbing reports as part of the containment."

"What do you mean?"

"Apparently this force cut a swath from the border. There were atrocities. Whole families murdered in their homes, anti-Anglo racist graffiti left behind. The screwed-up part is that it will work for us as part of the cover-up."

"Is that a problem?" Bolan asked. Platt had spoken through nearly clenched teeth.

"I don't like it, sir. I don't like it at all. The United States has been invaded by Mexican nationals, and we're covering it up to avoid a public panic."

"That's what we do, Commander Platt," Bolan said. "You knew that when you signed on with the Sensitive Operations Group."

"I know, sir." Platt shook his head. "And I'll do my job. It's just that, well, if we do our jobs, nobody will ever know that elements of the Mexican military have crossed the border and killed American citizens."

"No," Bolan said. "That's true. They won't. We put out small blazes before they become political forest fires. We stand between the United States and anarchy, Platt. We are the guardians. We fight terror so the American people won't be terrified. In so doing we save innocent lives."

"I don't question that, sir," Platt said. "But it still stinks. The people deserve to know who their enemies are."

"If there's one thing I've learned through the years," Bolan said, "it's that they already do, Commander. They already do. We protect the people from the worst of it, but they're not stupid. On some level they know who their friends and their enemies are."

Platt nodded. "I hope so, sir."

Bolan clapped a hand on Platt's shoulder. "Know so. Have faith in the citizenry of the United States, Commander. I do. It's what keeps me going, even though there's a dirty job to do."

"Understood, sir."

"Continue the containment. Make sure none of our terrorists escape the cordon you've set up. Run any interference you have to with local authorities and especially the press, but keep them all out of it. Enough people have died. It's time to remove the threat."

Platt nodded.

Bolan left him there. The man knew his job. Now it was the Executioner's turn to do his.

He stalked toward the barricades, reflexively touching two fingers to his left ear. "G-force, this is Striker. Do you read me?"

"Loud and clear, Striker," Grimaldi responded. The beat of the little Boeing's rotor blades was audible when he transmitted, but the earbuds' filtering circuits cut it to tolerable levels.

"What's it look like from up there?"

"I'm buzzing along the perimeter, Sarge," Grimaldi reported. "We've got the airspace to ourselves. The Farm, coordinating through our field communications, is warning off all air traffic from this part of the city. That means no news choppers to worry about."

"You're my ace in the hole, G-force," Bolan told him. "Be ready. I'm going to hit them, use you to draw them off as I go, then funnel as many as possible into your sights. Once I'm inside the facility, cover Platt's people until I work my way back out to you."

"And then?"

"And then it'll be over," Bolan said. "Let's get to work."

"On it, Sarge," Grimaldi said. "G-force out."

Bolan slipped through the outer barriers, checked his rifle and started trotting. He ran at an easy pace that was more like a jog, heading across the golf course. There were stands of trees and occasional outbuildings that he could use for cover, but there were also large tracts of manicured grass that were completely open. The darkness of night was the greatest ally Bolan now had.

From his war bag he withdrew a compact pair of night-vision goggles, another innovation for which he could thank Gadgets Schwarz. The Stony Man electronics expert had managed to design a commercial night-vision unit that was slightly more comfortable, making the whole thing more compact and less of a liability in combat. He put on the goggles and switched on the power. The greens stretching before him came to life in strangely flat shades of artificially enhanced illumination.

After the jungles of Honduras and the streets of

Tegucigalpa, the vast emptiness of the Arizona golf course felt alien to Bolan. In a half crouch, he moved silently nonetheless, once more an avenging, black-clad wraith.

His plan was to move across one corner of the golf course, eliminating those invaders he could while using that action to draw in any others stationed there. If he were running the invasion, he would concentrate most of his force in and around the government buildings to hold them, using the remainder of his men to provide perimeter defense as mobile patrols. The golf course and the park were two areas too vast to cover any other way, and thus they were the points of vulnerability a savvy military strategist would seek to protect. The key to breaching the government complex, then, was to make sure there was somewhere for the hostages to go. If they had no route for an extraction, either that park or this golf course, the complex could become an abattoir. Bolan wouldn't walk them into La Raza terrorists' guns.

Platt was convinced that the Mexican military was involved, and Bolan had no doubt that at least some of the fighting force against which he was now pitted was comprised of men drawn from military units south of the border. The presence of Zapata, however, guaranteed that many of them would be Zapata's own racist gunmen. Military personnel, even those who normally answered to a succession of notoriously corrupt governments, would chafe at the thought of taking orders from a civilian idealist, no matter how bloodthirsty that idealist might be. It was to be expected that Castillo would use Zapata, whom the Farm had determined was working with or for the Mexican government, to shield him from fallout should anything go wrong during this brazen foray. Zapata's psych profile, once again based on the dossier the Farm had transmitted to Bolan at the mission's outset, wasn't that of a stable or cooperative man. If Zapata was being allowed to run amok in Tucson, he had to at least believe he was calling the shots.

All of this meant he probably was doing just that. Capturing or killing Zapata would be the key to neutralizing this violent incursion onto United States soil. It stood to reason that Castillo would probably have committed only enough troops to help Zapata do that. The rest of the manpower would be La Raza true believers following Zapata for their own reasons…or even paid mercenaries, which wasn't very likely. Mercenaries tended to seek employment from those who could be relied on to pay them—men who were, in other words, stable and reasonable. By reputation, Zapata was neither of those.

With no firm numbers on the enemy, Bolan would have to play it by ear. He had a lot of experience in that sort of thing; he was nothing if not flexible in combat. He had the advantage of surprise, much as he'd had in the jungles of Honduras. They wouldn't expect a lone night-stalking demon in their midst. They were the men with the guns and power, after all, lording it over helpless men and women. To meet sudden resistance would put them off balance. They expected to be beset by authorities from outside, probably ineffectually, but they were no doubt braced for the possibility of armed attack from the perimeter. They would use the hostages as shields in that event, if Bolan was any judge. It was how predators thought.

Mack's plan was a simple one. A single motivated fighter, especially with the air support of Grimaldi in his little attack chopper, could infiltrate the enemy's lines, fight his way into the government buildings and then break the back of the terrorists from within, in order to free the hostages.

The night was nearly moonless, for which Bolan was grateful. If the golf course had any outdoor lighting, it was shut off, either by the terrorists or by the authorities outside. The specifics didn't matter. Bolan couldn't know if the invading force had night-vision equipment, so the darkness might not be his advantage alone. But his own night goggles were the best available. He moved confidently across the rolling contours of the golf course, his weapon ready.

He wasn't surprised to find his first patrol before he had moved very far. There were four men squatting on a rise above a sand trap. The smell of cigarette smoke tipped off the soldier long before he actually saw them. When he did finally have them in his sights, he was lying on his stomach on a close-cropped green hillock overlooking the bunker.

The four were dressed in BDUs, and they carried M-16 rifles. The uniforms bore no insignia that he could see at this distance, but if those men were ragtag nationalist terrorists, he would be very surprised. Granted, they were not sporting Mexican FX-05 assault weapons, which would have as good as signed Mexico's name to the incursion. Castillo and the people working for him weren't stupid. They would hardly have equipped their invasion force with hardware so distinctly traceable.

Nonetheless, the soldiers did, indeed, look like Mexican army to Bolan. Platt's instincts were good, it seemed. At the very least, they matched Bolan's own.

The distance was at the outside range of his Beretta 93-R, but he had made longer shots. He had, in fact, made shots at distances that would cause armchair firearms experts to scoff that the 9-mm bullet simply couldn't travel that far, or travel that far accurately.

Bolan had never put much faith in such pronouncements.

The suppressor screwed to his weapon's threaded barrel would make it less accurate, but he had fired countless thousands of rounds through it with the device attached. He knew what to expect.

The Executioner drew the machine pistol, flicked the selector switch to single shot and braced the 93-R in two hands, stretching out his arms.

He drew in a breath, let out half of it, paused and pressed the trigger with the pad of his index finger.

The 147-grain hollowpoint subsonic bullet took the first man in the head. He fell backward, landing awkwardly. The other men turned to stare at him, uncomprehending. While their brains tried desperately to process what they had just seen, Bolan put a bullet through the head of the next man.

The next two shots had to come faster. The terrorists—or Mexican soldiers, or invaders, or however these men should be classified—were now reaching for their rifles. A few shots would be all that was needed to expose Bolan's position and bring down the rest of the nearby patrols on his head. He couldn't afford that; he had to retain the element of surprise.

The third man took a round through the face as he turned. He fell forward, blurting out a dying sound that would be lost in the night. The fourth man had almost managed to bring his rifle up for a shot when Bolan drilled him through the neck. The Executioner put a second round through the man's face when the mortally wounded terrorist swayed in place; death was assured, but Bolan couldn't give him a chance to pull the trigger. Dead twice over, the corpse finally hit the green.

It wasn't quite a hole in one, but then, Mack Bolan wasn't finished yet.

CHAPTER ELEVEN

Bolan continued across the golf course. He found three more patrols, and in each case, he killed them to the last man with the suppressed Beretta 93-R. There was little chance he would be discovered, and even less chance he would be taken by the likes of these men; they weren't in his league.

He worked his way back around the golf course and toward the largest concentration of parked vehicles near the government buildings. Here, there was considerably more activity. He couldn't tell if an alarm of some kind had been raised, but he didn't think so. Apparently the jamming was effectively cutting off the field patrols from the invaders in the government complex. It was either that, or the patrols didn't check in often enough for Bolan's removal of them to raise a commotion, at least not yet.

As he went about his grim work, he could hear the rotors of Grimaldi's chopper overhead in the night sky. The noise waxed and waned as his position changed.

Bolan gave the invaders credit for fire discipline; none of them took potshots at a target they wouldn't be able to see well enough to damage to any degree. For his part, Grimaldi and the Boeing could have torn up many of the enemy with only a few trigger pulls and button presses. That wouldn't help the hostages that Zapata held, however, and it just might get them killed.

Bolan found a stand of trees opposite the road dividing the golf course from the government buildings. From there, he could observe the enemy encampment surrounding his primary target. Canvas-covered two-and-a-half-ton trucks were parked in a semicircle protecting the main entrance to the complex. Sandbag barriers had been set up in front of them, and gunners with bipod-equipped RPK light machine guns were positioned behind the bags. These men wore a greater variety of clothing, although all of it was military castoffs or paramilitary gear such as fatigue vests. The troops were sloppier; some had long hair, while others wore metal piercings that glinted in the headlights of the trucks, turned on to provide illumination in the parking lot. Apparently the authorities, or Platt's men, had indeed cut the power to the area.

It also made sense that, if what he had surmised was true and this invasion force was made up of Zapata's La Raza goons augmented by Mexican military men provided by Castillo, the roving patrols farthest from the perimeter would be the more experienced, better-trained soldiers. Sitting behind a barrier with a rifle was something anyone, even a haphazardly trained, ill-disciplined terrorist, could do with relative ease. Patrolling a stretch of ground to protect it from incursion by SWAT teams or the American military would be a job for the Mexican troops.

Not that they'd stood for long in that capacity. The best plans of men in combat were often nullified by unknown variables, and Bolan was nothing if not that.

He monitored the comings and goings of the guards outside the complex for a time. On his secure satellite phone he had a complete floor plan of the buildings and surrounding area, over which had been uploaded the positions of Platt's blacksuits. Bolan checked it now. Pushing his night-vision gear onto his forehead, he cupped his hand over the dimly lit screen to prevent even the faintest hint of illumination from giving him away.

He was preparing to stow the phone and plot his route over, around and through the enemy to the nearest entrance to the complex, when he realized the layout was working against him. The attackers' cordon was sloppy, but it was dense. He'd have a hard time getting past.

He needed a distraction.

"Striker to Platt," he said.

"Platt here." The voice in his earbud was tinny but audible.

"Platt, I need a distraction. Something to occupy the guards at the front entrance."

"Give me a moment, sir." Bolan waited for perhaps thirty seconds before his earbud came to life again. "Platt to Striker. Platt to Striker."

"Striker," Bolan said quietly. "Go ahead."

"I think I have just the thing, sir. I'm going to release a vehicle we've been holding. It is now inbound to you," Platt reported. "A news van."

"Is that advisable?" Bolan asked. "We're supposed to be containing reports of this."

"Tactic of opportunity, sir," Platt said, although he stopped short of sounding apologetic. "They're a squirrelly public-radio-looking news team operating from a little nine-volt news-talk station near the border. WKAL, it's called. The terrorists used a runner to bring us the request several hours ago. They asked for this station specifically. Said they were the least biased toward their cause and therefore their 'vessel of choice' to bring the truth to the masses, or some crap like that. I'm not sure how, but they got the word out beyond us, either by phone before we started jamming, or through some pre-arrangement. The news van showed up almost before we got the note. We've been holding them here since, and they're none too happy about it. Bitching about the Constitution and freedom of the press and so on. To be honest, sir, I don't really blame them. A small part of me wants to set them loose. Apparently somebody realized they might need to speak to these yahoos in Spanish. A translator they sent for just showed up. We checked him over and sent him in with the others."

"Understood," Bolan said. "Will they be broadcasting from inside?"

"No, sir," Platt answered. "Our jamming is still in place. Per what they think our arrangement is, and as instructed through me by Stony Man Farm, they'll record an interview. Then, on the way out, we'll stop them, strip them of all their equipment and send them on their way with a legal gag order arranged by the Justice Department. That will keep them from reporting anything too damaging until we've informed them what the official story is. As I understand it, the paperwork says that in order for these political dissidents to get a fair trial, reporting that hasn't been fact-checked will bias the jury pool."

Bolan almost laughed at that. He detected Brognola's very dry sense of bureaucratic humor in those words. To

Platt, he said, "Good thinking. It'll keep the terrorists occupied, maybe discourage them from shooting the hostages for a while longer."

"Yes, sir," Platt said. "You should see them any minute now."

The WKAL news van, a beige Ford panel model with an extending satellite rig on the roof, was already in view. When it reached the sandbag barriers, a couple of the gunmen stationed there moved a set of wooden sawhorses being used as a makeshift gate. The van was ushered inside and the sawhorses were replaced.

When the WKAL van passed his position, Bolan was no longer hidden in the stand of trees. He was running for it, using the van to cover his movement, following in the lee of the vehicle. The rotor sound overhead grew in volume as he did so. Apparently Grimaldi, trying to help cover his movements, was flying closer, using his Boeing to create a wash of white noise that would conceal any sounds Bolan might make.

The soldier got past the outer defenses fronting the government complex, and as he ran, he held the Beretta 93-R. His arm flashed out to full extension as he put a single suppressed slug through the face of one of the two guards by the sawhorses. Then he aimed across his own chest and shot the man on his left.

The van took a left turn, following a driveway that would take it to an access door around the side of the building now facing Bolan. The Executioner broke right, hoping to find some other means of entering the place before he was confronted by another guard.

The rotor noise grew louder still. Bolan couldn't understand why Grimaldi was coming so close. He looked up to wave the pilot off.

The first salvo of small-caliber bullets nearly tore his head off.

Bolan ducked and rolled. He had the fleeting impression of a helicopter inches away from his own face. As he hit the pavement, he realized that was an optical illusion. The helicopter had looked so large and thus so close because it was so small.

The UAV!

He ran back toward the front of the building, toward the semicircle of trucks. As he ducked and weaved, the ripping of automatic weapons followed him. Chips blown from the pavement pelted his ankles. The sound of the rotorcraft UAV was deafening as it closed in behind him, trailing him with the implacable, tireless, unblinking lens of its camera eye.

He started to detour toward a side parking lot, feinting as if he would charge that way. The UAV unleashed one of its rockets. The nearest car exploded, spraying hot shrapnel and raining flaming debris. The cars next to it were rocked and scorched.

A second rocket touched off another fireball among the cars, this time powerful enough to detonate the gas tank of the vehicle parked next to that one. Bolan, with no real cover nearby except a building he couldn't enter, ran toward the flames.

He picked his spot and rolled through, feeling his war bag flatten against his body as he did so. The M-16 scraped the pavement as he went. There was no time to worry about that. Automatic fire from the helical-feed guns mounted on the little chopper's skids was lighting up the moonless night, pursuing Bolan mercilessly.

The explosions had drawn the attention of every terrorist invader nearby. They were firing on him now, without a real idea of where he was. Aiming at the explosions, they were simply blazing away with their automatic weapons. At least one of the RPK light machine guns was being triggered in his general direction, too.

Bolan, ducking and weaving, shoved his Beretta back into shoulder leather and brought up the battle-scarred M-16. He triggered a 40-mm grenade into the semicircle of trucks, racked the action open and repeated the process. A third grenade thumped downrange before he was through obliterating military equipment, and by that time, everything in the vicinity of the front entrance was on fire. Men ran screaming, their clothing ablaze, and Bolan could spare no time for mercy rounds. He was going for broke.

He thumbed another grenade into the smoking launcher tube and turned to fire. The UAV, buzzing behind him, fired another rocket, which sailed past him and detonated far behind somewhere. Bolan didn't look to see what was struck. He fired.

The entrance to the government complex blew apart.

Through this molten, flaming maw came the Executioner. A pair of guards, dressed in what was most likely the ragtag paramilitary chic of Zapata's La Raza thugs, were blown apart by the explosion. Bolan stepped over the remains as he raised his rifle, sighted on a third man farther down the hall and pressed the trigger.

Nothing happened.

Without hesitating even a fraction of a second, even as the vibrations of that impotent trigger pull were still traveling from his finger up his arm, Bolan was ripping the magazine out of the rifle and removing a fresh one from a pouch on his combat harness. He was moving laterally as he did so, changing his position by habit, always shifting, always trying to avoid enemy fire. He rammed the fresh magazine home, pulled it to verify it was seated, yanked back the weapon's plunger with a single angry slap of his hand and returned fire.

Except that he didn't.

Bullets were ripping through the air as if in slow motion, and still his rifle wouldn't fire. The reptilian part of Bolan's brain processed the dump of fight-or-flight that surged through every fiber of his waking mind then, and as he was trained to do, he ignored it. He wasted no time staring at this reluctant weapon, shaking it, fighting with it, trying to make it work. He simply let it fall and drew the Beretta 93-R, still with its suppressor attached.

The 9-mm round blew a third eye in the gunman's forehead. He hit the floor.

Bolan was inside.

The UAV operator knew it. A rocket blew apart the wall as Bolan, responding to some sixth sense, hit the floor. Fragments of concrete, drywall and plaster flew everywhere. The UAV unleashed a torrent of gunfire through the gap it had just made in the building. Bolan glanced up at the holes in the wall behind the spot where he had been standing. Some part of his mind cataloged them as most likely nine millimeter. A vehicle-mounted, remote-activated, 9-mm automatic weapon wasn't something one saw every day. Bolan looked up just in time to see the UAV move from the hole in the wall to the blown-open doors, changing its angle so it could get at him.

He ran. The UAV's bullets strafed the floor behind him.

Then the helicopter was inside the building.

The entryway was just wide enough that the machine's rotors were clear. It couldn't come on into the narrower corridor, but it now had a perfectly lined-up shot down the hall. It would be like shooting fish in a barrel…except that Bolan didn't intend to stay there. He pulled the Desert Eagle left-handed, reaching behind his back to do it, and blew the lock off a nearby door. Then he bowled through it, just as a rocket turned the hallway behind him into flaming vapor.

Bolan hit the polished floor with rib-crushing force. Flames licked through the doorway behind him. The air was full of choking smoke. With the breath forced from him, Bolan hissed in pain, rolling away from the doorway as liquid fire started to splatter in. The rocket blast was so hot it had melted portions of the insulation in the walls and ceiling, and these were striking Bolan and the floor tiles around him with gobs of yellow-white pain and destruction.

"Jack," Bolan started to say, but he couldn't choke out the words. Pausing to press a clenched fist to his ribs as he rolled onto his back in pain, he could feel the metal of the Beretta against his flank. He drew in a deep, ragged breath and tried again.

"This is G-force." The familiar voice sounded in his ear. "Sarge, I do not copy. Say again?"

"G-force, this is Striker." Bolan croaked the words. His transceiver had "smart" audio circuitry. It would perceive the faintest whisper and amplify it for retransmission, or cut the sound of shouting to a less distorted level. It also filtered out the noise of gunfire.

"I read you, Sarge," Grimaldi replied. "I'm homing in on the explos—"

"I'm in trouble, Jack," Bolan interrupted. "The UAV... it's *here*."

"I copy, I copy," Grimaldi said quickly, determination in his voice. "I've got the bastard. Hold tight, Sarge. The cavalry's on its way."

The next beautiful, violent sound that Bolan heard was gunfire, but of a much more authoritative pitch. It was the minigun mounted on the left skid of Grimaldi's little Boeing. There was a tremendous gust of hot ash- and spark-laden air as the two aircraft churned the space outside the burning building.

"Nailed the son of a bitch," Grimaldi said, his channel still open. "I'm after him, Sarge, but..." He paused, cursed loudly and unleashed a torrent of invective about the machine he pursued and its cowardly, grounded operator. "Okay, he's moving away from your position, Sarge. I'll keep after him. He's so damned fast I can't hit him."

Grimaldi's armed scout was itself a very small, light helicopter, but the UAV was an engine, a weapons package, a camera and not much else. It had neither the relative weight Grimaldi carried, nor any constraints as to its physical behavior. Maneuvers that would leave a human pilot nauseous with vertigo or unconscious from the g's pulled had no effect on the unmanned rotorcraft.

"Do what you can, Jack," Bolan said. He pushed himself to his knees, a gun in either hand. Then he staggered to his feet. He reloaded both weapons and then holstered the Beretta, transferring his heavy .44 Magnum cannon to his right hand.

Time to end this.

"Striker to Platt. Striker to Platt," Bolan said.

"Platt here."

"We are blown, repeat, we are blown," he reported. "Move your teams in now, Platt. Tighten the perimeter and take out all resistance. The attackers know I'm here."

"The hostages," Platt said.

"The hostages," Bolan agreed. "I'm going right for them. There's no time to waste."

"We are on it, Striker." There was a pause. Then Platt said, "Good hunting, sir. We'll meet you at the center of our cordon."

"Striker out," Bolan said.

He walked out into the burning, blackened, cratered hallway. Striding purposefully down the corridor, he took long, deliberate steps, working the knots out of his tortured muscles. As he moved he picked up his pace.

The Executioner followed the route he had memorized from the floor plan. He was headed toward the core of the building, to a large, central conference room that was the most likely place for the hostages and their captors to be gathered. With the building on fire and war raging outside, the numbers had counted down. He wouldn't allow the captured employees to die, not while he could do something about it.

Through his peripheral vision he noticed the large

windows on the east side of the hallway he was taking. Then he caught the movement.

Bolan made a flying leap, landing on his stomach and ignoring the shooting pains from his already bruised ribs. The UAV rotorcraft, floating past the window outside, was a shadow in the flickering firelight of the consuming blaze that nibbled at the building. The UAV's guns opened up again and sprayed out the windows. Bolan covered his face with his arms as he was pelted with razor-sharp shards of tinted glass.

"G-force!" he shouted. "He's on top of me again!"

"On my way, Sarge!" Grimaldi's voice was taut. "There you are, you little son of a bitch. Now I've got you!"

The chain-saw roar of the Boeing's minigun was almost deafening, and Grimaldi's chopper was close enough that Bolan could hear the throaty, mechanical whine underlying it as the electrically driven barrels spun. The UAV moved off to avoid the devastating rain of fire Grimaldi had brought to bear.

Bolan pushed back to his feet and continued his desperate end run.

A guard rounded the corner and screamed something in Spanish. Bolan shot him through the face without breaking his stride. He cut that same corner, taking it wide to "cut the pie" and afford him shots at those on the other side, and was rewarded with a target: three paramilitary-dressed, long-haired men carrying automatic weapons, one of whom was holding a cigarette in his hand. The others were trying to get their weapons up; two had M-16s and one had a MAC-10 clone. All had obviously been taking some sort of break in the corridor. Bolan's shot had shaken them from their complacency.

His next shots shook them right off the planet.

The Desert Eagle barked. Hollowpoint .44 Magnum rounds howitzered downrange. One man took a bullet through the forehead, and he died as his brains exited the back of his skull. Another was hit in the chest, immediately over the heart. The man to his right saw death coming with methodical, whipsaw speed and threw his MAC-10 to the ground, raising his arms into the air.

The loaded submachine gun, its bolt cocked back, hit the floor and burped a stream of .45 automatic fire in the direction of its now-reluctant owner. The bullets tore through the former gunman's abdomen. He folded over on himself with a wet, despairing cry, the sound of a man who knows he's just suffered very serious damage.

Bolan had hit the deck the second he saw the MAC-10 flying through the air. The weapon fired from an open bolt; only the very stupid or the very ignorant would make a projectile of such a gun. He scrambled to his feet and was about to continue on when the writhing gunman called out to him in Spanish.

Bolan paused and looked down at him. The wound was very bad. The automatic fire had shredded his guts. Death would come for certain, but it wouldn't be quick and it wouldn't be pleasant.

"Por favor," the man pleaded.

Bolan brought the ugly, triangular snout of the Desert Eagle on target. As the doomed man found himself looking into the gaping maw of the gun, his eyes widened.

Apparently this wasn't the request he thought he was making.

Bolan showed him the Executioner's mercy.

The shot still echoed as he continued to run.

CHAPTER TWELVE

"With the hated Anglos driven back from whence they came," Tristan Zapata roared at the camera, "we, the proud people of Mexico, will finally achieve the greatness that has been denied us for so many years! Long have we suffered. Long have we waited. Long have we—" He stopped abruptly as the cameraman lowered his device. "What are you doing?"

"The tape is full, sir." Eduardo Lima shook his head.

"Put in another, then."

"Respectfully, sir, have we not enough of this footage?"

"We have enough when I say so!" Zapata yelled. He relented nonetheless. "Very well. Put it with the others. Pack up the camera gear. Ready your crew. And bring me the clothing."

At the rear of the conference room, three dozen men and women sat or knelt with their arms crossed. They had been ordered to remain in that position, and told that to look upon their captors meant death. Zapata had personally executed a shrill, screaming woman to make that point. It had taken only that single death to bring the others in line. Anglos. They were all cowards. It was a wonder their kind had ever managed to hold sway over La Raza, the Race, the people for whom his freedom-fighting organization was named. A pair of guards with M-16 rifles stood over them now.

Lima hastened to obey Zapata's orders. As much as Zapata berated the man, he was among his more reliable operatives. As much as he hated to admit it, the members of La Raza, while committed to the cause of reclaiming the occupied lands that were rightfully theirs, weren't a terribly disciplined band.

Tristan Zapata had always believed himself a distant relative of Emiliano Zapata, the famous and tragic revolutionary. The branches on the family tree weren't there, strictly speaking, but it didn't matter. He styled himself as the descendent of Mexican revolutionaries, and in revolution, in the fight for freedom, symbol was more important than substance. If he believed it, it didn't matter if it was true. And if he believed it, others would.

Born to wealthy parents who lived in Mexico City, Tristan had attended college at a prestigious university in California. There, he had learned to hate the Anglo way of life, to hate the lies told by those who believed it superior, to hate the racists he saw in every facet of American culture. The Anglos and their European forebears had dominated the world, always keeping the Mexican people under their heel. Those of Hispanic descent were destined to suffer as long as the Anglos held power. Capitalism, corporatism, mercantilism, imperialism… these were the forces Zapata came to hate more than anything, evils synonymous with the smiling, pale face of the Anglo.

Tristan dropped out of college, much to his parents' horror, in his junior year. Then he was off to travel

Europe, as so many dissipated, disaffected youth did when they had unearned money in their pockets and endless time on their hands. It wasn't until Zapata was arrested in London for attempting to bomb a subway stop that his parents disowned him. Thanks to a politically correct legal system that painted him as cultural victim rather than an aggressor, Zapata was able to escape those charges, and he vowed to be more clever the next time. His narrow escape from British justice only emboldened him; it reinforced his belief that the Anglos were weak.

He moved from radical organization to radical organization over the next few years, finding more extreme comrades in arms. From them he learned what he could of weapons, explosives, fighting tactics. He trained with knives. He learned firearms. And when he finally purchased his first submachine gun, the old Uzi he carried to this day and treated with the respect of a lover, he knew that he would never again be the youth who had left his parents' home.

He tried to find those who shared his vision of a restored Mexico. In this he was often disillusioned, for too many of them spoke of revolution as if it were an exciting, exotic hobby, something to be talked about in coffee shops or while bedding dark-eyed women. He managed to build his revolutionary group, yes, but it took much, much longer than he had originally thought. Over time, most of his notions about the path of the revolutionary were proved naive. He was disabused of misconceptions that had, at times, nearly gotten him captured or killed. But still he fought on.

The years of struggle had taken their toll on him.

He was fairly certain he had a bleeding ulcer. He had no friends. He had many enemies on both sides of the law. He was wanted by Interpol and by the Americans' Central Intelligence Agency and Federal Bureau of Investigation. He had twice almost been arrested while in Europe, thanks to Interpol or nations cooperative with its efforts. He had given up his freedom and possibly any future in any part of the world…if he failed. He didn't intend to fail.

A few years ago, Zapata had become aware that government agencies were attempting to infiltrate La Raza. He'd been both horrified and pleased. Horrified because a spy in their midst meant they might all end up in prison. In some parts of the world, they wouldn't even live long enough to see the barren walls of small cells; in those places, they would simply be killed by government death squads.

He was pleased, however, because if governments considered La Raza a sufficient threat that they sought to destroy him from within, it meant he was proving to be effective and powerful. Governments didn't waste resources or undercover operatives—he had rooted out no less than three of these, and slit the throats of all three personally—on "terrorist" organizations they considered of no consequence. Tristan Zapata was moving up in the world.

He didn't realize just how far, however, until the day that security agents of President Castillo's administration showed up in the small tavern he favored in the warrens of Mexico City. It amused him to live there, unknown among the masses, his own wealthy, uncaring parents somewhere in the city still, never realizing how close at hand was their prodigal son.

He had thought he was about to be assassinated when those security men showed up in the tavern, fanning out, their hands inside their suit jackets, their eyes concealed behind mirrored sunglasses. Zapata had placed his palms very carefully on the rough-hewn wooden table before him. His Uzi was in the room he rented above the tavern. He had in his pocket the folding straight razor he always carried, and there was a .38-caliber revolver tucked into his waistband, but there was no move he could make that wouldn't end in his death. He braced himself, wondering if he should sell his life dearly before the end. The idea of dying didn't scare him that much, in all honesty. He was only sorry that he was to die at the hands of his fellow Mexicans. It had been his dream to die fighting the hated Anglos, taking as many of them with him as possible.

The security men merely stood and stared at him from behind their mirrored lenses. Zapata had made up his mind to go for the gun and shoot the nearest of them, had almost persuaded himself that he could still go out in a blaze of glory, when the strangest thing happened.

President Gaspar Castillo had walked into the room.

He was dressed in a fine, tailored suit, with a light overcoat draped on his shoulders like a cape, even though the weather was warm enough that no such garment was required. Castillo, Zapata knew from seeing him on television, was a creature of affectations who always cultivated the image of a man of refinement and taste. His haircut was perfect. His tan, produced either by machines or a spray, was even and flawless. Not a thread of his clothing was out of place; not a speck of dirt or dust clung to him. He carried in his hands a pair of lightweight black leather gloves—another affectation—and he slapped them against his palm. Had he carried a crop the effect would have been no more pronounced.

"You are Tristan Zapata," Castillo had said to him.

"I am," Zapata had replied.

"We," Castillo said, looking him in the eye, "have much to talk about."

And so their association had begun, and for the first time, Tristan Zapata started to believe that his dream of the Reconquista, the reclamation of those lands stolen by the Anglos from Mexico, could be accomplished. The Southwest United States was occupied territory, and Tristan Zapata dreamed of a day when it could be taken back.

President Gaspar Castillo believed the same.

Castillo explained that he, too, had long been a follower of the philosophies and teachings of La Raza. He meant the Race as a system of belief, not the organization Zapata had founded. A man who rose to government power like Gaspar Castillo, however, understood the political landscape and everything in it. For some time, Castillo had been aware of Zapata's activities, and of late he had even come to support them surreptitiously.

Suddenly, many things that had seemed not to make sense now became clear. A traffic inspection that had resulted in Zapata being passed over without a second glance. A hint or tip from a man on the street that had resulted in the recovery, or purchase at a very low price, of weapons Zapata's organization could use. Increased media coverage on state-sponsored television highlighting the Race's grievances against the Anglos, and against the United States particularly, with mention of "freedom fighters" who worked to secure future independence for those of La Raza who suffered. Suddenly, these things all became part of a coherent whole, with no less than President Gaspar Castillo behind them. Zapata was awed.

Castillo explained that now that he held power, the time had come for Mexico to move forward. He wasn't a coward like those before him; he believed in action. And he would move on the Anglos in a way they would be powerless to oppose, ultimately. He would use their own political weaknesses against them.

To do this, he needed what he called "plausible deniability." He explained that there were certain "political exigencies" that had to be taken into account. So he needed a man who thought like he did, a man who understood the importance of the Race, and who would work tirelessly for freedom and self-determination. In short, Castillo explained, he needed Tristan Zapata. Would Zapata be willing, the president asked, to answer the patriotic call of his native land, and fulfill the revolutionary heritage of his ancestors?

Zapata would have walked barefoot over broken glass to say yes to such an offer. He did so, and his life became a whirlwind. Castillo gave him fabulous weapons, extended training to his people and provided them with government safe houses. In return, Zapata took his orders from the president, hitting where and when the man demanded. Often the orders were vague enough that Zapata and his people were left to their own devices, to kill or take hostage whoever they chose. It was enough, President Castillo told him, that Zapata was putting pressure on the United States. It was, he explained, all part of an overall plan, one that might ultimately enrich Mexico while it made her much more powerful.

Zapata was content to let the president concern himself with those details. He wished only to fight the Anglos and extend the Race's power and domination, restoring to Mexico those things that were rightfully hers.

This bold raid across the hated border into Tucson had been Castillo's idea. The orders, and even instructions for how to accomplish the affair, were given to Zapata. For his own part, Zapata had indulged himself as they crossed the border and made their way to the seat of government, burning and raping and killing as they went. It sent a bold message, and the spray-painted slogans left behind a warning, as well. Impermanent though such statements might be, they were burned indelibly on the minds of witnesses to the atrocities Tristan Zapata and his men had committed. He had done so knowingly, willingly. He had long ago learned that to unleash one's passions in this way was liberating. It was also enjoyable.

For the Race. Everything was for the Race. He always kept that uppermost in his mind. It made what he did the actions of a freedom fighter; it made him a noble hero; it absolved him of responsibility for any of the more vulgar things he might do in its name.

He could admit it to himself, privately, here in his

mind. There was no harm in that. He believed it made him a stronger person, after all.

Eduardo Lima was taking a blessedly long time to return with his change of clothing. Zapata would need the suit, the tie, the shirt and the shoes to successfully impersonate one of the "news crew." He still laughed at how easily that little deception had been accomplished.

The hard part of taking a portion of an American city wasn't the act of invading it initially. This, President Castillo had explained to him. The Americans were soft, and slow to respond. Their border was porous, and as much as they wailed about the harm illegal immigration did to them, they did little to stop it. Terrorists from the Middle East had used the very border Zapata had crossed this night. The Americans seemed incapable or unwilling to do anything about it. How, then, could they cope with a sudden military action the likes of which they had rarely if ever experienced in their national history?

No, the hard part was to escape back across the border when the operation had accomplished its purpose, which was to put the United States on notice. The border incursion would, Castillo had explained, be followed up with more invasions, this time targeting territories slightly less "high profile" than an American city's government houses. The plan was first to bloody the Anglos' noses, then take something they would miss less than the target originally siezed and given up. Much of this was military theorizing on a level far above Zapata's understanding, intelligent and educated though he believed himself to be. He simply did as he was told, for Castillo's orders had proved out time and time again.

He had been told, for example, to make the request for the WKAL news crew as soon as he was able. That team had been taken hostage the night before the attack by a specially designated contingent of Zapata's men. Members of La Raza impersonating the news crew would arrive and, when the American security operatives finally let them in—Castillo had assured Zapata that, yes, the Americans would eventually let a camera crew in, if they believed they could control the message sent, and that this distraction would keep the "terrorists" occupied for a time—they would enter unsuspected.

It annoyed Zapata that at the last minute Castillo had chosen to place a Mexican army observer on the news crew. That had been explained to him only after the fact, when the news van arrived with his men and an individual Zapata didn't recognize. Something in the stranger's carriage brought to mind the haughty arrogance of the Mexican special-forces men Zapata had trained with at Castillo's urging, so he had no doubt this man was who he claimed to be.

He said he had been sent to "help," though truth be told, he'd disappeared shortly after arriving. Zapata assumed he was out with the patrols. Castillo had ordered that the Mexican soldiers loaned to the invading force be used to patrol the grounds outside their inner fortifications, which suited Zapata well. The men were too quiet and too certain of their own superiority to his ragtag freedom fighters. Part of Zapata knew they were probably right as often as not, and that, too, bothered him. Thus he didn't expend too much effort wondering where President Castillo's watchdog had gotten to, once the news crew was on the scene.

Zapata had instead busied himself filling tape after tape with the video equipment. It amused him to use the Anglos' cleverness against them. Zapata wasn't naive, and neither was Castillo; both men knew that the Americans would likely try to keep news of what was happening from their people. It wouldn't do for the fat, lazy Americans, proud residents of what they stupidly called "the greatest nation on Earth," to know that their neighbors south of the border had finally slapped them in the face.

No, the Americans would do everything in their power to cover it up, which, Castillo had told him, ultimately would work in their favor when it came time to negotiate the release of certain portions of the United States to Mexico. The government of the Anglos would do what it could to make this pass by quietly. They would fail, of course. Their talking radio stations would berate them long and loud, and their people would eventually march in anger in the streets. That, too, was fitting. Let the Americans march and wave signs and impotently demand a change. The boot was on the other foot now, and soon it would be pressed against the other neck.

It was even possible that, if the Anglos confiscated the videotapes as the van left this place, those tapes would eventually be leaked to the media. That thought had helped inspire Zapata to great feats of rhetoric and oratory.

Meanwhile, he himself would trade places with one of his operatives and escape when the van left, ahead of whatever final military push the Americans would eventually attempt. Their tactics and methods were entirely predictable, and Castillo had explained to Zapata that he had made an extensive study of their hated enemies' ways. At every turn, they had anticipated what the Anglos would do, and the plan was working smoothly.

The man with whom Zapata would trade places looked very much like him, and for all that, the Anglos often thought they all looked alike, he was sure. With a trade of clothes, the deception would be passable. Zapata regretted that Lima was unlikely to survive, but the man didn't know that. He thought it was his mission to oversee the hostages until the Americans surrendered Tucson. He was gullible enough to believe this was possible. It was a pity; Zapata had always been fond of Eduardo, who was simpleminded but loyal.

There was a frantic rapping on the door to the conference room. It was thrown open by Tomas Flores, another of Zapata's men. He was almost breathless. "Sir," he said with deep gasps, "I think…I think the building is on fire."

"What?"

A sudden explosion rocked the structure. Zapata could feel the vibrations through his feet. There was another blast shortly after that one.

Swearing, Zapata picked up the Uzi that lay on the conference table.

Lima returned then, his walkie-talkie in his hand. "Sir," he said, "Emilio says there is a man in the building! He is trying to kill him with the helicopter, but there is an American helicopter chasing him, and he must be careful."

"Tell him to do it without destroying us all, fool!" Zapata snapped. Lima and Flores fled.

Zapata eyed the hostages. With the reassuring weight of his Uzi in his hand, he was suddenly inspired simply to shoot them all and be done with it. None of them were destined to survive this operation, after all.

The little helicopter was another matter. It wouldn't do to lose so fine a weapon. It had been a gift, of sorts, from Castillo's allies abroad, the president had said. Zapata didn't begin to understand everything about it. One of his men had been trained hour after hour in the operation of the little helicopter, by scowling Mexican special-forces fighters and some scrawny technicians who clearly understood the electronics and mechanics of the thing. Castillo had warned that this first test of the machine would prove just how useful it could be, and thus the man running it must be kept safely away from the bulk of the fighting. He had to be able to escape when the conflict was over, bearing the little helicopter with him on the control and transportation truck designed for that purpose.

The chosen "pilot" of the unmanned helicopter was Zapata's trusted friend Emilio Diaz, whom Zapata knew had the intelligence and the reflexes to undertake the mission. Diaz had spent hour after hour learning to fly the machine, and playing a video-game simulator. When the signal was given, Diaz, equipped with forged documents, would slip back across the border in the truck, which was camouflaged to look like a simple cargo vehicle. It even had a false rear facade that would appear to contain densely packed cartons of whatever goods had been chosen for the disguise. Castillo had explained that

Emilio had every advantage, and that his return with the truck and the helicopter was both assured and vital to their cause. Castillo envisioned using the UAV for a series of attacks on American interests. In time it would become the feared mechanical master of their skies.

But first Diaz had to kill their enemies without burning down the damned building around them.

Zapata shouted orders to his guards, who took up positions at either side of the doorway. He caressed his Uzi, running two fingers across the scarred wooden stock. Then his eyes narrowed and, with a flush to his cheeks that was as close to pleasure as Tristan Zapata ever got, he leveled the barrel of the 9-mm submachine gun on the crowd of helpless hostages. With the flat of his left hand, he yanked back the cocking knob on top of the weapon.

One of the women looked up, saw what he was doing and screamed. At that moment, there were shots outside.

Even as he turned, Zapata's finger began taking up slack on the trigger....

CHAPTER THIRTEEN

Mack Bolan spotted the two men leaving the conference room. He raised his weapon and ended their lives in quick succession.

A woman screamed.

Tristan Zapata was aiming an Uzi submachine gun at a cluster of bound civilians. Bolan punched a .44 Magnum round at the terrorist leader.

Zapata was turning at the same moment that Bolan fired. He shrieked and dived to the floor in a spray of blood. Bolan, still moving, threw himself forward and swiveled as he fell. The gunmen guarding either side of the door, whom he'd spotted in his peripheral vision, were bringing up their weapons. Their spray of automatic fire went high—fortunately, high enough that none of their bullets hit the prisoners. Bolan landed heavily on his spine, letting his shoulders and upper back take the brunt of the impact, and triggered off two quick blasts.

The .44 Magnum hollowpoint rounds blew a crater in the face of the man on the left and drilled a gaping second mouth where the right-hand man's nose had been. Bolan rolled over, searching for his next target and narrowly missed a burst of 9-mm fire that ripped up the tiles where he had lain. There was no cover in the large conference room except for the obvious: the giant table dominating the center.

Bolan crab-walked under the end of it, then surged to his feet. He took the edge of the massive wooden table on his shoulder and pushed for all he was worth. Like a heavily armed Atlas, every muscle in his body screaming at this abuse, he managed to lever the mighty table up and over. It rolled at a forty-five-degree angle once in the air, landing on its side, effectively blocking him from view.

Bolan pulled a folding knife from his pocket and threw it in an arc. "Cut yourselves free!" he shouted. He could see that the hostages were bound with duct tape. A single sharp edge would be all they needed, and once one or two were free, they could start freeing the others.

Zapata was scrambling for the door now, screaming into a walkie-talkie he had produced from somewhere. He'd dropped his weapon. Blood streamed from what appeared to be a bullet graze on his forehead. As Bolan leveled the Desert Eagle he heard rotor blades.

Bolan had enough time to hit the floor again on his back, raising his pistol to point to the sky. There, through the black square of the skylight above, he saw the silhouette of a hovering predator.

The UAV had returned.

The Executioner rolled out of the way as the submachine guns on the unmanned rotorcraft pushed back the darkness with yellow-orange twin muzzle-blasts. The bullets ripped into the floor and sprayed everyone in the conference room with razor-sharp, glittering pieces of the skylight. Zapata screamed and lurched;

he had apparently been hit. He disappeared through the doorway, leaving a trail of blood as he went. Bolan was helpless to follow. The UAV poured on the fire, creating a curtain of death Bolan dared not breach.

Before he could ask for him, Grimaldi's voice was in his ear. "I'm on him, Sarge, I'm on him." The ace pilot cursed a blue streak, obviously intent on pursuing the little remote-controlled chopper. The UAV took off, and the sound of the larger Boeing washed overhead, its passage raising a windstorm through the broken sky-light. Then the two vehicles were off on their protracted dogfight.

Bolan suspected that Zapata himself had called in that strike, though he'd taken a hit in the process. The Executioner stood, popping the magazine from his Desert Eagle and slapping home a fresh one in almost the same motion. He checked the hostages, mindful of any among them who could be terrorists shamming. The dazed civilians were working at freeing themselves, he was pleased to see. One had the pocketknife he had thrown, and was cutting the tape off another, while two women already free were ripping tape away from their neighbors.

"I am with the federal government," Bolan announced. "My name is Cooper. Remain calm and follow my instructions." He looked them over. "Are any of you injured?"

"No, sir." A man in a rumpled suit, his tie at half-mast, spoke up. He had a fat lip and a bruise spreading across the lower corner of his mouth. Obviously he'd been quick to say something before, and the terrorists had hit him or pistol-whipped him for daring to do so.

Bolan was glad he still had the guts to speak up when necessary.

"Can anyone here use a firearm? Anyone here with any weapons experience?"

The man who had spoken raised his hand tentatively. "I can, sir. I own several guns." There were a couple of other murmurs of agreement. One fellow volunteered that he was a member of the National Rifle Association, the NRA. Bolan nodded and separated them and the two women from the others a few paces.

"This building is on fire," Bolan said. He kept a watch on the door. "There are an unknown number of terrorists still inside. Government forces are now moving on our location, but we have no way of knowing what sort of resistance they face." As he said this, they could hear gunfire from somewhere in the distance. To Bolan's trained ears, it seemed to be coming from multiple directions. Platt and his blacksuits were moving into range, and mopping up the invaders as they went. Bolan couldn't hear any rotors, and wondered what that meant. He didn't expect Grimaldi to let a grounded jockey with a remote joystick get the better of him.

Bolan began searching the dead men. He found a total of three pistols in the room and passed them out on a first-come, first-served basis. He gave the M-16s to two of the former hostages, a man and a woman who had served in the U.S. military and had qualified on similar rifles. "Keep it to single shot," he cautioned. "Don't get fancy. We're not fighting a war—just getting the hell out of here in one piece."

Under normal circumstances he would have holed up and guarded the hostages himself until help could arrive. That wasn't going to be possible. The building was burning. While its fire-suppression systems might be enough to douse the flames, which might even burn out on their own accord, Bolan couldn't risk keeping the former prisoners here.

"Striker to Platt," he said.

"Platt here. We're closing perimeter, inbound. Should reach you in five minutes."

"Resistance?"

"Resistance is light," Platt said. "We've broken their lines. We're doing mop-up at this point. Is your zone hot?"

"My airspace is," Bolan said. "That chopper just took another run at me."

"This is G-force." Grimaldi broke in. "I have no sign of that UAV, Striker. Repeat, UAV is no longer in the air. I don't know where he went, but I sure can't find him anymore."

"Understood," Bolan said. "Platt, I'm on my way out with the hostages."

"Survivors?" Platt asked.

"I have at least one confirmed down." Bolan glanced at the body lying against the wall in a pool of blood. "The rest appear to be all right." He looked over the former prisoners. "Is everyone accounted for?" he asked. "Anyone missing?"

"Uh, there is one, sir," a member of his armed party replied. "Sheila. Sheila Sands. She was taken away at the beginning. I..." He trailed off and would not make eye contact.

"That bastard you shot at," another woman told Bolan angrily. "That Che Guevara type who loved his camera so much. He had her pulled out when this all started. They took her somewhere."

Bolan motioned the woman over and took a few steps away from the group. "Miss…?"

"Richards," the woman said. "Melissa Richards."

"Miss Richards, was Sheila…"

"Pretty? Damned straight she was. She was a runner-up for Miss Arizona a few years back, in fact."

"Did they say anything?" Bolan asked. "Give any hint where they might take her?"

"No." Richards shook her head. "Although…"

"Anything you know might help."

"Well, there is a room with a couple cots in it. Some of the staff use it when they're working late nights. I imagine…" She shot him a meaningful, horrified glance.

Bolan removed his phone and called up the floor plan of the building. "Can you show me where?"

She examined the little image for a moment and finally pointed. "There it is."

"Thank you," Bolan said.

"Mr. Cooper? Can you rescue her? You don't think they've killed her, do you?"

"I don't know, Miss Richards," he said, "but if she's alive, I'll bring her back. You have my word."

Bolan led the hostages through the burning wreckage at the front entrance, concentrating his "deputies" at the rear of the group to watch for terrorist stragglers. He encountered Platt as he exited the building with his charges.

"Commander," Bolan said, "please take care of these people and see that they get to safety."

"And you, sir?"

"Unfinished business," Bolan said.

"We've got fire and rescue on the way, sir," Platt reported, "but I've got to check and clear this area before I can let them in. We can't have them blunder into the middle of a war zone."

"Use your best judgment." Bolan nodded. "I'll be inside regardless."

"But, sir—"

Whatever Platt wanted to say, Bolan couldn't hear him. He was already running back into the burning government building.

Melissa Richards, not an unattractive woman herself, had known what some of the other hostages hadn't wanted to face: Sheila Sands had been taken away to provide entertainment for the terrorists. They had singled out an attractive female to rape, separating her from the others to prevent outrage from emboldening the prisoners.

Following the route he had memorized as he looked at the floor plan, Bolan ran as fast as his battered body could carry him. He rounded a corner, cut through what looked like a classroom or perhaps a court facility and found himself facing the hallway leading to the glorified closet Melissa Richards had pointed out to him.

There was no reason to play it cool; there was enough noise, enough combat, enough fire and smoke and destruction to mask his approach. Bolan simply planted the sole of his combat boot against the door, slamming it open and practically ripping it from its hinges.

He stopped so abruptly his boots squealed on the polished floor.

"Well, well, well," said the tall, hatchet-faced man who stood inside the room. He had a Browning Hi-Power pistol pointed at the temple of an attractive blonde woman who was desperately trying to cover herself with what was left of her skirt and sweater. Her face was bruised; she had been beaten, probably to force her cooperation.

Rarely was Bolan surprised by what he encountered in battle. This was an exception.

"You," he said simply.

"Forgive me," the tall man said, "for not extending my hand to greet you. We have not been properly introduced. I am Roderigo del Valle, late of the Honduran government. But then, you probably know that already."

Bolan said nothing. The barrel of his Desert Eagle was pointed straight at Del Valle's face. Del Valle, in turn, was using the woman as a shield. He had one arm around her neck and was almost, but not quite, choking her. She was turning red as she squirmed in his grasp.

"You are wondering how I come to be here, I imagine," Del Valle said. "Well, I see no reason to tell you that. But I *can* tell you that, once I arrived, and I overheard those cretins working for Zapata speak of the girl they had liberated…well, the rest was simple, was it not?"

"Drop the gun," Bolan said. He had been surprised, but that was all; he was a combat realist. Del Valle couldn't be here, but he *was,* and therefore Bolan would deal with him.

"You are taking all the fun out of this." Del Valle grinned his sickly, insincere grin again. "You see, I remember. I remember when we met, and I received reports after you departed. I know you, and you personally, rescued those villagers I held captive on the Guatemalan border. Even if I did not, your *hero* sense radiates from you like heat. You are one who believes he does noble work. I knew that, sooner or later, you would learn of the girl's plight, and then I knew it was certain you would come for her. So predictable."

"Last chance," Bolan warned.

"I entertained myself as I waited." Del Valle paused to breathe into the captive woman's ear. She whimpered in abject terror. "It was a simple matter to while away the time here, while Zapata and his idiots went about their business. The added benefit was that I did not have to spend too terribly much time in their company. This woman's was so much more preferable. You know, it has been some time since I even felt the urge to indulge myself so, but something about the circumstances made it seem the thing to do."

Bolan's eyes narrowed. This man was on the edge of hysteria. He had cracked; that was certain. That made him extremely dangerous, for those who weren't stable could act in ways no rational person could predict.

"I know, I know." Del Valle grinned, as if he had been reading the Executioner's mind. "You are going to shoot me. In fact, I imagine, given what little I have seen of you in action, that you plan on shooting me right past this poor girl. You could probably even make the shot."

"You're right about that," Bolan said through clenched teeth.

"The hammer of my weapon is cocked," Del Valle

said, "and this particular pistol has a fairly light single-action pull. If you kill me, I will still take her life. If I gave you no other alternative, you would probably trust your skills and take that gamble, would you not? Be honest, now."

Bolan could sense where this was going. The pain in his ribs was worse the longer he stayed on his feet. Every part of him ached. He didn't relish what was to come.

"I would," he admitted.

"Then we understand each other," Del Valle said. "You took everything I built, American. You *are* American, aren't you? You have nothing to say? No matter. I do not intend to live in fear for the rest of my life, wondering if you will come through the door and put a bullet through my head. No, American, I intend to end this here. Now."

"I'm listening."

"Put your gun down. I will do the same. We will do it simultaneously, in fact. I, of course, will do so from behind this woman. When both our guns are on the floor, I will release her. Then we will fight. It has been a very long time since I matched someone hand-to-hand. To be honest, I consider it beneath me. But you so enrage me that I will make an exception. I wish the pleasure of taking my revenge blow by blow. I will kill you, American. Now. Make your choice."

There was no choice. Del Valle was just crazy enough to go through with it. Under normal circumstances Bolan would never give up his gun, but looking into the pleading eyes of Sheila Sands, already starting to glaze over with a kind of resignation to the evils she had undergone, Bolan knew he wouldn't allow her to come to more harm. He couldn't, not while there was even the slightest chance he could pull her from the jaws of death.

"All right," Bolan said. "You got it. Put your gun down and face me."

"Together," Del Valle reminded him. He moved his gun slightly away from Sheila Sands's head as Bolan lowered the Desert Eagle a fraction of a degree.

They continued like that, slowly moving their guns out of position. Bolan watched Del Valle closely to make sure the man offered no treachery. Del Valle, sensing the nature of the man he faced, watched just as intently, staying well behind his hostage so that Bolan couldn't get off a shot. Both men knew that without Sheila Sands between them, Bolan could easily have fired off a round, even from hip or thigh level, that would end Del Valle's life.

A tremor ran through the floor. They heard an explosion in the distance. Somewhere in the building, a fire alarm began to ring. Sheila Sands whimpered again.

"We don't have much time." Del Valle smiled yet again. He eased his pistol to the floor as Bolan's own Desert Eagle came to rest there, as well.

"Now," Del Valle said, "let us begin!"

He shoved the woman to the ground and went after Bolan with sudden, almost unbelievable fury. The tall man became a whirlwind of incredibly powerful chopping kicks. His first few blows Bolan managed to fend off, but when Del Valle finally connected with a roundhouse kick to his rib cage, the big American felt renewed agony blossom, and colored lights flashed through his vision.

The blow threw Bolan backward, knocking him to the floor. The relentless Del Valle pressed his advantage, kicking the soldier over and over again as Bolan struggled to overcome the shooting pains that had temporarily incapacitated him.

Knowledge of what was to come brought him back from the brink of unconsciousness. He was on the ground, helpless, as an enemy pounded him repeatedly with heavy boots. He would die like that, stomped to death, and he would die at Del Valle's leisure. Bolan couldn't permit that. He had to focus.

His indomitable will reasserted itself. He brought up his legs, fighting from his back, and lashed out, hitting Del Valle with a savage blow to the shins. Suddenly it was Del Valle who was on the defensive. As he attempted to move in for another kick, Bolan stomped him viciously in the shin again, and this time something cracked. Ignoring the pain, Del Valle tried to circle for another shot at Bolan's flank. The soldier used his free leg to scoot around, always keeping his heavy boots between himself and Del Valle.

The Honduran, favoring his injured leg, backed off a few paces, and Bolan rolled over and shot to his feet. Del Valle, who had apparently trained in savate or a similar boxing style, would be vulnerable inside kicking range. Bolan rushed him, caught a brutal kick on one lifted shin and then worked his way past the effective range of his adversary's weapons. Once there, he rained down a series of blows, using the edge of his hand to batter Del Valle about the neck. Then he started punishing the tall man with hammer-fist shots, as if pounding him into the floor like a nail.

Del Valle tried to fight back, but he was rusty and it showed. He had the tools, but not the instinct or reflexes to use them fast enough. He tried to throw an elbow, but Bolan blocked it, pushed the arm up and passed it over, and then slammed his own elbow across the man's face. There was a sickening crunch as cheekbone gave way.

Del Valle went to his knees, his nose bloody, his gaze dull. Bolan cracked him across the face with a knee strike.

"Wait," Del Valle said.

The gunshots were very loud.

A series of scorched holes appeared in the man's shirt. Bolan threw himself to the side. The gunfire continued until the slide of Del Valle's discarded Hi-Power locked back.

It was held in the small fists of a weeping Sheila Sands, who was still trying to pull the trigger as Bolan gently took the weapon out of her hands.

CHAPTER FOURTEEN

Mack Bolan sat in the back of an ambulance outside what was left of Tucson's government offices. The sun was rising, turning the eastern sky a beautiful series of oranges, striating the clouds with beams of yellow. A cool breeze had come up. It felt refreshing, but it smelled of ash and smoke and death.

Bolan frowned as he surveyed the activity around him. The freed hostages had long since been taken to the nearest hospital to be checked over, at which point some of Platt's blacksuits would ride herd on local law enforcement while the group was debriefed. Several fire departments had been scrambled to deal with the burning building, and their crews were still putting out hot spots. The rumble of diesel engines and the sound of the fire hoses spewing water cut through what would otherwise have been a pleasantly cool, tranquil morning.

Sheila Sands had been taken away in an ambulance. After she'd recovered Del Valle's gun and emptied it into him and the wall behind him, Bolan had taken it from her and held her until her sobs subsided. He certainly couldn't blame her for what she had done. His own war against the forces of evil had begun from similarly personal stakes, and was dedicated to the idea that people who preyed on others should pay for their crimes.

He thought she hadn't quite believed him when he'd

told her there would be no charges against her, and that, in fact, he would tell anyone who asked that he had shot Del Valle. But she had nodded when he told her not to tell anyone about the shooting, but just go with the medics. He would ask Brognola to have someone reach out to her with counseling ASAP.

Del Valle, for that matter, wasn't dead, although that wasn't for lack of trying on the young woman's part. He had been wearing a ballistic vest under his shirt. It was a relatively light device and hadn't stopped one of the slugs completely, but the wound wasn't too serious. An unconscious Del Valle and a blacksuit guard had been dispatched to the hospital in a separate ambulance.

The jurisdictional arguing had started almost as soon as the combat was over. There was no difficulty with the federal organizations, for they received peremptory marching orders from on high, thanks to Hal Brognola's work behind the scenes. Local and state law enforcement were on scene in droves, however, and there had been more than a few spats among them and the Feds before Platt and his people had finally stepped in. The fact was, Tucson was a mess and was going to stay that way for a little while, until the cleanup could be completed.

"There you go, sir." The paramedic nodded. He had taped Bolan's ribs, which helped with the pain. He also gave the soldier some over-the-counter painkillers. "Take two of these with two of these—" he gestured with the bottles "—every four hours as needed. And try not to get kicked in the chest for a few days."

"I'll see what I can do," Bolan grunted. He pulled the top of his blacksuit back on, shrugged into his combat harness and holsters, and slung his war bag over his shoulder and across his chest. The paramedic looked impressed by the display of hardware, but didn't say anything. Bolan got out, closed the ambulance doors and gave one a hard couple of slaps. The ambulance driver tapped the horn and drove off; this was the last medical team on-site, the others having left for the hospital long before now.

Bolan walked across the parking lot. Grimaldi was going to meet him at the far end and provide him with transportation. The pilot had a few circuits of the perimeter to complete, however. He'd lost the UAV in the dogfight high above, and the fact obviously bothered him. He hadn't admitted it to Bolan, but the soldier presumed he was making a few last passes to see if he could determine where the unmanned device had landed. Such a craft would likely have a service vehicle that would serve as its control center. Grimaldi was high overhead trying to find that. The problem was if he hadn't found it by now, he wasn't going to, and Bolan imagined the Stony Man pilot was very aware of that fact. Still, he gave Jack credit for refusing to give up. It was what Bolan would do, too.

The flagpole in the center of the drive-around had been cracked in half. The American flag lay on the ground, covered in debris. Bolan bent, unhooked it from the end of the pole and shook it clean. Then he carefully folded it. Platt found him there, and Bolan handed him the flag.

"Sir?"

"Take good care of it," Bolan said. "You did good work here today, Platt."

"Thank you, sir." He looked down at the flag and

handed it back to Bolan. "I think they would want you to have it, sir. The hostages, I mean. You don't know how much they've had to say… Well, sir, they're just very grateful."

Bolan accepted the flag and put it gently in his bag. "Thank you." He would return it to the Tucson government.

"Your pilot is on his way, sir." Platt held out a printout of some kind.

"What's this?"

"News from the Farm, sir. Satellite imagery confirms a concentration of troops just south of the border, possibly staged for a follow-up attack. The data just came in. Would you like to call them, sir?"

"No." Bolan shook his head. "Just give me the coordinates. Jack!"

"Already on my way." Grimaldi's voice sounded eager in his ear. "Let's kick some ass, Sarge."

WITH BOLAN ABOARD, Grimaldi paused the Boeing at a small commercial field nearby only long enough to fuel up. Then they were on their way. Bolan conferred with the Farm by satellite phone while they were in the air, and Price transmitted to him the information they had just relayed to Platt.

"Jack," Bolan said from the copilot's seat, "will these rockets take out light armored vehicles?"

"Absolutely," Grimaldi said.

"I'm looking at a short column here," Bolan said. "Deuce-and-halfs here and here." He held up the printout so Grimaldi could read and fly. "What looks like armored personnel carriers and a couple of armed amphibious wheeled trucks here. There's no doubt that's Mexican military."

"How can you tell, Sarge?"

"Hi-res satellite imagery, enhanced for analysis," Bolan said. "The trucks are unmarked, but the armored vehicles have Mexican military insignia. My guess is they're holding this force back along whatever line of retreat their people were planning on using if their armed force managed to extract in the trucks we saw. The route that would take them here is different than the one intel says they took to get into the country, but not by much."

"So the Mexican military is guarding the back door, probably looking to provoke an international incident if any of our guys pursue the hitters across the border."

"Exactly," Bolan said. "The game Castillo is playing is built on what he thinks is our unwillingness to use direct action."

"He doesn't know you very well," Grimaldi cracked.

Bolan said nothing to that. He appeared lost in thought for a moment. Then he said, "Take us low across the column and don't spare any of your rockets, Jack. Get me behind them, set me down and then use your minigun to show them the error of their ways. I'll be on the ground, doing much the same."

"You got it, big guy." He paused and looked at Bolan from the corner of his eye. "You, uh, okay there, Sarge?"

"No, Jack," Bolan said. "I'm not. These people hit American citizens on American soil, and they're counting on an international game of political maneuvering to shield them from the consequences. Well, that stops now."

"Right on, Sarge."

It wasn't long before they were approaching the border. Grimaldi had arranged for the Farm to run interference for him, in case he popped up on any municipal radar systems and somebody started asking questions. As for the Mexicans and their government, well, if they noticed anything, it really didn't matter. Bolan was long past caring what they might say or do. He was out for payback on behalf of the American people, and the corrupt government Castillo was running was going to pay the ultimate price for Castillo's dangerous acts.

"There they are!" Grimaldi said. He and Bolan could see the column of men and equipment below them. This section of terrain was relatively barren, with clearings on either side of a dirt road that ran parallel to the border fence. There was no cover. Once Bolan's boots were on the dirt, he would have to use the vehicle column itself to shield him from the enemy's guns.

The vehicles were arrayed for fast deployment, while men carrying assault rifles stood in formation nearby. They were simply waiting—either for targets to come to them in pursuit of Castillo's invading force, or for the order to back up their comrades and cross the border themselves. The border fence—here just a simple chainlink affair topped with barbed wire—had been flattened for several hundred yards, probably by one of the amphibious armored vehicles. The heavy transports were ungainly, but they were equipped with .30-caliber machine guns set in mounts in the rear decks. Most of these were manned.

The sound of the helicopter had drawn attention. Both men could see their quarries turning and pointing into the sky.

"Let's give them something to worry about, Jack," Bolan said.

Grimaldi nodded, then fired his rockets.

The Boeing unleashed hell, smoke trails connecting it to each of the armored vehicles in turn before those vehicles exploded in balls of orange fire and black smoke. Men scattered everywhere. Small-arms fire began to hit them, and Grimaldi danced out of its way, moving the chopper deftly to keep his minigun on target. He triggered it and sprayed the men below with electric, rotary death as Bolan silently urged him on.

"Another pass first, Sarge?" Grimaldi asked.

"Do it," Bolan said.

They wheeled about and the Stony Man pilot bent to his work again, this time bobbing and weaving as he moved along the column, avoiding the worst of the ground fire while walking the gout of bullets from the skid-mounted minigun through the ranks of soldiers on the ground. They fell, and sometimes they fell apart, as the electric might of the multibarrel gun chewed them to pieces.

"Now, Jack," Bolan said, reviewing the carnage they had wrought. "Get me on the ground, fast. Midway to the column, over in that field."

Grimaldi did as he urged. The skids barely kissed the ground before Bolan leaped from the machine, crouching low to steady himself, and then Grimaldi was skyward again. A few stray rounds pursued him, and a few hit the dirt many paces from where Bolan stood, but that didn't matter. No enemy fire was going to find either of them this night. Mack Bolan and Jack Grimaldi were on a mission of vengeance…and ultimately a mission of justice.

Bolan sprinted for the column, using the line of now-burning trucks and armored vehicles to shield himself from the frantic Mexican soldiers shouting to one another in confusion. He drew the Beretta 93-R with one hand and his larger combat knife, the Japanese-style short sword blade, with the other. The wrapped and resin-stiffened handle of the big blade felt firm and lethal in his grip.

The Executioner hurled himself into battle, and beneath his calm, some part of him still felt outrage at what had been done to his country. The United States had many enemies, and he had dealt with countless foes both on and off American soil. Something about the brazen attack on the citizens of Tucson, however, and the casual victimization of people like Sheila Sands went against the grain.

With the Beretta on single shot, he chopped down the nearest gunners like a lumberjack trimming small branches. Suddenly he was surrounded by soldiers, as the confused and terrified Mexican backup force tried to rally and swarm the deadly threat now in their midst.

That was a mistake.

Mack Bolan waded into them. He fired his Beretta with one hand, wielding his knife with the other, moving among the enemy in an almost choreographed kata of vengeance. When the Beretta went dry, he dropped it into his war bag's open primary pouch. The blade of his knife plunged deeply into the hollow of the throat of a nearby enemy, and then he had wrested the M-16 assault rifle from the man's hands.

He fired the rifle, aiming low, deliberately chopping the legs from under the men who faced him. They fell on one another, screaming, impeding the men behind them, and as it happened Bolan was already on them. He ducked under one man, slashing him as he went, stabbed his knife through the armpit of another, shoved that man off him with a kick and fired the M-16 one-handed to blow away yet another.

Grimaldi made a strafing run then. So precise was his control of the little chopper and of the minigun that Bolan could feel the spray of dirt on his legs as the minigun's rounds tore a deep furrow into the ground. It tore that furrow through the ranks of the men closest to the Executioner, spraying him with their blood and pulping them beyond recognition.

With the two knives in his hands he began fighting his way through the ranks of the soldiers who, in blind panic, could do nothing but swarm him. Many of them forgot their weapons in their primal drive to grab him, to drop on him, to pile onto him, anything to stop this deadly monster who had appeared in their midst.

Bolan disappeared under a pile of frantic uniformed men, all of them intent on killing him to save themselves.

Grimaldi walked the trail of his minigun's fire as near as he dared, chopping off parts of the clump of enemy fighters. The weapon's high rate of fire made it a ballistic chain saw. Men screamed in mortal terror as the shock of what had been done to them reached brains soaked in fight-or-flight impulses.

Bolan punched a hole through the pile of bodies with one fist, leaving his Japanese-style short sword blade buried in the chest of the man unlucky enough to be in the way. Snarling, Bolan grabbed a bayonet off the belt of another man and, with a stolen knife in each hand, worked this way and that, slicing and cutting and slashing and stabbing, climbing as if using pitons to work his way up a cliff face. Wherever his hands landed, men screamed. Wherever his knives met flesh, men died.

The Executioner was upon these enemies of freedom, these invaders, these predators. There would be no escape.

The closest truck had escaped being burned or blasted by the two-man mechanized attack. Bolan fought his way to it. He grabbed another rifle, this one a Mexican special-forces assault type, and checked its load. Then he sprayed it empty, clearing enough room for him to leap onto the truck and into the cab.

The military-model vehicle had no key. He started it up, shoved the big shift lever into gear and turned the large wheel over and over.

The heavy two-and-a-half vehicle rolled toward the soldiers and crushed several of them under its tires. Survivors began shooting back, and Bolan ducked as the return fire spiderwebbed the windshield and began peppering the seats behind him.

When Bolan's vehicle struck one of the wrecked amphibious personnel carriers, he threw himself from the cab, landing on a soldier who was trying to climb in. He spared the man a single thrust through the neck with one of his borrowed knives.

Picking up another M-16 from a fallen enemy, Bolan

fired it dry after only a few rounds. Then he grabbed the weapon by the triangular handguard and began swinging it like a club.

Grimaldi dived into the melee yet again. Bodies flew through the air as the minigun hosed them down. Then Bolan could hear the electric whine of the device cutting through the sound of the chopper's spinning rotors as the Stony Man pilot completed his pass. His minigun was empty, his rocket pods exhausted. There would be no more air support.

Bolan bashed a Mexican soldier across the face with the M-16. The weapon's plastic stock broke. He continued hammering away at the enemy gunner with the barrel of the weapon.

And then there was nobody moving.

Bolan paused, suddenly exhausted, the pain in his ribs like the points of screwdrivers being levered and twisted into his body. He threw away what was left of the M-16 and stood with his hands at his sides.

His breath came heavily. Bolan had a great deal of stamina, but it had been a very long night, and he had been fighting, running and gunning for what seemed almost every minute of it.

Grimaldi had landed the chopper and now joined him, his cut-down M-16 up and ready to assist. "Damn, Sarge," he said, looking around. "This is…"

"I know." Bolan nodded. "But we had to do it."

Dead men lay, in scattered rows, in haphazard clumps. Almost every vehicle in the column was on fire.

"Hal is going to have a coronary," Grimaldi said.

"No," Bolan said. "I don't think so. Our job is to stop the threat of this invasion and forestall full-scale war with Mexico. By halting them here we stopped them before they could get across the border and create the very incident the Man and Hal don't want."

Grimaldi nodded. "What now?"

"We go back. We'll need to resupply, make some preparations. Then we go to Mexico City. It's time we brought this fight to Castillo's doorstep. But there's something I want to do first."

"What's that?" Grimaldi asked.

"The problem isn't Mexico," Bolan said, reaching into his war bag. "The problem is Castillo, and his corrupt, illegitimate, extremist government. These men weren't Mexicans. They were predators, members of a gang, basically. They were part of Castillo's gang, and they were massed to attack the United States. We stopped them. But more importantly, people need to know we stopped them."

Bolan took out the American flag that had flown on the pole outside the seat of Tucson's city government. He walked up to the lead vehicle in the column, which had burned itself out by now, and attached the flag to the whip antenna of the otherwise charred and color-less hulk. The wind picked up the red, white and blue of the stars and stripes. The American flag fluttered in the breeze, its bright colors contrasting sharply with the blackened, ruined truck.

Bolan paused for a moment, regarding the flag. Then he shook his head as if to clear it, and started walking toward the helicopter.

"Come on, Jack," he said. "Let's roll."

CHAPTER FIFTEEN

Waning red-orange sunlight streamed through the windows of the presidential residence in Chapultepec Forest. The area was a sea of soothing greenery that contrasted sharply with congested Mexico City. It had always seemed to Gaspar Castillo that the city confronted the forest; that the two sat forever baring their teeth at each other, with the city and its fumes and its teeming masses and its cars ever more daring, ever more likely the victor. As he stood staring out the window in a drawing room of what the odious Anglo tourists often called "the Mexican White House," Castillo suppressed a sneer and produced a silver cigarette case from inside his suit jacket.

The harsh, black clove cigarettes weren't the most expensive brand available, though surely the president could afford such if he chose. The brand, however, was one to which Castillo had become thoroughly addicted long ago, when he'd worked the streets of Mexico City as a common criminal.

The remains of a sumptuous dinner sat on a silver tray on his desk. He could ring for its removal, but a servant would be in shortly to do that no matter what. Gaspar Castillo was now a man of fairly regimented habits, and the staff knew that he smoked after a meal. They also knew that he didn't like to be disturbed as he paused to reflect on the day. They had become quite good at timing their entry to take the dinner dishes. He wondered if perhaps they were not spying on him in some subtle way, so as to avoid displeasing him by arriving too early or waiting too long.

He reached into his pocket and produced an ornate silver lighter hand-engraved with elaborate scrollwork. Raising it, he brought the cigarette to his lips and drew in a deep, grateful puff of the warm, caustic blue smoke.

He was alone in the room. Well, he was alone in the room except for his two enormous bodyguards, whom he had come to regard as furniture. They were well paid, not terribly bright and very, very loyal; they had been specially selected for these qualities. They had names, but he'd dubbed them Zeus and Apollo, a private joke to himself that had its roots in an old American television show. The program had special meaning to Castillo, for it was the first one he had ever watched in the privacy of his own hotel room. The first time he had managed to earn enough money for a night in a cheap hotel, with his own soft bed and shower and even cable television, he had been overjoyed at the wondrous new world of luxury in which he found himself. The fact that the "luxury" he remembered so fondly was in reality the cheapest of cheap motels meant nothing; it made the memory all the more poignant. That was why he hadn't changed cigarette brands. He liked these little reminders of his past, and of how far he had come since then.

The son of a prostitute, Gasper Castillo had been turned out by his mother to starve or to eke out a living as he chose when he was nine years old. He had no idea what had become of his mother and he didn't care.

He carried a memento of those days still, in the tailored pocket of a suit that was itself worth more than he had managed to make for himself all together in those first few years on the street. It was a gigantic Navaja clasp knife, honed to a razor edge. He had taken it from a drunken fool outside a dive bar in the worst neighborhood of Mexico City when he was thirteen years old.

At fourteen, he killed his first man. "Man" was probably not fair; his victim had been another boy his age, but that boy had been intent on first raping him and then taking what little money he had. The clasp knife had done its work well, and Gaspar Castillo had his first taste of power.

He would kill many more people through the years. As he grew older, he got smarter, and he started tackling bigger and bigger forms of crime. At fifteen, he was running messages and parcels for Mexico City's largest drug gang. At seventeen, he was carrying a gun for the same group. At twenty-one, he assassinated the gang's leader and took the reins of power for himself.

As he gained power and wealth, he learned that he liked both more than anything. Oh, Gaspar Castillo enjoyed the pleasures of women…but even that paled in comparison to holding sway over his fellow man. The only other force that held meaning for Castillo, the only other belief he held that was as powerful as his desire for control and for affluence, was his hatred.

Gaspar Castillo *hated*.

He hated many things casually, such as the crushing poverty that he associated with the miserable years of his childhood. He hated his mother to this day and regretted that he had never had any means of tracking her down, for were she alive, he would surely make her wish she wasn't. To be betrayed and abandoned, left to die or to succeed on his own power at so young an age… that, too, he hated.

But he hated the Anglos more.

The United States and its riches represented everything Gaspar Castillo resented. They lived fat and happy off the products of poor nations' labors. They denied poverty-stricken Mexican citizens entry into their land, and when those citizens entered the country anyway, they used them and abused them as little better than slave labor. As he immersed himself in the racist literature of groups like La Raza and he learned of the movement toward the Reconquista, he thought perhaps he finally understood what his destiny was to be. He would use his power to right the wrongs that had been dealt Gaspar Castillo, yes, but he would also use his power to right the wrongs that had been dealt to the Race. The Mexican people would no longer be anyone's slaves. They would be independent and powerful…and free, just as long as they did exactly what Gaspar Castillo told them to do.

He was in his early thirties when he discovered that politics was a means of waging power, and soon he had purchased several members of local and federal government. But it wasn't enough to wield power through others. He wished to hold it himself. He wanted to be the man to whom others answered. He would never again be the poor, starving, victimized boy on the streets, the youth who held a knife to his chest as if it were a teddy bear and cried himself to sleep as he huddled in garbage-filled alleyways. He would become the man in charge.

He would become the president.

It took years for him to get the education he knew he needed. To use his connections, his money, his willingness to indulge in violence to gain his resulting power base, and thereby manipulate the political system. Corrupt as Mexican politics were, one did not simply throw a pile of cash on the table and declare that one was buying the presidency. The process was much more complicated, and once in office, only a shrewd president could wield power in the face of upstarts, rebels and mavericks who thought the government was a joke. Respect for the presidency was the lowest it had ever been when Gaspar Castillo first started working his way toward that office. He remembered well the "shadow government" of dissenters that had plagued his predecessor, who'd won an election and yet was powerless to lead when dissidents essentially told him they refused to acknowledge his authority.

Thus it was that while Gaspar Castillo laid the groundwork for his presidency, he also laid the groundwork for controlling the military. In Mexico, the army was power. He was going to make sure that power was his, and that the Mexican people and those within its government would learn to tremble in fear at the thought of his displeasure.

Money bought power, but indirectly most of the time. The exception was the military. Pay enough soldiers enough money long enough, and you held their loyalty. Pay their officers more, promise them more, and you owned them and those under their command.

Castillo spent years building his career on supporting the military overtly, running for lesser offices, always with his eye on the presidency. He spoke out in support of armament expenditures, of raising soldiers' pay, of the Mexican military above almost all other considerations. In the popular press, he was caricaturized as an anthropomorphic hawk. As long as that hawk looked powerful and dangerous, he didn't mind so much.

Seeding the military with men loyal to him, co-opting its power structure, took time, but wasn't very difficult. When finally he was ready to rise to political power, to run for the presidency, he did so with the full knowledge that he controlled the military and thus he controlled the people.

His first act as president was to declare martial law. Mexico had suffered long enough under the yoke of corruption, inefficiency and waste, he declared on now state-controlled television. His administration would bring about order at last and, to that end, the Mexican army would be taking up stations throughout Mexico City and in other urban centers in the country. They would establish the type of peace and orderliness that Gaspar Castillo wished for his people, and in so doing they would help initiate a new age of Mexican prosperity.

Or else.

Castillo had no illusions. He knew he was a dictator. He was entirely comfortable with this fact. Only the power wielded by a dictator could accomplish the bold tasks that lay before him. Actually making the Reconquista happen was one of those things.

When Orieza had contacted him, he had been flattered. Then he had deployed his spies and learned that Orieza was the puppet of this Del Valle. Well, that was all right, too, and truth be told, Del Valle was a potentially useful man to have on hand, given his skill and political savvy. The thought that these men wanted to make a deal with him, a pact that would help bring about the Reconquista and make him richer, was certainly a flattering one. Even the fact that another nation took the scheme seriously had been enough to spur Castillo to move forward, regardless.

It was good that he hadn't waited for the Hondurans and their ridiculous timetable. Again, being honest with himself, he had never really expected their elaborate plan to succeed. Castillo had spies everywhere he could maintain them, and he was very proud of the espionage network he had developed among Third World nations. He hadn't had much confidence in Orieza succeeding simply because there was too much to do, and because Guatemala, nominally a United States ally, would inevitably bring the hated Americans into the fray. Del Valle had skill and he had will, but these weren't going to be enough. Certainly Orieza himself brought little to the bargain, which was clear when Castillo's operatives investigated the old fool and figurehead thoroughly.

When Orieza's plan fell down around his ears, Gasper hadn't been surprised. He would miss the money, but he did have Orieza and Del Valle to thank for the gift of the UAV helicopter. The weapon had proved its worth in the attack on Tucson. It had, in fact, been the only part of that plan that had not ultimately been a miserable failure. The thought produced a frown.

Things in Honduras, meanwhile, were rapidly deteriorating, as one would expect in a total power vacuum. There would be nothing to salvage from that connection. Castillo dismissed it from his mind. Yes, it would have been useful to procure some of the wealth available in Guatemala, and the oil money would surely have helped, but perhaps the absence of these found riches would help spur his people to fight harder to reclaim what was theirs from the hated Americans. It held similarities to the ancient practice of burning one's boats after landing an army, so that the soldiers could only go forward, never back, until victory was theirs. Surely there was no turning back here. He would never be able to sustain action against the Americans unless he gained and held territory. His whole plan was built on that.

He stubbed out his cigarette in a silver ashtray on his desk. As if on cue, a pretty young woman in the uniform of a maid came to clear away the dishes. Castillo favored her with a smile and she dropped her gaze demurely.

"Have Zapata summoned to me," he said, turning to look out at the sunset once more. He clasped his hands behind his back.

"Yes, Mr. President," the young woman said, and was gone.

The would-be revolutionary had to have been waiting nearby for the summons he surely knew would come, for he skulked into the room not fifteen seconds later. Castillo waved for him to sit down, produced his cigarette case and went through his elaborate ritual again. When his cigarette was trailing blue smoke, he moved to sit on the corner of the desk and look down at Zapata, who was squirming uncomfortably in a chair before him. Behind the desk in the alcoves dedicated to this purpose, Castillo's large bodyguards hulked. They could have been statues or even bookends for all they moved. There were times when Castillo thought he should check them to make sure they were still breathing.

He made a note to watch them practice the following morning. Both men were powerful grapplers who trained with each other and with a coach twice a week. It was as close to a private sporting event as one got, and Castillo enjoyed seeing just how dangerous these men were. It was a reminder that his attack dogs were lethal and they were *his*. That was a giddy thought to him, even now, as president.

Zapata had a bandage on his head. He twitched often. His dirty, stringy hair had been pulled back, and he wore jeans, sandals and a formless beige shirt. He looked, in other words, like the disaffected college dropout he had been when Castillo first found him and determined to make use of him. His confidence had been shaken by the operation in Tucson. If Castillo were to continue to use him as a stalking horse for his racially motivated attacks on United States territory, he would have to make sure the man was at least not afraid of his own shadow. Castillo had no use for a man terrified of the consequences of his actions.

"Would you like a cigarette, Tristan?" He proffered the silver case.

"No, thank you, Mr. President," Zapata shook his head. "Please forgive my failure across the border. I was…I mean I…"

"Will you stop worrying about that, Tristan?" Castillo lilted, raising his hands in a soothing gesture. "You may think it was a failure, but it was not."

"But, sir," Zapata protested, "we lost our men. We lost the hostages. I was forced to flee."

"But we dealt a serious blow to the Americans," Castillo countered. "We shook them, Tristan. We made them realize that they are not so safe as they thought they were, not so mighty, not so invulnerable. We reminded them of just how impotent they can be."

"Will that not make it harder for us in the future, sir?"

"Were it Mexico, or some other proud nation, yes, it would," Castillo said. "But remember, Tristan, that the Americans are weak. They have no nerve. They will hold their breath in fear of us coming. And when we hit them again, we will crush their spirits so totally that our plan will work perfectly. We will hit them hard and take more than we want, so that when we withdraw, when our demands become less, they will be much more palatable to the weary Americans. By that time we will have begun the Reconquista in earnest, and the first of what will be many American territories will be firmly under our control."

"I of course would like to see that day, Mr. President."

"I know you would, Tristan," Castillo said. "That is why, in perhaps two days, no more, I will have you lead another attack on Tucson. I will give you more troops this time."

"Another attack, sir?" Zapata sounded horrified. "But is that wise?"

"Of course," Castillo said. "It is the last thing they would expect. We shall hit weary, long-suffering Tucson, this den of usurper Anglos, and we will do so with fresh troops. I have men and equipment staged outside Chihuahua. When you are sufficiently rested and the men have been briefed by my special-forces operatives, you will go there and see to it that the raid is heralded as being for the Race. You can do that for me, can you not?"

"Yes, of course, sir," Zapata said dubiously. "It is just that—"

"I know," Castillo said smoothly. "You suffered much at the hands of the Anglos and you are not eager to repeat the experience. I know the cost will be heavy and has been so. Surely the loss of so many men, as well as our border troops, was a high price to pay, but in truth it was not altogether unforeseen. The Americans are a powerful foe, even in their current lethargic state. No doubt they sent a unit of their special forces against you. That is why we will use more men this time."

"I am not…" Zapata began, and then stopped.

"What? You are not what?"

"I…I am not convinced, Mr. President, that we faced a unit of their special forces. I think perhaps there were only a handful of men. Perhaps only two or three."

"Are you mad?" Castillo said. "Why would you say that?"

"I saw only one man," Zapata said. "And there was the pilot flying their helicopter, who dueled Tomas in the skies. But I saw no one else."

Castillo waved a dismissive hand. "These are special-forces soldiers, Tristan," he said patiently. "Of course they did not let you see them, or perceive their full numbers. That is how they operate. But I can see you are still unsettled."

"I have fear, sir. I will not lie. What if this man—these men—come here? What if the Americans decide to train their might on us? What if another attack draws them out and prompts them to do just that?"

"It is good that you do," the president said, placing his hand on Zapata's shoulder. "That is normal and natural. Do not let it get the best of you. I saw to your safe return, did I not, by providing for Tomas and his truck to safely cross the border under subterfuge?"

"Yes, sir," Zapata said. "Tomas came to my rescue when the American special-forces troops invaded the building. He used the helicopter to free me, and I was able to escape in the truck with him. I hid in the secret compartment with the helicopter, and we were passed by the border patrol."

"Thus do the Americans aid us in their own destruction." Castillo smiled and shook his head. "How is your wound, speaking of that?"

"It is all right," Zapata said, touching his bandaged forehead. "The doctors tell me it left a furrow, but it is not very bad. I have some pain but I am not troubled overmuch by it."

"Good, good. Rest well here in my house, my friend. Surely you are safe here, with my military camped in the forest surrounding us, with my patrols and garrisons throughout the city?"

"Yes, sir."

"Go now, Tristan," Castillo said. "Get some sleep. You will need it. I am counting on you to lead the next incursion."

"Yes, sir." He got up and left Castillo's office.

Poor fool. He was obviously brain-addled from the

fighting, to think that a single man or even a half a dozen men could have done as much damage as was done to their resources in the night and morning. Castillo was still very angry about the destruction of the reserve troops over the border south of Tucson. That wasn't supposed to happen. The men had been massacred, for lack of a better word. Worse, his operatives reported that someone had left an American flag on the scene, conspicuously placed on one of the destroyed vehicles. If that wasn't a message, Castillo didn't know what was. The problem was, exactly what did it tell him? How far could he push the Americans? He was becoming less sure of himself, but he wasn't so foolish or cowardly as to give up his plan. He simply would have to make allowances for pockets of resistance.

The reports crossing his desk all day had, in fact, been uniformly bad news. When the ornate desk phone began to ring, he expected it would be more of the same. He was, therefore, surprised when he picked up the receiver and Del Valle's voice came faintly over the line.

"Mr. President," Del Valle said weakly.

"Roderigo?" he asked. "How in this world... I was told you were captured."

"I was wounded," he said. "Taken to a hospital and treated. There, I managed to kill my guard and escape."

"Where are you now?"

"Somewhere in Tucson. I am at a pay phone. I do not have much time."

"No, I imagine you do not." He rattled off an address. "Can you get there?"

"I believe I can, Mr. President. What will I find?"

"It is an auto-body shop run by one of my operatives,"

Castillo said. "Give him the code word *Ferrari* and he will assist you. Tell him I sent you. He will see to it you are given transportation across the border and thence to Mexico City."

"Yes, sir. My men—"

"A lost cause, I am afraid," Castillo reported. "Your men waited at this WKAL station to guard the prisoners and await your safe return?"

"They did," Del Valle said. "Just as you told me, I used the ruse of the news crew to gain entry when they were finally admitted, per your plan to extract Zapata when his part in the events were over. They suspected nothing and I was able to gain access. I left my men behind to help your own guard the prisoners. There was no way to insert more than one additional man without raising suspicions."

"That is why you are free and they are not," Castillo admitted. "The plan would not have worked, it seems, and poor Tristan was fortunate to leave the scene by other means. Something we did made the Americans suspicious. A team of military or law-enforcement operatives raided the station and freed the employees we were holding. I have no further word on what became of them. The local news reports some 'terrorists' holding WKAL were killed in the counterterrorist assault, and that all the hostages survived. I can only assume your men were murdered or captured."

"That is unfortunate."

"Indeed."

"Is there still a place for me in your administration, Mr. President?" Del Valle asked bluntly.

"I do not see why not," Castillo said graciously. "You

have proved yourself a survivor, and you have proved you can follow instructions. I can use a man of your skills and abilities."

"Thank you, Mr. President," Del Valle said. "I will report to you shortly."

"Yes," Castillo agreed. "See that you do." He replaced the receiver in its cradle and considered that.

Zapata would eventually outlive his usefulness, and when that happened, Castillo would have to have him killed. Perhaps this Del Valle could fill that role. At least until he, too, had to be eliminated.

In the meantime, Castillo would be a fool not to take precautions. There were certain defenses he could arrange to put in place here at his residence. The UAV had been returned to him. He could station the control somewhere convenient, have it linked to the security sensor grid and make sure that its operator had specific orders for dealing with intrusions.

To augment that—for Castillo rarely trusted a single mechanism, no matter how remarkable—he would have his men form contingency plans for armed resistance. These would likely not be needed. It wouldn't do to be caught by surprise, however. There were other measures that might prove useful, too, but still others that wouldn't. His men had had to stop some of the La Raza idiots from digging spike-filled tiger traps in the forest. Tiger traps, for pity's sake! Who would think such a thing would be helpful here?

In the event that the American commandos somehow grew bold enough to come here and attack him, which was laughable, he would have the means to repel them. He would rely on the UAV first. Sent home with their tails between their legs, the Americans would report their defeat to their government and the Anglos would be more eager than ever to come to the table with him, for fear of suffering more humiliation at his hands.

Castillo had nothing to fear. He told himself that several times. There was nothing to fear, and nothing to worry about. He was safe in his headquarters, secure here in Mexico City, assured in the power he wielded. A strong leader couldn't afford to have doubt. A strong leader couldn't allow petty personal fears, or even fears for his own safety, to interfere with his exercise of power. That was, after all, *strength*.

He kept telling himself that, too, in the hope that if he said it often enough, he would eventually believe it.

CHAPTER SIXTEEN

The sun was climbing higher in the sky on this bright, hot morning when Mack Bolan pulled over. The stolen Jeep in which he traveled he had picked up on the outskirts of Mexico City. The vehicle was running roughly. It had been a hard ride from the outskirts into the depths of the largest city in Mexico, which boasted something like nine million residents, or perhaps twice that depending on how much of the sprawling metropolitan area was defined as Mexico City for purposes of the census. Ranked in the top ten by gross domestic product among cities in the world, the Mexico City region accounted for perhaps one-fourth the gross domestic product of Mexico. It was also polluted, congested and riddled with crime, and had an insufficient fresh-water supply for its needs.

Bolan had decided on a blitz through the city that would ultimately take him to the very offices of the Mexican president. The Farm's intelligence sources had verified that, yes, Castillo was in residence, and that had been good enough for Bolan. Grimaldi had flown him to the outskirts of the city, and Bolan had HALO-dropped under cover of night. He hadn't been spotted. Wearing another Panama hat and a light, white, tropical-weight overcoat, he had found a Jeep, hot-wired it and used it to get him this far.

The roadblock had come up unexpectedly. He had anticipated security; he simply had put that concern aside.

As Bolan picked his way through the congested and narrow streets of the maze that was Mexico City proper, he marveled at the poverty and the decay. Commercial and residential concerns abutted one another and were interspersed almost at random. Children and animals roamed the streets. Street beggars were everywhere. Yes, Mexico was a large, powerful and dynamic city, but Bolan now traveled through its seamy underbelly, and the picture was a bleak one.

He made no attempt to avoid the roadblock. Encountering a security checkpoint had been inevitable. The brazen manner in which he approached it was something else again.

The soldiers surrounded his vehicle. There were five of them, stationed at a temporary barricade that had a sign that read Police in Spanish even though these men were nothing of the kind. They wore some new digital-pattern camouflage Bolan hadn't seen before, and carried FX-05 Xiuhcoatl assault rifles with the stocks folded. They wore dark blue berets. They also wore dark armbands that bore a single word: *Castillo*. These were Castillo's version of shock troops, and Bolan could guess what they were here to do. The way the pedestrians averted their gaze as they passed by, the way the other drivers glanced up and then away in fear… Mexico City was an armed camp. This was direct evidence of that fact.

The Mexican soldier leaned in the open window of Mack Bolan's Jeep, a smug look of self-satisfaction on his face. He reached out his hand and, in Spanish, informed the Executioner that this was a toll road. Before he could come through they would have to inspect his vehicle, and when they were done, he would have to pay the fee for the inspection. The man also remarked that Bolan's hat was quite nice and that he thought it just might fit him. At that crack, his fellow guards laughed.

"You know what you are?" Bolan asked in passable Spanish.

"What am I?" the guard asked, too incredulous to take offense just yet.

"You're a bully," Bolan said. He'd had to search for the word for a moment. Then he switched languages. "Do you speak English?"

The guard's face turned hard. "An American tourist?" he demanded in accented but fluent English. "Just who in hell do you think you are, you son of a whore? Get out of the vehicle!" He reached in the open window to grab Bolan by the lapels.

Bolan had a small tactical folding knife clipped to the pocket of his blacksuit pants. When the guard reached in, he pulled it out, and as the man's fingers curled around the lapel of his overcoat, Bolan snapped the knife open using its built-in thumb stud. The viciously serrated hawkbill blade clicked and locked. He brought it up and carved around the outside of the man's arm, practically filleting him like a fish. He shrieked in horror and fell back.

The other guards at the roadblock opened up with their FX-05 rifles, spraying the windshield of the Jeep with 5.56-mm NATO rounds. Bolan ducked, then slammed the vehicle into gear, rode out the loud bang as its transmission caught and stomped on the gas pedal.

The Jeep surged forward, running down two of the roadblock guards. Not satisfied, Bolan threw the engine into Reverse, peeked up and over his seat and slammed into a third man with the tires still squealing.

More automatic gunfire blew the tires on one side. Bolan slid across the seat and kicked open the passenger door, dropping down and hitting the street. Bullets strafed his Jeep.

More soldiers raced to join the guards Bolan had originally engaged. He didn't know where they were coming from, but the densely packed neighborhood was disgorging them with disturbing rapidity.

The Executioner got rid of his coat and went EVA. He spun around the rear of the Jeep, clotheslined a running guard and took his rifle. The FX-05 was a fine, advanced weapon, and Bolan put it to good use, spraying its magazine in measured, aimed bursts at the attacking gunners.

He took a man in the throat, shot another through the face and stitched a third in the chest. Traffic stopped in the street and drivers fled their cars. Bolan was careful to avoid putting innocent people in the cross fire; the citizens of Mexico were victims just as surely as had been the residents of Tucson, the villagers of Guatemala and the civilians in Honduras. The situation was rapidly becoming untenable, however, as more soldiers arrived on scene. One group arrived in an army jeep, which was marked with a dark blue symbol bearing Castillo's name. It seemed that dictatorial fashion leaned toward blue these days, unless Castillo's enforcers and Orieza's blue-tagged bullies had somehow compared notes before the fact.

Bolan dismissed the random thought from his mind. He ran for it, finding a narrow alley and ducking into it.

The laneway was full of refuse and obstructed by metal trash containers, large cardboard boxes full of garbage and broken furniture. Bolan vaulted this like an Olympic track star. He reached the end of the alley, brought his borrowed rifle to his shoulder and waited.

The first of the Mexican army pursuers entered the mouth of the alley at the opposite end. Bolan fired, putting a shot precisely through the man's left eye.

Another soldier made the same mistake. Bolan dropped him, too.

The rest of the gunmen figured out the danger and took up positions on either side of the entrance. They started shooting blindly, poking their rifles around the corner and pulling the triggers, unable to see what they were firing at.

Bolan took careful aim and, as chips of stone and brick from the walls of the buildings sprayed him, he fired once, then twice, then again. He scored clean hits on two of the rifles before the third man yanked his back. There was much cursing in Spanish from the opposite end.

The big American took off up the street. He elbowed past confused citizens and those who were looking on in fear, having realized that a firefight was raging half a block away. Bolan turned several times, picking new alleys as he went, zigzagging to make sure that he wouldn't be easy to spot, follow or line up for a shot.

Always, as he ran, he was aware of the general direction he needed to head. He was moving inexorably toward the forest around which Mexico City squatted, the forest that was home to the president. No doubt Castillo thought himself safe at his home. Perhaps he thought these security measures throughout the city made him doubly safe, secure from those who meant him harm.

Well, fascist troops in the streets and ominous posters on the walls—Bolan passed yet another giant picture of Castillo's grinning face, with the slogan in Spanish He's Watching Out for You—were no match for a determined operative who had right on his side. Bolan was going to teach Gaspar Castillo the dangers of waking the sleeping giant that was the United States.

As so many had learned before.

He emerged from yet another alley onto a larger street at a dead run. A soldier smarter than the others had angled to cut him off, and Bolan practically rolled right over the man. Both of them hit the pavement.

Bolan was up first. He had lost his rifle, but that was all right; there were many people here in the street and he wouldn't risk a shot. He brushed the coat aside and drew the smaller of his two fighting blades from his harness, bringing the weapon out, up and over in an arc in one smooth, fluid motion. The needle-pointed, subtly curved blade slashed across the soldier's throat as he tried to bring up his rifle. Blood sprayed as he went down, gurgling, and Bolan shot out with his right foot in a brutal front kick that pistoned into the man's lower abdomen. The kick folded the man and pushed him back, away from the rifle, which clattered harmlessly to the ground. Bolan shoved his knife back into its sheath.

The big American bent long enough to snatch up the rifle and continue his dash.

At the next intersection, two more military jeeps were converging on his location. Bolan, not missing a beat, emptied his rifle into the one on his left, breaking right to angle for the other vehicle. He jumped up and onto the hood of a car parked nearby, which gave him enough height to leap into the rear of the military jeep he was now targeting.

The vehicle had an old M-60 machine gun mounted in the back on a swivel.

Bolan drew his large knife and nearly beheaded the gunner. As the driver and his passenger turned to try to get at the sudden invader in their midst, Bolan reversed the knife and drove its point down into the subclavian artery of the nearer man, digging the blade back and forth before he yanked it free. His left hand found his Desert Eagle and he jerked it from its Kydex sheath, pumping a .44 Magnum round into the other soldier. The knife flashed back into its sheath as he reholstered the hand cannon.

He took in the scene before him quickly, processing his targets and what lay beyond them. There were no innocents in the line of fire.

Bolan jacked back the cocking handle of the M-60, snugged it to his body and let fly.

The firestorm of 7.62-mm rounds showered the occupants of the first jeep, burning through them, through the vehicle itself and into the pavement. Bolan kept up the blaze until he was satisfied the threat was neutralized.

Then he reached down, yanked the pivot pin and picked up the entire M-60, complete with its attached ammo box.

The neighborhood was a warren, and there was no shortage of new alleys and side streets he could duck down. Sirens were blaring from all directions as word of the violence spread; the soldiers were likely calling in support. None of that mattered. Bolan wasn't worried about the resistance slowing him. He was a man on fire, a man burning with a mission, and he would accomplish that mission regardless of the obstacles thrown in his way.

There was, despite this seemingly casual, berserker charge, a method to his madness. He wasn't simply hurling himself heedlessly into danger without thought of the consequences. He was instead relying on his superior skill and experience as a soldier, as a lone warrior in an endless war, to carry him through this bold phase of his admittedly brazen plan.

The more unrest he created in Mexico City, the more soldiers would be called to respond to it. If he could move the focus to the surrounding neighborhood and away from the president's residence, it would make his penetration of the latter that much easier.

He just had to survive this part of the plan. That was more or less the weakest part of this operation.

Not that there was any doubt in his mind he would succeed. It was just a lot of work.

He trotted down a wide thoroughfare, carrying the M-60 before him. People screamed in Spanish, then ran for cover. Bolan found an inconspicuous doorway, kicked it in and followed the M-60 inside.

The Executioner found himself in the back room of a small restaurant. He made his way past the dry goods in storage, beyond a cooler whose metal door was dented with age, and then through the kitchen. People shouted at him, but he ignored them. He emerged from the front of the little café to the sounds of gasps from the customers. He nodded at one particularly attractive young woman in a summer dress; she was probably in her mid-twenties and had a truly remarkable figure. She smiled, despite her shock at his appearance and the weapon in his hands.

His movements were being tracked through a grid of streets familiar to his enemies and not to him. That was fine. Bolan could anticipate moves like this. When he saw a group of Mexican soldiers waiting on the other side of the street from the restaurant entrance, he hit the deck. Rolling to make sure he didn't draw fire at an angle that would endanger the civilians in the restaurant, he took the M-60 with him, and to its credit, it survived the maneuver intact and functional.

He tested its function at great length.

The weapon chugged and churned and smoked, hammering out heavy 7.62-mm rounds and splashing his would-be killers over the concrete wall behind them. The rounds chipped the heavy cement but didn't penetrate, blasting the plaster facade and raining white dust onto the bloody bodies of the men Bolan had just dropped.

An army truck turned and moved up the alley, the diver foolishly thinking the vehicle was some form of protection. He ducked down, and Bolan sprayed the engine block with the M-60. He worked the weapon up the hood and across the cab, under the level of the windshield. The driver never got up again, and by the time Bolan was through burning up the canvas-covered rear, the soldiers attempting to pile out into the alley weren't in any condition to give him any trouble.

The M-60 was empty and there were no reloads for it. He looked around, ducked behind the truck where no one could see him and threw the weapon onto the pavement. The Army would recover it, most likely. He imagined the locals' fear of Castillo's forces would prevent some shrewd citizen from appropriating it. Bolan had no desire to leave military hardware lying around for the neighborhood children to play with, nor did he wish to make the drug gangs in this part of the world any better armed than they already were.

He crossed a busy street, weaving in and out of traffic, then rounded a corner. His guns were holstered, but they were visible, and a black-clad soldier wasn't exactly going to blend in, walking through such a neighborhood, under the best of circumstances. It was therefore a testament to how badly the people of Mexico had been beaten into submission by Castillo's rule that nobody challenged him. More than a few noticed him, however, and gasps and shouts followed him.

He had a small wristband compass clipped to his harness and he glanced at it. To continue in the correct direction he had to turn left. He turned the corner—

Three Mexican soldiers were standing there.

They froze and looked at him. He looked at them, and as he did so, he checked behind them. There were no civilians in the line of fire, provided he was careful.

The man on the left had a pistol in a flap holster on

his belt. The man on the right looked terrified. The man in the center simply stared Bolan in the face. Then his eyes narrowed.

Bolan's hand flashed to the Kydex sheath that held his Desert Eagle. He snapped the weapon out in a smooth gunfighter's draw, dropping into a Weaver's stance as he half crouched and leaned into the shot.

He put a .44 Magnum round through the head of the man in the middle. Then he tracked right, pressed the trigger and sent the man there to hell with a single bullet through the brain. The soldier on the left was still clawing at his weapon, trying to drag it from its flap holster. Judging by his rank insignia, Bolan knew he was an officer. When the man realized the fight was all but over, he looked up hopelessly.

"Should have left it in your desk," Bolan said. He took the few steps necessary to bring him closer to the man.

"Por favor—"

Bolan had heard that one before and was in no mood. He pistol-whipped the officer savagely, dropping him unconscious to the pavement.

He was about to continue on when he heard the trucks.

They were more army-issue deuce-and-a-halfs. They were troop carriers, with canvas-covered beds, and they were full of soldiers. Hundreds of them.

Bolan picked the closest, smallest alley he could find and ran for it, holstering his weapon as he went. He couldn't face that many and live. Sooner or later, they would overwhelm him with their numbers, or he would simply run out of ammunition. Bolan wasn't superhuman. He was just a man well trained to handle the extraordinary. Forty to one, sixty to one, a hundred to one... These weren't odds any sane man attempted, not even the Executioner.

As he ran for it, he kept his goal in mind. He wouldn't retreat. He wouldn't give up. He wouldn't fail to bring justice to Castillo. If he didn't stop the man here and now, more American lives would be at stake. There was no end, quite literally, to the deaths Castillo could cause in his mad plan to forcibly annex portions of the United States, and his racist hatred for Americans would spur him on to ever greater acts of horror and predation.

Bolan knew the type well. He despised racism in all its forms, and the philosophy of La Raza followed by Castillo and his operatives, such as Zapata, turned his stomach.

No, they might pursue him. They might hurt him, but he wouldn't stop. He wouldn't quit.

He was going after the president.

CHAPTER SEVENTEEN

Bolan discovered sooner than he expected that he was running out of inner-city maze. He was making good time through the densely packed neighborhoods, and he had taken down several squads of Castillo's beret-and-armband-wearing enforcers. A few times he had run into contingents of what appeared to be regular Mexican army, usually performing routine neighborhood security checks, but these men didn't seem terribly interested in him. They pointed and they spoke into walkie-talkies as he passed, but it quickly became apparent that the word had been handed down: Castillo's enforcers were on the trail of this interloper, whoever he might be, and apparently they wanted no interference.

He stopped short as a truck bearing the Castillo enforcer logo pulled up at the end of the narrow street ahead. More of the men piled out. Bolan was fast running out of options.

He passed several closed doors and shuttered windows. One of these opened after he'd gone by.

"Over here!" a voice called. It was a young woman's; he could tell that much.

If it was a trap, he would have to trip it. He barely had time to enter before the soldiers converged on the street.

The woman's fragrance hit him as she closed the

door behind them. She was in her mid-twenties, most likely, with a breathtaking figure and long, dark hair that framed a heart-shaped face and large, dark eyes. Her skin was dark; her red, lightweight dress clung to her in all the right places. Bolan had just enough time to look her up and down once and be impressed when she whirled, her face full of fear.

"Quickly! Inside!"

"Aren't I already—" Bolan started to ask.

"Through here, through here," she urged. She pushed him through the modestly furnished little apartment, through the kitchen, where an older man and woman sat staring in stark terror. Bolan caught just enough of a glimpse of them to place the young woman's features. The woman was obviously her mother, which meant the man was most likely her father.

"I am Maria Catlan," she said quickly. "These are Rosario and Sandro, my parents." She pointed. "In here, now!"

She opened the ancient refrigerator. Actually, Bolan realized, she had moved the entire refrigerator, revealing an alcove behind it dug into the plaster walls, just large enough for a decent-size person. Barely.

Bolan knew a spiderhole when he saw one. He moved without complaint or argument into position. Catlan pointed to a small device extending from the "roof" of the spiderhole, which was at first glance a cardboard tube. When she rotated the refrigerator back into place on its hidden hinges, the light from the tube caught Bolan's attention. It was a homemade periscope, with a vantage somewhere above the fridge, looking out into the living room. It had a good view of the front door, which made perfect sense.

Catlan took up a station near the refrigerator. She spoke without looking at Bolan, while her parents continued to sit at the table. "The BA are everywhere," she said. "They are sweeping the neighborhood. You must wait for them to pass over and through, and then wait some more. Then it will be safe."

"The BA?" Bolan asked. His voice was most likely muffled, but she seemed to be able to hear him just fine.

"Bastardos azules," she said. "The Blue Bastards, you would call them. President Castillo's secret police, dressed as the army."

"Castillo's enforcers, you mean."

"Yes," she said. Her English was close to perfect. "Who are you?"

"You don't know?" Bolan said. "Yet you helped me."

"We would help anyone who fights the BA," she said. "Word travels fast in this city, *señor*. Neighbors have come by to spread the word that one who fights the BA, a big man who spoke English to them at the roadblock, is coming through. More say that the BA has sent out what must be every soldier in the garrison. We knew you needed help. But some…some are not so brave. I am not so brave, either, but there was no one else. So I helped you."

"You're doing something very dangerous."

"*Sí.* I know this. But my family…we hate the BA. Anything that hurts them is good. You fight them?"

"Yes."

"You are American?"

"Yes." There was no harm in telling her.

"Why do you fight these enforcers, these men of Castillo?"

"Castillo has done terrible things in the name of power," Bolan said vaguely. "If he's not stopped, he'll do worse. I've come to do that. I've come to stop him."

"But you fight his men in the streets of the city. He is not here."

"No," Bolan said. "He's not. I'm trying to draw attention from where I know he'll be."

"You talk of his residence."

"Yes."

"You are a soldier, then? You fight Castillo's men, and you will fight him…. So you are American military?"

"I'm a soldier," Bolan said truthfully. "For a very long time now."

"You have told me what you intend to do. I could betray you."

"But you won't," Bolan said. "Or you wouldn't be hiding me in the first place."

"That is true." Catlan looked down, and through the periscope Bolan could see she appeared thoughtful. "Things in Mexico City have not always been easy. Very seldom were they so. But we have a happy family. We are simple people. I hope to go to college. I want to go to America, when I can afford it. To California. For school. I had a job at a café here, but it has closed. So many things were closed or shut down by Castillo. Sedition, he called it. Places where sedition takes place. He rules us through the BA. Many people have disappeared. Many more have been beaten. We know he is murdering us. He will kill us all before he will let us be free. Things are much worse, now."

"I can do something about that."

"But first you must wait," Catlan said. "Wait until the patrol has passed. Then you may go."

"Why do you have a hiding place in your kitchen, Miss Catlan?" Through the periscope, Bolan could see Marie's parents glance at her sharply. They were clearly scared out of their minds. Bolan got the impression that this young lady was used to doing as she pleased. She had a strong will and a good way about her.

"For my brother," Catlan explained. "He is not here right now. He is at school. But when he comes home, the PR Corps will try to take him. They come often. It is a youth corps. My history teacher, before the BA came to take him, they told me it was like Hitler. The Hitler Youth. We don't want Lino, my brother, to join this Hitler Youth, this PR. So we hide him when they come through looking for boys."

"What is 'PR'?"

"Puño de la Regla." The youth corps of President Castillo.

"I see," Bolan said. He was amazed at this young woman's quiet confidence, and her willingness to take in a stranger and hide him without a moment's notice. "Maria," he said, "what is the address here?"

She rattled it off and he memorized it. "Why?" she asked.

"I need to know roughly where I am, so I can calculate where I need to go and how fast to get there. It's part of my mission."

"I see." She echoed Bolan's tone, and the soldier smiled despite himself.

There was a loud knock at the door. Someone shouted outside in Spanish for the occupants to open up. They called themselves the police, but when Catlan's father went to open the door, men in the military fatigues of Castillo's enforcers entered.

Without a word the men began tearing up the modest apartment. They looked in closets. He could hear them looking under beds. They peered under the threadbare sofa in the living area. One even came into the kitchen and checked all the cupboards before opening the refrigerator door right in front of Bolan. Through it all, his hiding space remained undiscovered.

It was clear from the resigned look on the faces of Maria's parents that this type of search was entirely routine. The casual contempt on the faces of Castillo's muscle brought the righteous anger back to the pit of Bolan's stomach. To see good people like this, brave people like Maria Catlan, suffering under the indignity of a dictator's whims made him reach for the butts of his weapons.

The Catlans would be none the worse for wear, however, as long as he simply held his peace. He was in no position to have a gunfight, not here in their home with them watching. He didn't wish to endanger them, and they would have to live here long after he was gone. It wasn't Bolan's place to make their lives harder.

He contented himself with watching. That was, he watched...until something changed.

Four men were crowded into the room when three more arrived. Then yet another came in, which meant eight soldiers were packed into the Catlans' little apartment. One of them whispered to the others. He then walked over to the kitchen table and, without a word of warning, tossed it aside. Mrs. Catlan yelled out and the soldier slapped her.

Bolan's jaw twitched.

The soldier grabbed both the elder Catlans and ushered them out of the room. The laughter started among his comrades. One of the seven remaining soldiers closed and barred the door, using the worn wooden block the Catlans apparently used to secure their home.

Maria Catlan stood in the kitchen, and now it was her turn to look terrified.

The laughing and vulgar jokes in Spanish increased in volume. The soldiers were grinning and elbowing one another.

There could be no mistaking their intention.

The young woman turned and look directly into the periscope. Her back was to the soldiers, whose eyes were crawling up and down her lithe figure in the formfitting summer dress. She mouthed four words in English for Bolan's benefit: *Do not do it.* She shook her head slightly to emphasize the point. She didn't want Bolan to interfere. She didn't want his help.

She turned. One of the soldiers dragged the kitchen table into the center of the living room. The men laughed more loudly, and one slapped the table roughly with his hand.

Maria Catlan's bravery, her willingness to do anything to hit back at Castillo's regime, suddenly made sense.

Bolan felt anger ignite in his belly. He thought of

the look on Sheila Sands's face, the look of a woman whose life would never be the same, whose emotions would never quite be whole ever again. He thought of the things men like Castillo and his enforcers routinely took away from others, things that could be so easily broken and never be fixed. He thought of the countless ways the poor people of Mexico were made to suffer under a dictator, and the ways that dictator threatened to make things even worse for them. If Castillo succeeded in initiating his insane scheme, there was no way it could succeed. To take portions of the United States might seem plausible, but ultimately it could only lead to war, no matter how ineffectual Castillo and his henchmen thought the Americans' collective political will might be.

No more.

Bolan pumped his combat-booted foot into the refrigerator, slamming it aside.

The soldiers had Maria Catlan spread-eagled on the kitchen table. Two held her hands and two held her legs apart; another was positioning himself before her. Her eyes were already glazed over in defeat; her mind was somewhere else, wherever it was she went to spare herself from these atrocities. Bolan had seen *that* before, too—men and women made to suffer so badly they retreated into worlds of their own making, usually temporarily. He had also seen some who entered such a world and never came back again. Torture would do that. No one was immune, and everyone could be broken. Everyone had limits.

The Executioner had his limits, and they had just been reached.

The big Japanese-style blade filled his hand.

The first soldier never knew what happened. Bolan grabbed him by the shoulder, pulled him from the spot between his victim's legs and shoved the point of the knife straight through his neck. He screamed, then his eyes rolled up into his head, his throat geysering blood.

The other soldiers were slow to respond, distracted as they were. Bolan lashed out with a side kick, snapping the knee of the man closest to him. He screamed and collapsed, for his leg would no longer hold him. Bolan crouched just long enough to reverse the big knife and drive it into his neck, forcing it out the other side before he pulled it free.

Bolan put his hand on the kitchen table and vaulted over it, clearing Catlan's leg and landing heavily on the other side, square on the foot of another man, who yelped and tried to turn. Bolan beat him in the head with the butt of his knife, then pinned his arm to the table with the big blade. He left it there.

Four remained. They were clawing for weapons, handguns they carried in holsters at their hips. Bolan drew the Beretta 93-R with its attached suppressor, snapped the selector to single shot and pumped a round into the forehead of the nearest would-be rapist. One man turned and tried to run for the door, so Bolan punched him in the back of the head with a bullet. He shot the third through the side of the head as he tried to reverse direction. The fourth froze in place.

"Por favor," he said, holding up his hands. Then, in English, he whined, "I no resist. I no resist. Surrender. *Por favor."*

Bolan walked up to him and snatched the pistol from the holster on his belt, then reversed the weapon and handed it to Maria Catlan.

"Maria?" he asked as gently as he could. "Do you want—"

"No, *señor*." She shook her head, and then, amazingly enough, smiled at Bolan. "We tried. We tried for many months to hide me as well as Lino. Papa knew what they would do. We tried to keep this from Mama, but a woman knows. It has been very bad, and many times, I wished to die, but, no, *señor*. I will not do this thing. It is not my way."

"I understand," Bolan said. "It's my way. Do you want me to let him go?"

"He will give you away if you do." She shook her head. "He is filth. Do as you must with him."

The soldier made a break for it, obviously afraid Bolan's next step would be to slap him with a suppressed bullet. He dived for the floor, and when he came up, he had a switchblade in his hand. He grabbed Maria by the throat with one arm, holding the knife before him to point at Bolan.

Anger flashed in Catlan's dark eyes. As Bolan watched, she stomped the soldier's foot with one low heel, then drove an elbow back into his crotch. This gave her enough room to grab his knife arm. She levered it down and, in one quick motion, drove it into the man's stomach. With a shove she pushed the keen edge of the blade across his abdomen. He shrieked in pain and collapsed on the floor.

Bolan stood and looked at her.

She glanced down at what she had done. "I have told you something that is not true, I think."

"What do you mean?" Bolan asked gently.

"It *is* my way." She held out her hand.

Bolan passed her the 93-R after making sure it was set for single shot. She held the heavy, suppressed weapon in both hands, aimed at the mortally wounded man's head and pulled the trigger. The recoil startled her, but she didn't otherwise flinch, and she looked down at the man she had killed with something like satisfaction.

Bolan reached out and took the gun back. "Are you all right?" he asked.

"*Sí, señor.*" Marie nodded. "*Sí.*"

Bolan looked around at the slaughterhouse the living room had become. "This isn't good," he said. "They're going to want to know where these soldiers went, and they're going to find a lot of blood here if they search."

"We will leave," Catlan said. The door opened, and her parents stood there, in the company of the eighth soldier. Bolan took three quick steps, grabbed the soldier by the collar and dragged him out. He spun the man and slammed his face into the plaster wall. The soldier fell, unconscious.

"My parents and I will go," Catlan repeated. "We will pick up Lino at school. We can go to my uncle's across the city. They will not quickly find us there."

"What can I do to help your family?" Bolan asked. "You saved my life, made it possible for me to continue."

"That is what we would wish," Catlan said. "That

you finish what you have said you will do. Make this Castillo pay. Free us, *señor*. That is our wish."

"Is there anything I can do to ensure your family's safety right now, though?" Bolan asked. "You've endangered yourselves for me."

"Not unless you can destroy the garrison two blocks from here," Catlan said.

"What is this garrison?" Bolan asked.

"The BA have fortified an apartment building two blocks south," she explained. "It is their base, their station, their place of rest when they are not on duty. From there they spread Castillo's will through neighborhoods like this one. If that garrison was destroyed, we would have time to clean and repair here, make it so that no one knew what happened. There would be no more patrols for a time while the garrison was seen to."

"Then that's what I'll do," Bolan said.

"You cannot!" Catlan breathed. "*Señor,* it is suicide! It was a joke. I never meant for—"

Bolan put two fingers to her full lips. "I'm going to make sure your family is okay," he said. "And when I'm done there, I'll be close enough to the president's home to take the final step."

"You do a brave thing."

"Not compared to you," Bolan said, and he meant it.

The Executioner helped Catlan's father drag the bodies of the dead men out into the alley, then down to the end of the street. They were careful to make sure nobody saw them. It would make no difference if someone did, however, for a member of the military police would make himself known immediately, and thus walk into Bolan's guns, while chances were that any of the Catlans' neighbors wouldn't want to get involved. Some of those neighbors would probably cheer them on, from what Catlan said of the day-to-day living conditions under Castillo's enforcers.

When they returned, Bolan found Maria and her mother already scrubbing blood from the tiled floors. He made a quick check for bullet holes and found only one round that had gone completely through its target, burying itself in the wooden strut of the couch. He left it; there was no way to repair it and the hole was inconspicuous enough.

Now he just had to take care of his part of business.

He turned to say goodbye to the Catlans. "Thank you for your help," he said. "I'm going to make sure this doesn't happen again. I'm going to make certain Castillo and his men hold no more power over you."

"Come here, brave American," Maria Catlan said. She stood on tiptoe in front of him and drew his chin down enough that she could kiss him. Her lips were warm and supple. When she opened her eyes again, she patted him on the shoulder and made a mock salute. "Do your work well, American soldier," she said.

Bolan was touched in a way he couldn't explain. He nodded, smiled at her and nodded to her parents. "Keep Lino safe," he cautioned. "Stay low until this is all over."

"How will we know?" Maria Catlan asked.

"You'll know," Bolan said. "The whole nation will know."

CHAPTER EIGHTEEN

Tristan Zapata sat at the desk in the small drawing room at the president's residence. He could feel himself going mad.

It was a strange thing, to feel your sanity slipping away. A man's mind was his only true possession. There was no such thing as property, after all, only the exploitation of the workers, especially the exploitation of them by Anglo property owners. When one's mind went, one's claim to any belongings in this world ended and one became less than useless. Zapata was unrooted. He was adrift in a sea of nothing. There was nothing. There would be nothing.

He was so very afraid.

He had seen it in those few seconds. He had seen death in the eyes of that man, that Anglo killer. That white devil. The Anglo murderer was a demon sent by God to make Tristan Zapata pay—first and foremost, for not believing in God.

He began to laugh for no reason.

He wasn't sure why or when his sanity had broken. He knew, however, that something inside him was very, very wrong. It had been slowly going wrong since he came back from Tucson and the president had said he wanted him to go once more into those blood-soaked fields, to attempt once more to wield the sword of President Castillo's might…. Zapata couldn't bear it. He couldn't think it. He was…he was… What was he? It was becoming very hard to think.

He wanted to go home. He missed his parents. He had missed them for a long time, he realized, and it made him sad to be unable to go home. It was then that he remembered, something he had worked long and hard to forget. He had called them once. A few years after leaving for good, a few years after embarking on his path of the revolutionary, he had phoned them. He had asked them if they would forgive him, if they would take him back into their home. He was sorry. He didn't want to fight for revolution any longer. He just wanted to be with his family. He just wanted to stop feeling so… empty. He didn't want to hurt anyone. He didn't want to forge a new nation. He just missed home.

"I have no son," his father had told him on the phone.

That was that. Some part of him had died there. Zapata wasn't sure, then, what part it was, but it had happened. It was gone. It had left him, as surely as his sanity had left him much more recently.

He thought of taking his own life. The idea of picking up a gun repulsed him. He could cut his own throat with the straight razor he carried. He could do that. But it would hurt. He didn't want it to hurt. He didn't want anything to hurt. He couldn't do this anymore. It had all gone bad. It was all wrong. Castillo wasn't a good man. He wasn't a benevolent man. He didn't help the people. Tristan Zapata had become a revolutionary for the Race because he wanted to help the Mexican people. What good was fighting for the Race if the man for whom he worked wasn't also helping the people?

Zapata had thought only hours ago, before the fight in Tucson, that he understood. He had rationalized what he believed and what he did. He had justified President Castillo's actions. He had thought himself at peace. He had thought himself happy. But he wasn't.

He was miserable and wanted to die.

It was the evil white devil Anglo's fault. That was it. He could blame the monster. The creature that had come for him and rained fire and death down on him.

But wait… Hadn't he called the helicopter himself? That wasn't the American murderer. That was an accident. Wasn't it?

No, no, no. He was wrong. He had been wrong then. He was mistaken. Clearly, everything bad that happened had been the evil devil Anglo white man's fault. The Americans were to blame for all that had happened. If he killed enough of them, he could be happy again. He just had to make sure he got enough.

Tristan Zapata sat down at the desk before him. He tried to write on the paper provided, using a borrowed pen. He discovered that he had forgotten how and he didn't know what to say. That seemed strange. He had always known it before.

The white devil! He had stolen from Zapata the ability to communicate! In this way would he isolate him from his supporters. It was all part of some evil scheme. Yes, that was it. There was only one thing to do.

He would have to wait. He would have to wait for the white devil to come. For come such demons always did. The creature would follow him to the ends of the earth.

It was ordained. It was predestined. It was assured. It was...

His mind stopped racing. Suddenly, he saw the face of the girl from Tucson. The girl he had selected for his own, the girl he had used. She had cried. He had held her, tried to comfort her, tried to tell her that it was really okay, that he was really a very nice person, and he could make it nice for her, if only she'd cooperate....

He hadn't meant to slap her. But he had. He had hit her again and again, and then he couldn't stop, because she was screaming and he didn't want her to scream, and if she screamed it meant he was a bad person and he couldn't allow that—

There was a sound outside the door. He grabbed his straight razor and flicked it open. Its weight was cool, reassuring. The white devil was in the hall right now. He was sure of it. He was coming for Tristan Zapata. He was going to devour his soul and leave him to think only of the girl and her screaming, and how bad a person he was. Zapata wouldn't live in that hell. He wouldn't give the demons dominion over him.

He threw open the door and found a female servant there. She had come to change the towels, she said. He raised the razor to kill her for that, for there were no towels in the drawing room....

But no one was there. Zapata looked around. What was wrong with him? He didn't feel well. Strange feelings of remorse and anxiety tugged at him. He pushed them away and sat down at the desk to write.

The scrawls on the paper surprised him. Who had written this? It looked like his handwriting, for the most part. But he hadn't written it. He certainly didn't think the things he could make out here. What was going on?

Then the memories started to flood back, and once again his sanity tore away from its moorings.

He would do it. He would kill himself. The girl came to him again. Screaming. Crying. Begging him to stop. He told her he wasn't going to hurt her, didn't he? He told her he would be nice to her if she would be nice to him. He begged her. She hit him and slapped him and clawed him, so he had to make her quiet, didn't he?

Then that Del Valle. That Del Valle had done worse to her. Zapata knew that. His men had told him. Del Valle wasn't a normal man. He found pleasure in strange things. Cruel things. Zapata remembered thinking that something was wrong and he should put a stop to it. But he had done nothing. He had thought it best not to interfere.

He wasn't a very good person, was he? He was a very bad man, in fact. He wasn't a hero of the people, though he had always wanted to be. Why wasn't he their hero? Why was he bad? What had he done wrong?

He started to write. He would write his last will. Someone had been scribbling out notes on his pad. Who had done that? He frowned. Was the white devil here now? Hiding in the closet? Under the desk? Waiting to ruin his notes and confuse him?

Zapata screamed. He put his hands to his head and shrieked. Something deep in his head was clawing to get out. He couldn't stand it. He couldn't take it. He wanted to die. He was afraid to die. He wanted to go home. He could never go home. He wanted to meet God. He was convinced that God had damned him.

Why? Oh, why was it so hard?

Shocked at himself and terrified at his inability to check his own thoughts, Tristan Zapata held his head in his hands and wept.

CHAPTER NINETEEN

The garrison was as Maria Catlan had described it. Sandbagged machine-gun emplacements lined the front of the multistoried building, and the muzzles of still more machine guns poked out here and there from windows on the upper floors. Mack Bolan looked the place up and down, assessed the men moving around behind the barricades and considered the target.

Well, he had wanted a distraction. It was time to create the biggest one yet. Consulting the street address and quietly checking the coordinates on his GPS map application as he flipped his sat phone open and closed, he verified that he could easily make the final leg of his journey to the president's residence from here. First, however, he had a promise to keep.

No reason not to walk right in the front door.

He had fresh magazines in both pistols, and of course he had his knives. With weapons exposed for all to see, he walked past wide-eyed citizens straight for the enforcer's building. He wasn't sure, but he thought perhaps he saw a couple of people nod or smile almost imperceptibly.

A pair of soldiers lounged outside the doorway, which had sandbag emplacements on either side leading up to it. Bolan walked right up to them and, in Spanish, greeted them cordially. Then he switched to English.

"Hi," he said. "In case you didn't hear, I'm the guy all your fellow rapists and murderers are looking for."

They gaped at him. One of the men finally got his wits about him and went to pick up the FX-05 rifle leaning against the building.

Bolan drove a palm heel into his face.

He slammed his knee up into the groin of the second soldier and, as the man doubled over and vomited, he drove an elbow into the back of the soldier's head. Then he ripped the Beretta from its holster, shot the man he'd palm-heeled and delivered another round to the man he'd kneed, who was trying to pull a pistol from a belt holster.

Bolan kicked in the front door to what had been an apartment building.

Soldiers ran in all directions. The hallway opened up into a television lounge, and beyond this, flights of stairs led up on either side. There were offices at the rear, probably once used for administration of the building. Bolan transferred his Beretta to his left hand and drew his Desert Eagle with his right.

It was time to go to work.

There were heavy pieces of furniture in the lounge area, made of thick, aged wood and covered with overstuffed cushions. Bolan, sensing the storm that was about to converge on his location, dived for cover behind a chair, landing with his weapons folded across his chest. He popped back up and leveled the pistols, firing first one, then the other, the flat, soft chugs of the suppressed Beretta's 3-round bursts contrasting with the pealing thunder of the Desert Eagle hand cannon.

He snapped one man's head back, then put a hole

in the chest of another. He punched a 3-round burst through another gunner's throat. He stitched a fourth and a fifth across the heart with follow-up bursts. A pair of men carrying assault rifles were punched to the floor by .44 Magnum slugs.

The Executioner had the initiative. The men he fought were retreating, unsure how to cope with this sudden onslaught, their morale fading as their ranks thinned and more of their number dropped like dominoes. Bolan marched toward the rear of the ground floor, determined to clear the entire level. He ducked into the administration offices, still marked with a faded, laminated sign, and almost walked into a hail of bullets. He drew back and took cover at the last moment as the soldier hiding under the desk popped up to fire an ancient-looking Makarov through the doorway.

Bolan waited for the panicked fire to stop, which meant the shooter had exhausted his ammunition. He ducked around the corner just long enough to put a single .44 Magnum bullet through the man's face.

He checked the other rooms on the level but found no one. Then he made for the stairs. They were old, rickety and patched in places with scraps of plywood and other mismatched lumber. He mounted them two at a time, bounding upward and taking the second level by storm.

He kicked in the first doorway that presented itself and shot the soldier inside as he reached for a rifle. Across the hall, Bolan kicked again, and repeated the process. Gunfire began to rip through the flimsy wood of the doors farther down the corridor. The apartments had been turned into billets for the soldiers, many of whom were now shooting blindly through their doors in an attempt to stave off their impending executions.

Bolan supposed he couldn't begrudge them that. Few men willingly shook the hand of the grim reaper when he reached out for them.

At this rate, however, it would take so long to clear the building that he would risk losing the combat momentum that had carried him this far. He holstered his Beretta, reloaded the Desert Eagle and positioned his war bag for easy retrieval of its contents. Then he started moving from door to door.

At each one, some now pocked with bullets, he kicked the flimsy wood aside. Then he reached into his bag, found a grenade, armed it and chucked the bomb inside.

The hot, hollow thumps of the grenades scrambled the interiors—and the occupants—of the billets. The blasts came one on top of the next, shaking the building so badly that it spurred the men on the upper floors to hurry their own response. They had been moving down the steps cautiously, weapons in hand, prepared to face the enemy below, but when explosions rocked the structure, they, too, threw caution to the wind.

Bolan reloaded, waiting at the bottleneck. The fatal funnel the stairways created was perfect for his needs. With a pistol in each hand, he knelt at the bottom, just out of sight of either landing. As soldiers stomped and tripped and stumbled down the steps, falling over one another in their haste, Bolan shot them. He fired almost without looking, his performance a perfect act of Zen marksmanship. The weapons were part of him. They were him, and he was them, and few living men had ever achieved a level of attunement with their weaponry that rivaled Bolan's own.

Dead bodies piled up in the stairwells. The enforcers of Castillo's ironfisted regime toppled like bowling pins and sprawled among one another, in death no longer able to abuse their power and misuse the people their leader was supposed to serve.

As he cut them down, Bolan felt nothing. He wasn't numb; numbness of that type signaled a disconnection with one's emotions and presaged mental breakdown or, worse, mental *break*—as in a break from reality. What Bolan felt was an utter calm, a complete equanimity with the righteousness of his actions and his ability to carry them out.

Then it was over.

The slide on the Beretta was locked back. Bolan shucked the magazine and slid a fresh 20-rounder home, racking the slide to chamber the first round. He waited.

Nothing and no one moved.

He made a search of the upper floors, checking each room, but there was nobody left alive in the garrison. Scratch one nest of killers, rapists and thugs. It was time to take the fight right to Castillo's doorstep.

Bolan was coming back down the rickety steps from the second floor when his boot went completely through the rotted wood. Suddenly, the platform gave way and he was stuck to the waist in the middle of the wooden riser.

A pair of soldiers entered the doorway from the street. Bolan shot them with the Beretta. Two more ducked their heads in, and they were taken out in swift order.

The roving patrols were returning in staggered groups to the garrison. As they approached, it was occurring to them that something was wrong. The growing pile of dead men in the doorway left no doubt.

Bolan struggled to free himself, but each time he tried to push himself up, another chunk of the rotted wood gave way. He finally gave up on it, lifted his arms and fell through the stairway to the first floor, landing heavily on his combat boots and rolling past the blaze of automatic-weapons fire that followed him from the front door. The returning soldiers had regrouped and were now trading off from the doorway, firing side to side as they switched off, standing over the small pile of corpses there.

Bolan threw a grenade at them.

The bomb exploded in midair; he had pulled the pin, popped the spoon and given it a long count. The shrapnel wiped the enemy out of the doorway and left Bolan with a clear exit. The only problem was he hadn't been able to give himself quite enough distance from the explosion, and his own grenade had his ears ringing. As a result, he didn't hear the men who sneaked up behind him.

The blow to the back of his head came just as he sensed the presence behind his back. He tried to roll with it, but was only partially successful. The gun barrel hit him hard and he went down to his hands and knees. The kick to the ribs that followed had stars blazing in his vision, as his tortured, taped ribs rebelled. He wasn't sure, but he thought perhaps something had broken that time.

The Mexican soldier standing over him kicked him in the head. He saw more stars that time, and his vision started to gray out around the edges. Suddenly arms were under his, dragging him, taking him toward the administration offices.

The enforcers were yelling back and forth to one another in Spanish, so rapidly that Bolan's command of the language wasn't up to catching it all. The pain and the repeated blows to his head probably had something to do with it, too. They pushed him into a chair and one of them started to strap his hands to the armrests with a length of telephone cord that he ripped straight from the wall. Bolan's guns were taken from him and set on the desk across the room.

Another Mexican soldier appeared in the doorway to the office; he was red with fear or anger or both. He started shouting, and this time Bolan picked up enough words to know what it was about: the soldier had discovered just how total the massacre throughout the building was. The eyes of the man nearest Bolan widened and he actually backed up half a pace.

"That's right," Bolan said in English.

"What is right?" the soldier asked. His accent was heavy, but his words were clear enough.

"I killed them," Bolan said. "I killed every last one of them. I cleaned this building out."

"Silence!" the man roared. "You will answer only those questions I ask you!"

"What's it going to be?" Bolan asked, his head clearing as he fixed his captor with a firm gaze. "Are you going to threaten to pull my fingernails out? Or maybe you'll reach for a knife and start playing with it, wave the blade in front of my face a few times, something like that."

"I said be quiet!" the enforcer yelled. His voice cracked; Bolan was getting to him already. The American soldier's attitude was simply too casual, too contemptuous. This, combined with the irrefutable evidence of the dead men lining the floors of the building, had made Bolan the devil incarnate to the poor man. He called for help, and the word was passed through the doorway. Soon there were four soldiers standing in the little administrative room, all of them holding FX-05 rifles.

"So that's all that's left, eh?" Bolan asked, his bravado deliberate. Inwardly, he thanked Mr. Murphy, the impartial demigod of combat. It could have been a lot worse than four. Bolan was already free, in his mind; all that was left was to act on the impulses percolating in his brain.

"Your kind are all the same," Bolan said with a sneer. He wanted to get them talking, get them distracted. Otherwise he was in for a very bad time. He had no desire to die at the hands of one of Castillo's enforcers playing the role of interrogator.

"Who are you?"

"Just a messenger," Bolan said.

"Message? What message?"

"Time to die," Bolan said. He felt the chair beneath him start to give way under his weight. He'd thought it felt fragile. Now he was sure.

"You will be quiet or we will kill you!" the first soldier shouted in a trembling voice.

"How about," Bolan said, "*you* be quiet, and *I'll* kill *you*." He stood, throwing his butt back, and the rickety wooden chair he'd been strapped into cracked against the floor. With a violent, stretching motion, as if he were trying to hug himself, Bolan brought his arms up and across and snapped the back of the old chair. The loops of telephone wire gave, and his hands went straight for the handles of his knives, still in his combat gear. The soldiers hadn't thought it necessary to take them, with Bolan's hands bound, and that was their mistake.

Bolan brought the two blades together like a giant pair of scissors and practically gutted the neck of the closest man. He kicked him away and leaped on the next, spearing him with both knives. Releasing the handles, he surged to his feet, grabbed his pistols from the desk and shot the third and fourth man as they tried to make a run for it.

Bolan drew in a ragged breath.

He was hurting. His respiration came in labored gasps, and with every intake of air he could feel ribs scraping together. He was tempted to cough, but he suppressed it; he might just cough up blood, if he was any judge of that feeling, coughing was very much likely to hurt his ribs even more.

This wasn't going to be easy.

The tape helped, and he paused to swallow a handful of the pain pills the paramedic had given him.

There was a closet, its door hanging open, not far from the front entrance. He found a lightweight overcoat here, similar to the one he had discarded before. He pulled it on over his weapons, careful not to jostle himself too much. As he slipped past the small mountain of dead enforcers that was his handiwork, he braced himself, then took the first step out onto the street.

He walked the streets of Mexico City as casually

as he could. Several times, patrols passed by, but they
didn't notice him. The coat helped him blend in, but he
was also hunched over, moving with the gait of a man
who had suffered significant injury. He was deliberately
exaggerating the effect, but didn't have to work hard to
find inspiration for his acting.

As he walked, getting closer and closer to the president's residence, he studied the neighborhoods he
passed. The nearer he got, the more giant posters of
Castillo there were. Then Bolan passed the first of the
statues.

It was of cast concrete and finished to look like
marble. It showed a triumphant Castillo standing atop
a pedestal with a child under one arm and two more at
his feet, pointing into the future as if according to some
grand vision and design. Bolan read the inscription on
the base of the statue: For the Race. Something about it
struck him as grotesque. As he looked up at the figures,
an old man came to stand behind him. He glanced up
at the statue in turn, looked at Bolan and spit on the
ground.

Bolan greeted him in Spanish. The old man gazed
at him, considered that and then pointed at the statue.

"He's a son of a whore."

Bolan blinked. "You don't say?"

"No, I usually don't," the old man said. "Not since I
lost my job teaching. I taught English, and also history.
Your accent tells me you are American."

"I don't seem to be having much luck hiding that."

"No," the man said. "I hear someone fought in the
streets today. An armed American. The state-sponsored
television is saying that we must all be on the lookout for

an American devil who means to murder us all. Strange, but few believe this, and still fewer comply."

"Yeah," Bolan said. "Strange."

"I am going to clear these people away," the old man stated. He waved to indicate those moving around the area. "This was my favorite plaza. I like to come here, drink coffee, read. It is not so bad to be retired. I spoke out against Castillo before the election. I was fired after he took power. It was not a coincidence."

"Probably not," Bolan said.

"I would like to enjoy my plaza again," the man said. "You would be doing me a favor, sir, if you did something about that." He spit again, jerking his head toward the statue. Then, without waiting for Bolan to answer, he left, yelling for everyone to move away from the statue.

In less than a minute, Bolan was alone with the concrete figure of Castillo. He looked left, then right. A sign at the far end of the plaza indicated that the president's residence wasn't located in that direction.

Bolan reached into his war bag and produced several grenades. He pulled the pins on them all, scattered them at the base of the statue and ran.

The overlapping explosions shook the plaza behind him. He paused to glance around and was rewarded with the sight of the top of the statue cracking off and toppling. People moved back into the area almost immediately, a few of them laughing. A group of children held hands and started to sing together, circling the decapitated concrete head.

Bolan pressed on.

If he'd ever been tempted to doubt the mission he had

undertaken, these experiences in Mexico City would have convinced him. All around him people suffered under Castillo's boot, people only too willing to help someone who represented a chance to stand against the dictator. It was a testament to the indomitable nature of the human spirit. Maria Catlan, especially, represented this well. None but those murdered had suffered more under Castillo's regime than had she, and doubtless many young women like her. Yet she refused to back down. She refused to give up. She refused to be broken, to be defeated. That was true power. It was a kind of power those hungry for domination would never understand. It was a kind of power that Castillo would never possess.

Bolan looked up. He had reached his destination. He stood at the entrance to the access road that would take him through the Bosque de Chapultepec.

Castillo's time had finally come.

Bolan consulted the data contained in his phone. Castillo had men camped like an occupying army throughout the grounds of his residence. The Executioner had done what he could to draw off some of these soldiers, who were sure to be enforcers and not regular Mexican army. There was nothing more he could try. Now he had simply to fight his way through the forest so that he could work his way back around to the residence itself.

He left the road, found a stand of trees for concealment, and checked and reloaded his weapons. He swallowed a few more painkillers, dry, and took a sip of water from the small bota bag he carried.

Bolan marched into the forest, creeping along as best

he could, balancing speed with stealth. He didn't want to walk into a contingent of soldiers without warning, but he also didn't want to be out here all day. His diversions, if they proved at all helpful, would be useful for only a short time. He had much to do, and all of it depended on getting through Castillo's security and finally to the man himself.

Bolan never anticipated the end of a mission. There was always something to be done and, if he wasn't engaged in this mission, he would be engaged in another deemed just as important, which would in turn probably be just as dangerous. As he contemplated the building that lay at the end of this particular leg of his journey, however, Bolan couldn't help but envision a Mexico free of Castillo.

The Farm had transmitted to him what information it could about the fallout in Honduras, and he had read it on the short plane flight into Mexican airspace. While there was currently a certain amount of chaos, the reports were edged with hope. There was a real chance that the Honduran people could put in place a government that was not totalitarian, a presidency that wasn't simply a cover for a dictator. Bolan was proud to have been able to accomplish that. No one would ever know, which was how it had to be. He didn't fight for justice and in defense of the innocent because he expected to be lauded.

He did it because it was right.

The thought buoyed him despite the aches and pains he suffered. He kept on, marching toward fate, marching toward freedom for Mexico.

He didn't notice the electronic trip wire his boots

set off. The invisible infrared beam he walked through tripped an unseen relay connected to a camouflaged receiver, which transmitted the location to a technician station in the president's residence.

Mack Bolan walked on.

CHAPTER TWENTY

The snouts of machine guns pointed in three directions from the sandbag enclosure. Mack Bolan saw from a low rise above them the group of men crouched there. He was on his stomach, ignoring the pain that caused, with his Desert Eagle in his fists. The range was too great for the Beretta; he needed the .44 Magnum's power. There was no way to get closer without breaking cover and being cut down himself by the machine guns the guards manned.

Bolan let his mind go blank. With the hammer back, the single-action pull of the Desert Eagle was quite light, crisp and manageable. He let the gun fire itself.

One man down.

The machine guns within the emplacement opened up, but the men were firing blindly in directions that brought their fire nowhere close to Bolan's position. He let them hammer away for a while until they were thoroughly confused, and then he shot the second man in the head. The third, now with some idea of Bolan's relative location, swiveled his 7.62-mm weapon and fired, but he was short of Bolan's position and still no threat. The Executioner triggered a bullet that bored through the front of the guy's head and out the back. He fell over backward.

Bolan marched down the slope and through the

emplacement. He had taken several others like it, all with a level of resistance no worse than that offered by the patrols at the golf course in Tucson. Bolan was no supersoldier; he was a warrior with good training and a lot of experience, a man whose will and whose skill certainly put him in the top one percent of combat operatives. He was, however, mortal. He was just a man. If one man could make a difference like this, could put a stop to the minions of a cruel dictator, there was no reason men of Castillo's ilk couldn't be thwarted each and every time they took power.

The rest of the world could never be permitted to know what truly took down Gaspar Castillo, but the resistance against his tyranny would be noted, and it was *that* the world would remember.

Finally, he reached the president's residence and closed on the structure. There was no point in tempting fate by walking up to the front entrance. Instead, he would skirt the building and come at it from the rear, finding an access point—or making one—and then blazing his way through the facility.

He was approaching the back of the building, surprised that he hadn't yet encountered any guards on the grounds, when he heard a familiar sound.

Rotors.

The familiar vibration of the deadly little rotorcraft UAV chilled his blood.

Bolan was concealed by brush and scrub leading up to what was essentially the back lawn of the building. He wasn't sure how the UAV had found him, but there were any number of possibilities. It might have been a routine patrol he had blundered into; he might have tripped some kind of sensor; he might have been tracked by the UAV from above ever since he entered the woods. It didn't matter. The little chopper was after him now, and this time Bolan wasn't going to let the aircraft stop him from accomplishing his goal.

He popped up and leveled the Desert Eagle at the UAV. Firing, he succeed only in drawing its attention. He knew enough to avoid the armored body of the craft, which was designed to withstand small-arms fire. He had hoped to take out its camera eye, but even though he scored what he thought was a pair of clean hits, it wasn't damaged. Apparently it was reinforced in some way.

The UAV belched flame from its pair of helical-feed submachine guns. Bolan hit the dirt, narrowly avoiding the twin lines of deadly lead. He made a break for it, but not for the relative safety of the tree line.

The absence of guards indicated that Castillo's forces were trying to be clever. They had pulled out to give the UAV a clear playing field in which to hunt Bolan. Well, he would ruin that play. He made for the residence, and as he neared a rear doorway, he saw the first signs of movement. Guards were concealed behind the half wall delineating the entrance. He didn't alter his stride. He simply kept running, with the UAV hot on his heels.

Bullets dug into the ground behind him as he ran, moving abruptly left and right as he did so, trying to stay out of the machine's sights. The UAV itself was very agile, but the pilot was only a man. The guns were fixed to the skids, so to hit Bolan, the entire machine had to turn. That took time and was subject to inertia.

Thus Bolan's fast, zigzagging moves were likely giving the UAV operator fits.

Running toward the residence served another purpose, too—it prevented the chopper's operator from using his rockets. If Bolan had given in to the urge to run for the trees instead, he would have been easy pickings for the rockets' explosive payloads.

A guard raised himself into position to fire. Bolan shot him, vaulted the half-height wall and landed on the other side. Bullets from the UAV raked the wall, but didn't penetrate.

The guard had carried a MAC-11 submachine gun. Bolan took this and the spare magazines. He also found a key card, and used it to swipe the electronic lock. The door popped open.

He was inside.

He consulted his secure phone, which contained a floor plan for the building. He would need to work his way toward the president's office, but the route he took might not be a direct one. There were a lot of offices and other areas in the building, and any one of them could house the UAV operator. If he could find the man, he could end the threat of the rotorcraft once and for all, either destroying it or using it against his enemies.

Bolan weaved through a variety of small hallways, obviously access corridors for servants and support staff.

He emerged in a killing bottleneck.

They had set a trap for him.

Gunfire converged on his position from three directions. He ducked behind a table, which was whipsawed apart by bullets. Bolan kept moving, staying one step ahead of the enemy fire as he went. On the run, he reached into his war bag and again began pulling out grenades. He was running low, but if ever there was a time when it was appropriate to use them all, that time was now.

Pulling the pins and letting the spoons spin free, he started to throw grenades in every direction. He bounced them off the ceiling. He banked them off the walls. They scattered and bounced and clattered among the enemy, landing behind the temporary barricades of wood and metal that had been erected.

The explosions came one after another after another. They echoed through the wide corridor and rattled the windows of the stately building, shattering a few of them. Men screamed and died as shrapnel tore into them, in some cases rending them limb from limb.

The dreadnought that was Mack Bolan continued on. He stalked past the first line of barricades. As he did so, some unseen hand initiated an alarm, and a siren sounded throughout the building.

He ignored it. As he reached the end of the corridor, more of Castillo's men bracketed him. He threw the last of his grenades. The explosion tore through these men and left them smoking and broken.

Bolan fired the MAC-11, burning through the spare magazines. He sprayed out one, then another, then another, working his way through each and dropping as many men as he could tag. The weapon eventually cycled dry and he discarded it.

Drawing both his pistols, holding the Desert Eagle in his right and the Beretta in his left, Bolan ascended a spiral staircase. Guards were posted on the second floor, and they were well positioned. He had to roll through a somersault at the top of the stairs to avoid being hit, and still he felt bullets burn past his shoulder and his thigh. The grazes weren't serious, but they added to the landscape of pain he was already enduring.

He pushed through a pair of doors to his right, hoping to get out of the line of fire.

The Executioner narrowly avoided the glittering straight razor that flew past his throat.

Tristan Zapata, his eyes wide and sweat covering his face, leaped onto him and bore him to the floor. Bolan lost his guns as the pain of the impact shot up through his ribs and chest. Zapata slashed at him again and again. As he tried to fend off the mad jabs, slapping aside Zapata's arm each time the straight razor came near, he was able to take in some small part of his surroundings. He was in a sort of drawing room. Zapata had either been sitting at the desk near the door or merely holed up in this room. He appeared to have no gun.

He was very clearly not well.

The La Raza leader was almost foaming at the mouth. His pupils were dilated. He might have taken a drug of some kind, or he might simply have cracked under the pressure. The straight razor slashed and slashed, and slashed again. Bolan finally managed to catch the man's wrist and twist, sending the razor flying across the room as Zapata yelped in pain. He tried to free himself, but Bolan increased the pressure on the wristlock.

"Don't," the Executioner warned. "I'll break it."

Zapata wrenched his arm free, breaking his own wrist. The sickening crack of bones was surprisingly loud.

The Mexican turned into a snarling wild animal. He bent to Bolan, trying to bite him, or claw him with his good hand. The soldier was forced to roll over and slam a knee into Zapata's stomach, then capture the man's arms and hold them above his head. He used one hand to grab both wrists. The pain had to be excruciating, given the broken one, but Zapata barely seemed to notice.

"You're the white devil! You're the white devil!" he chanted. "You've come to take me to your Anglo hell! My people will never know freedom as long as the intergalactic Anglo-Saxon predators reign! I will kill you! I will kill you, white devil! White devil!"

Bolan punched him across the jaw.

The blow dazed him and shut him up, for which Bolan was grateful. He grabbed Zapata and kneed him in the stomach, doubling him over.

The Executioner retrieved his weapons and pocketed the straight razor. Then he curled his fingers in a bunch of the man's shirt, dragged him to a standing position and put the big snout of the Desert Eagle under his chin.

"You and your people enjoy taking hostages," Bolan said. "Maybe it's time you learned what that's like from the other side. Come on. We're walking."

"The white devil has me in his clutches! Woe am I, for the white devil taketh me beside the still waters, and he leadeth me beside—"

"Shut up or I'll pistol-whip you," Bolan said flatly.

Zapata shut up. Bolan walked him out of the room carefully, keeping the gun under his chin with the hammer cocked back. He made sure to maneuver the terrorist in such a way that Zapata's body was between him and the shooters clustered behind various makeshift barricades, around corners and at the ends of connecting hallways.

"Lead the way to Castillo's office," Bolan instructed. Zapata looked at him goggle-eyed, but seemed to be heading in the right direction. Bolan stayed close.

In truth he wasn't entirely certain anyone here cared about Zapata enough not to shoot through him to get to an intruder like Bolan. He was gambling that Zapata's position of favor among Castillo's people would make him a person of some value, but there was no guarantee of that. At the very least, though, he could use Zapata as a human shield—and Bolan couldn't think of a better person for that job.

Bolan rounded the corner with Zapata in front of him.

A hail of gunfire met them.

It was like walking into a curtain of lead. Zapata's body shook this way and that as it became riddled with bullets. Bolan did indeed use him for a shield as he ducked into a doorway to get out of the direct line of fire.

As Zapata's body fell to the ground, Bolan swore he heard the man say something like, "Thank you, God."

There was no time to wonder about that now. From the doorway, Bolan returned fire. A squad of Castillo's gunners were ensconced behind barriers at the end of the hall, and a large picture window dominated the wall behind them. Bolan ducked his head out long enough to take aim at one and tag him with a .44 Magnum bullet.

The UAV rose into view in the window.

The men turned and tried to wave the machine off. It didn't work. The remote chopper opened up with its twin submachine guns, moving laterally to spray the end of the corridor with a long, flat blast. Those men who didn't duck were scythed mercilessly.

Bolan ducked out to fire again, and saw the trail of a rocket as it flew toward him.

So much for the theory that the building was safe. Bolan had only fractions of a second in which to act. He threw himself from cover and ran toward the rocket. He could feel the heat as the weapon passed him, or he imagined he could.

As he ran toward the surviving shooters, he triggered blasts from both pistols. Castillo's soldiers fired back, but Bolan was the better shot, and more used to firing on the run. Man after man fell before him.

The explosion of the rocket approached him from behind now as a physical wave of heat and light, a bubble of concussive force that expanded and pursued him. He fired one last shot from each pistol, tagging enforcers left and right, and hurled his body out the shattered picture window.

The drop from the second floor wasn't a pleasant one, but it was survivable. Bolan took the impact and rolled with it.

The enforcers stationed on the grounds opened up again, soon joined by the UAV. The remote helicopter, aimed vaguely in Bolan's direction, unleashed another rocket. This flew past his position and blew a crater in the ground some distance away, killing several of the enforcers.

Bolan couldn't figure it. As he ran, again weaving,

now heading for the nearest trees, he couldn't fathom why the UAV operator would take such reckless chances. Didn't the man care? He was killing his own people and even endangering the president, presuming Castillo was still inside the building. Bolan hoped the dictator hadn't evacuated. He didn't think so; Castillo was a proud man, and the defenses around the building had obviously been put in place to eliminate threats such as Bolan represented. Castillo would want to be able to show anyone, most of all himself, that he wasn't a coward and that he could face the threat of death, meeting it head-on with force. That was how such people thought.

The UAV buzzed overhead. It danced and weaved, bucking this way and that, barely under control. Bolan wondered at that; suddenly the machine seemed much less stable and much more wild in the air than it had when he had seen it in Tucson. There was no doubt this was the same machine. Could the operator be having a problem of some kind?

He hit a trip wire and every muscle in his body responded to the sudden tension. He hadn't counted on booby traps in the forest; to use them would endanger the men stationed out here. Anyone willing to rocket the president's residence on the off chance of hitting Bolan, however, probably didn't care about collateral damage from lethal mantraps.

All of that went through Bolan's mind as he hit the dirt, his boot still tangled in the wire he'd tripped over. When no explosion came, Bolan rolled onto his back. Soldiers were converging from three sides. Lying there in the grass and underbrush, he extended both pistols and began to shoot.

His enemies died acrobatic deaths, falling or sprawling and seeming to fly through the air as they did so. He kept shooting, tagging enemies in the air, rolling away from the mine he'd stepped on, in an effort to play it safe if the "dud" turned out to be merely "delayed."

When no more enemies presented themselves, Bolan looked back the way he'd come. What he'd tripped over wasn't the wire to a mine or mantrap at all. It was a power cable.

The cable connected something from the president's residence to a location in the forest, if the direction it ran meant anything. Bolan picked up the cable and started pulling, watching behind so he didn't end up taking a slug while he was otherwise occupied.

He ripped the cord out of the ground as he walked, able to follow it for several dozen yards before it got so deep he couldn't pull it up anymore. If the power cord led out into the woods, it just might be connected to the controls for the UAV. And that gave him an idea.

He flipped open his secure sat phone. With one thumb he pressed the speed-dial number for the Farm, then took off at a run again. More soldiers with submachine guns were pouring lead onto his part of the world as he tried desperately to find a safe place. He finally managed either to shoot or elude his pursuers, however, and ended up crouched in a hollow behind the trunk of a particularly thick tree.

Barbara Price picked up. Before she could say anything, Bolan said in a whisper, "This is Striker. Get me Bear or Akira or one of the specialists, fast. I need satellite assistance."

"Roger that," Price said. She wasted no time on greetings; this was an urgent-code call.

"Tokaido," said the Farm's top hacker.

"Akira, I'm being chased by our UAV friend," Bolan told him.

"The armed rotorcraft?" Hal asked. "What do you need?" He sounded both excited and worried.

"I need you to pull up satellite imagery for this location," Bolan explained. "Somewhere on this property is the control shack, or truck, or skid, or something. It's going to be a big power draw, obviously, and it's pumping out RF of some kind in order to stay in touch with and control the UAV. I can't do anything about the helicopter itself, but if you help me, I just might be able to poke out its brain."

"I'm on it," Tokaido reported. "Give me a few moments, Striker."

Bolan hoped he had a few moments. Some of the pursuing enforcers located him among the trees and started to shoot. The thick trunk he hunkered behind began to be chipped away as bullets thudded into it, spraying bark.

Right then, Tokaido would be cross-indexing Bolan's GPS location with the satellite feed from whatever spy satellite was most likely to be of service to them. The Executioner didn't doubt there would be a satellite they could use, or one they could at least use soon. Appropriating satellite feeds was one of Stony Man Farm's specialties, at least among the cybernetics wizards who worked under Aaron "the Bear" Kurtzman, and there were plenty of satellites in orbit to choose from. At least, there were plenty when almost no security system on earth could stop you from taking temporary control of the satellites. Such were the privileges and benefits of access to Stony Man Farm's technology.

Bolan didn't like the situation one bit. While he sat here in the forest, fending off gunners and trying to find the UAV's operator, Castillo could very well be leaving the scene. Again, the Executioner had to hope the man's pride would hold him here. If he trusted to the psych profile, there was almost no chance Castillo would flee on his own, not from the office that was symbolic of his rise to power—and of his total control over Mexico's citizens. His regime might withstand the public-relations blow that would result from fleeing the scene, even temporarily, but Bolan doubted the man himself would be very forgiving of himself if he gave in to what he would see as cowardice.

Bolan was concerned that a lot of this mission was starting to hinge on "ifs."

"I have your coordinates," Tokaido said over the phone, snapping Bolan out of his reverie. "North-north-east of your location, Striker." The young man rattled off precise GPS coordinates. "I'm transmitting the data to you now. Thermal imaging clearly shows a square trailer of some kind with a fairly serious heat signature. It corresponds precisely to what we project the UAV's support facilities would need to be."

"I'm on it," Bolan said.

"Good hunting, Striker."

Bolan closed his phone.

A grenade landed in the grass next to him.

He was already on the move when the detonation came, but he lost his sat phone to the blast. The explosion knocked him over and sent him rolling through the suddenly cracked and smashed trees. It also sprayed the air with deadly shrapnel, some of it jagged pieces of wood.

Without the phone he had no GPS tracking ability. He did, however, still have his button compass, and he knew the general direction he needed to go.

He would play it by ear.

First he had to deal with this new enemy. There were no more grenades being thrown his way, but the forest was abuzz with gunfire. The UAV wasn't close by, but it was prowling about; he could hear it in the sky, darting to and fro like an angry, oversize bumblebee. Clearly there was no coordination between the men on the ground, the forces in the president's house and whoever was running the UAV. The pilot of the remote vehicle was so reckless that Bolan wondered if perhaps he didn't have a death wish for Castillo and everyone who worked for Castillo's cause.

There was no time to plumb the psychic issues of the UAV pilot. Bolan weaved through the thick woods, moving left, then right, then left again, following his compass and trying to stay on target despite the difficult terrain.

The forest was alive with unnatural noises—the screams and shouts of men, wounded or dying, or simply pursuing their quarry. The sounds of the deadly rotorcraft UAV as it continued its erratic domination of the skies. The sounds of fire, unnatural here only because it was the result of the UAV's rocket fire. Bolan could detect no serious blazes, but was genuinely concerned that continued use of the rotorcraft's rockets might result in burning the residence or the surrounding Chapultepec Forest to the ground.

He ran. He had spent so much time on this mission running toward danger, running toward his targets, that he could feel his side start to ache, adding to the misery of his damaged ribs and the muscles he had treated so cruelly over the past few days. He shut all this out.

The UAV found him again. In the dense tree cover, Bolan had an advantage, for the machine couldn't see him clearly, couldn't get close enough to fire on him. He dodged and weaved among the trunks.

The UAV unleashed the remainder of its store of rockets.

Bolan could do nothing but throw himself flat and hope. The wave of heat from the explosions washed over him, leaving him feeling parboiled. Trees exploded and others cracked in two near their bases. The forest suddenly had a gaping hole in its canopy, and through that hole dropped the buzzing, inhuman death machine with its unblinking camera eye.

Bolan managed to pick himself up and keep going. The UAV pursued, shadowing him as he moved in and out of the trees.

The spaces between the trunks were wide enough now that the UAV could match Bolan turn for turn. The Executioner kept running, sure of his goal, certain of his plan. He pumped his legs for all he was worth, and the seemingly unstoppable, unmanned helicopter chased him.

Just a little farther, he told himself.

CHAPTER TWENTY-ONE

Roderigo del Valle stood next to the La Raza terrorist, Tomas Flores, atop the open carriage of the support truck in which Flores operated the UAV. Stripped of its disguise, the truck was remarkably Spartan, without even a metal enclosure. Given the heat, Flores had opted to have the canvas cover pulled back. The result was that he sat on the back of the truck in the command-and-control chair, exposed to all the world. The vulnerability of the UAV's operator had been foremost in Castillo's mind, no doubt, when he had arranged to have the truck stationed here, far into the forest, away from his residence and from obvious targets for attack.

The Browning Hi-Power in Del Valle's fist was pressed against the base of Flores's neck, and thus he did as Del Valle commanded.

Del Valle had awoke that morning determined to end the threat that this miserable American death-dealer represented. He had had a dream that night, as he tossed and turned, still terribly sore from the injuries he had sustained. He had dreamed that the big, dark-haired, steely-eyed American had come for him, and Del Valle had pleaded and begged for his life like a coward. The very idea had brought him awake covered in sweat.

He had conferred briefly with Castillo about the security measures the president was implementing. Armed with that information, he had simply made sure he understood where the control point for the UAV could be found. When the security alert was triggered, Del Valle had some sort of premonition: the big American killer was here. Knowing that, he found it a simple matter to go to the spot, threaten the life of the operator and turn the UAV to his own ends. He wouldn't rest until the American was dead.

Since his last encounter with the big soldier, he was convinced that this monstrous foe wouldn't stop until Del Valle was dead. Even if not for Del Valle, it was very likely this vengeful specter set upon them by America would come for Castillo, who had been working with Orieza toward their supposedly mutual goals. Either way, if he discovered Del Valle here in Mexico, he would attempt once more to end his life. Roderigo del Valle didn't intend to let the American hunt him to the ends of the earth. He would use the best weapon available, the rotorcraft, to kill this man, and do so from a safe distance. Once the American was dead it didn't matter if Castillo was annoyed. Nor was it any great loss, in Del Valle's opinion, that Zapata had been killed. The idiot Tomas Flores had seemed upset by that unintended consequence, but the fool seemed more worried that he would be blamed for the incident than that Zapata was dead and going to stay that way.

Better to get forgiveness than permission. Castillo would forgive Del Valle's appropriation of the machine if it ended in the destruction of the largest threat the regime was likely to face anytime soon. At least, Del Valle certainly hoped the big American was relatively rare among his kind. The former Honduran master enforcer shuddered at the thought of facing an entire army made of men such as this enemy.

"There!" Del Valle cried out in surprise. "There he is again! Follow him!"

"I am trying, I am trying," Flores replied. "I cannot get through the trees here, sir. They are simply too thick."

"Then use your missiles to make them *less* thick!"

"But, sir, the risk of burning… Already I have fired on the president's house! We must stop this madness—"

"Fire everything!"

Del Valle jabbed hard with the barrel of the pistol. The terrified man hit the rocket button, unloading the remainder of the UAV's explosive payload. The explosion was near enough their position in the forest that they could feel the vibration through the ground and hear the blast through the trees.

"That's it," Del Valle said. "There he is now. There's that big son of a whore.… Now get him! Lower the chopper and follow him!"

Flores did as instructed. They both watched on the screen as the rotorcraft descended through the forest canopy.

"Now," Del Valle said. "Forward. Forward! Catch him! Use the guns!"

Flores pulled the trigger, and the rotorcraft, hot on the heels of the fleeing American, spit flame. The sound, normally strangely muted, seemed louder. Del Valle looked around. Something wasn't right. He couldn't determine what. Then, cursing himself for being an old woman about things, he forced himself to focus on the screen. The big American was running through a particularly difficult stretch of trees, and it was all Flores could do to navigate them without striking a rotor blade on one.

"Left," Del Valle ordered. "Now go through there. Now right. Straight, follow him! Turn there, sharp corner... No, you will not fit there! Go back and around, to the left, to the left!"

If Flores minded this backseat driving, he didn't let on. The two men watched on the screen as the flying machine drew ever closer to the big man's back. Flores was having a very difficult time lining up the nose of the rotorcraft for a shot at their quarry because of the constant maneuvering, and no doubt the American knew that. But time was on their side. There was nowhere he could go. They could chase him from one end of the continent to the other.

"What is that?" Del Valle asked. In front of the fleeing American, a large, metal structure was visible. It had to be somewhere close by, for they could hear the rotors of the machine very well now. The American couldn't be far. If they could determine—

Flores drew in a deep breath. He had apparently realized, just as did Del Valle, that he was looking at a zoomed camera shot of the back of his own head. There was a thundering crash.

Red-black liquid splashed across the screen.

The last thing Flores saw in life was his own image from the rear, just before the big American put a bullet through the back of his skull.

Del Valle wasted no time on recriminations. He threw himself over the bed of the trailer. Metal clanged as a bullet struck the frame of the trailer where he had been a moment before.

He dropped down on the other side, then scooted under the trailer, in the gap created by its leveling jacks. The big American hit the ground right after, in pursuit.

Del Valle tripped him. He reached out and grabbed one of the man's legs, sending him sprawling. The American had lost his gun, but recovered with incredible speed, rolling over and jumping to his feet. Del Valle brought up his own handgun.

Bolan stepped in so quickly Del Valle wouldn't have believed it possible. He slapped the gun out of Del Valle's hand. The Honduran, suddenly afraid, threw himself on top of the enemy.

They rolled across the ground in the shadow of the support trailer and the dead man on it. Beyond them, the rotorcraft spun out of control, struck a tree, attempted to whip its rotors into the ground and broke apart. Pieces snapped off and tumbled through the air like saw blades. In the scuffle, Del Valle wrenched one of the pistols from his enemy's holster. Bolan again slapped the gun away with brutal force. The two now stood before each other, hands empty.

Del Valle reverted to his savate training again, but Bolan was ready for that. He dropped an elbow onto Del Valle's leg as the kick came in. Del Valle felt the limb spasm and go numb. He fell back, reached for the sheath on his belt and snapped up the Fairbairn-Sykes combat knife. The long, thin dagger had been provided by Castillo's armory. Del Valle intended to put it to good use.

"You are finished!" He lunged with the blade.

The Executioner produced not one, but two massive fighting knives. The edges of the blades gleamed in the sunlight. "Maybe you should rethink that," he said.

"Die!" Del Valle exclaimed. He charged, his technique deliberately sloppy. When Bolan went for a simple cut to deflect, Del Valle changed angles and very nearly scored a hit. The American leaned back, just missing Del Valle. The Honduran counted himself lucky in that exchange.

"You can walk away, Del Valle," Bolan told him. "Cut a deal. Tell us everything you know about how the attack on Tucson went down, give us a full debrief and surrender into U.S. custody. Inside information on Castillo's operation, whatever you have, could mean the difference in years for you. You're going away no matter what."

"I will never go to prison," Del Valle hissed. "I will see you dead first!"

"If you do this," Bolan warned, "you're going to die. Put down the knife."

Del Valle turned and ran.

He pumped his legs harder than he could ever remember, sprinting, fleeing, trying to leave behind the demon who haunted him. He risked a look back—

The devil was still fast on his heels, running almost effortlessly, a killing blade in either hand.

Del Valle stopped. He simply slowed and stopped. He couldn't do this. He couldn't run from this monster forever. That was no life. Better a death while on his feet than a life fleeing, or worse, a life on his knees. He turned.

The American wouldn't relent.

"Drop the blade," Bolan ordered, and Del Valle realized he still held the combat knife.

"No," he retorted. "I will not surrender. You will have to kill me."

"Don't do this. You don't have to die."

"Are you so afraid of taking life?" Del Valle laughed at this grim reaper before him. "You, who have killed so many? What is it, American? Do I threaten to overflow your book of names, your list of the honored dead? Surely there is room for one more."

He thrust with his blade. Bolan easily dodged. Del Valle lunged again, attempting to fence with the knife as he had been shown. The Executioner easily parried his attacks, using the spines of his knives as he slapped away the Fairbairn-Sykes each time. Each time Del Valle attacked, his adversary deflected him effortlessly. It soon became clear to Roderigo del Valle that, at any time he wished, his enemy could move in for the kill.

Del Valle stopped.

The American halted and backed away a pace, wary of a trick. "Are you giving up?" he asked.

"I cannot match you," Del Valle said.

"Probably not, no."

"Tell me something, American. How many men have you killed?"

"That's not important."

"But it is. I see in you nothing but death. It pervades you. It emanates from you. How many has it been? Hundreds? Thousands? Tens of thousands? Not this last, surely. But something about your way makes me think you kill as easily as breathing."

"Surrender," Bolan said. "Give up and I won't kill you."

"A meaningless vow," Del Valle answered. "You would keep it until some security consideration overrode your personal notions of having made promises to one such as me. Would your government honor such a promise?"

Bolan didn't respond.

"I thought not," Del Valle scoffed. "No, American, I think this is it. Goodbye." With that, he turned and began walking away. He threw the dagger to the ground. It landed point-first.

"Del Valle!" Bolan shouted. "Stop!"

"I am walking away now," the Honduran said. "You will not shoot me in the back. It is not your way."

"Don't move!"

Del Valle took another step—and plunged through the brush that had been used to conceal a trap. At the last possible moment, he managed to catch on to an exposed tree root. He held on for dear life.

Bolan appeared at the lip of the pit in which Del Valle now found himself. The hole was very deep, and at its base were sharp spikes carved from wood.

"Give me your hand!"

Del Valle fell farther as the big man reached out for him.

The Honduran managed to grab another tree root, but now he was far enough into the deep, deadly hole that the American couldn't reach him with an extended arm. Del Valle looked below and then up at the man who had pursued him.

"Goodbye, American. Goodbye, demon. I would have liked to have known your name. Now I shall not."

Del Valle looked up then down.

He let go.

The spikes speared his body, bringing sharp pain of an intensity he had never experienced.

As the darkness closed in around him, he heard the American speak. "My name is Mack Bolan."

CHAPTER TWENTY-TWO

Bolan looked down at the crudely crafted tiger pit. What it was doing here, he couldn't say. He had realized what it was, realized what the oval of dead undergrowth meant, just before Del Valle had stepped into it. The pit had done its work well enough; it had taken a human life.

Bolan recovered his weapons. There was no time to clean them, but he removed the slide of the Beretta and used a bandanna from his pocket to wipe it clean of dirt as best he could. The Desert Eagle hadn't taken too much in the way of debris, so he simply wiped it and checked the action. With both weapons reloaded and once more on his body, his knives in their sheaths where they belonged, he was ready to return to the president's residence to finish what he had started.

The UAV was burning itself out behind him, leaving a plume of smoke. Bolan glanced back at it. He hoped a forest fire wouldn't result. Nothing seemed to be blazing out of control, though. Apparently the forest wasn't so dry that a conflagration was a concern.

Small favors, Bolan thought.

He let himself into the residence, the Desert Eagle in one fist. Somewhere in the building, fires crackled, and somewhere else, sprinkler systems sprayed water. He registered the sounds as he moved quietly through the ground floor.

Dead men and wreckage were everywhere. The gun-fire, the rockets from the UAV, Bolan's own grenades—the cumulative effect had been to demolish much of the interior of the stately building, and that was unfortunate. Bolan wasn't insensitive to the cultural and historical heritages of the nations he visited. His job wasn't to sightsee, to stop and enjoy the places he went, but he was no "ugly American." He understood there were certain possessions, certain relics, certain places that nations held dear to their national identity.

The house could be rebuilt. It was unfortunate that it needed to be, but the Mexicans could rebuild it better and stronger than ever. With luck, they could do the same with their presidency.

Gaspar Castillo was living on borrowed time.

Bolan heard the stomping of feet. There were rein-forcements, or simply a last, reorganized troop of men somewhere in the building. He braced himself for the attack that had to come.

They filed down the spiral staircase, some of them throwing themselves down to avoid enemy fire. Bolan drew a bead on them and began emptying .44 Magnum rounds into the descending enforcers.

The first man took a round in the chest and collapsed to the floor. The second took one to the head, twisted as he fell and landed perpendicular to his fellow. A third took a bullet to the heart and staggered back, his arms and legs splaying as Bolan put him down, hard. The fourth and fifth took rounds through the face while still standing.

Whenever possible Bolan fired for the head or the heart, depending on the target offered and the angle of the shot. He was a trained, experienced sniper who had logged many, many more thousands of rounds on his chosen weapons than any one weapon could expect to endure. His guns were custom-tuned for him by the Farm's armorer, their high-wear parts replaced frequently. Everything the Farm did to support the Executioner was done with one goal in mind: to make Mack Bolan the most efficient, most reliable and most lethal soldier imaginable.

Castillo's enforcers didn't have a chance.

Bolan crushed them and pushed them aside like falling leaves. He fired the Desert Eagle empty, reloaded it as he moved and triggered several more blasts, until the men above finally stopped coming down the stairs to be funneled under enemy gun sights.

The Executioner finished with these shooters and ascended the spiral staircase. He surged up and out, rolling, then coming to his feet at a dead run.

He stopped cold.

Four men, dressed as Castillo's enforcers, stood in the middle of the loftlike space, which Bolan presumed was an area designed primarily for entertaining. Each of the four had duct-taped a grenade to the mouth of a household servant. Three of the hostages were women, two of them young; the fourth was an older man who might have been a steward. The enforcers, to save their own lives, had resorted to this human-bomb tactic. Each stood with his index finger through the ring of the devices shoved partway into the mouth of his victim. The tape securing the grenades would make it hard to remove them without setting them off, which of course was the idea. Each man's index finger was a crude deadman's switch, for shooting him would cause his body to drop, and most likely to yank the pin from the weapon.

Bolan remained still. Inwardly, he was hefting the weight of the Desert Eagle. There was still a chance to prevent any of this.

"You don't have to do that," he told them. "Do any of you speak English? Even a little?"

"Sí," one of them said—the enforcer who held the man before him.

"Tell your comrades that they don't need to pull those pins. I'm not here for you. I'm interested only in Gaspar Castillo. Walk away from this. I won't pursue you. It can stay here, between us."

"Lay down your weapon, *señor.*"

"I can't do that," Bolan said.

"Then we shall lay you down, *señor.*"

One of the enforcers went for his gun with his free hand.

Bolan threw himself to the floor and rolled through an awkward, painful somersault. As he came up again, the Desert Eagle was extended in his fist as if were a part of his arm. Almost in slow motion, the Executioner targeted the first man, fired, targeted the next man, fired, then the third, the fourth.

Screams filled the air. The four hostages stood in shocked disbelief.

Each enforcer, sprawled on the floor, held the bloody stump of his hand where Bolan had blown off his index finger.

The Executioner ripped the tape free from each hostage, took the grenades and sent the servants on their way. The first of the gunmen was trying to recover from the pain of his injury and pick up a gun with his left hand. Bolan stood over him.

"Can't do the left hand, eh?" he asked. "There's something to be said for ambidexterity." The man on the floor sneered as he managed to grip the revolver. Bolan shot him in the face.

As two more gunners went for their weapons he repeated the process, before the fourth and final man, still moaning over his lost finger, staggered from the room. Bolan waited, wondering how predictable the enforcer would be.

He reappeared, charging, holding a rifle awkwardly before him.

Bolan shot him down. Pretty predictable, as it turned out, he thought.

On the upper level, he finally reached what was labeled the suite of offices held by El Presidente. He paused, placing his ear to the wall next to the door. He didn't, of course, put his ear to the door itself. People in his profession too often got their heads blown off that way.

He checked his ammunition supply and then his war bag. He was running out of rounds. There had been no time to scrounge, really, while he fought so frantically against so many foes. Now he was very close to being out of ammunition for both weapons, his .44 Magnum especially. He had just enough, he thought, to fight his way into the room beyond.

He heard the clack of sticks beyond the door and knew that sound. It was a nervous habit, the sort of thing a person with a nightstick or billy club did when trying to work off nervous energy. Bolan could hear the men beyond the doorway telling one another, in Spanish, to hold the line, to refuse to surrender, or words to that effect. Apparently they were the last line of defense, or at least thought they were.

Time to see what they had to offer.

Bolan rapped on the door.

"Who are you? What do you want?" one replied.

"Give me Gaspar Castillo," he said simply.

"Go away or we will open fire!"

"Give me Gaspar Castillo," Bolan demanded.

There were no shots, despite the sort of provocation that normally had lead punching through wooden doorways.

They were out of ammo!

The battle had taken its toll on all of them, it seemed. He tested his theory one last time, slipping to the other side of the door and trying the knob. Still nobody fired, so he backed up with his pistols in both hands, planted his foot and kicked the door free of its lock. A small piece of molding hit the floor before he stepped inside.

A group of perhaps two dozen men armed with truncheons, and dressed in the uniform of Castillo's enforcers, rushed him en masse. The room where they stood had been cleared of furniture. It was intended to be a killing floor. The enforcers swung their clubs with the easy familiarity of men who have beaten others to death before.

Bolan didn't intend for them to get that chance this time.

He fired once, then twice, then again. He emptied the Beretta, too. Men fell, but there were still too many left, still a mob intent on braining him with the clubs they carried.

Bolan went feral.

He roared in fury, a tactic that startled a couple of the less committed fighters, the ones who were hanging back. Swinging his pistols like clubs, he began to beat them mercilessly. He pistol-whipped his opponents as he moved in and out among them, dodging a blow here, using the heavy frame of the Desert Eagle to block a strike there, stomping ankles and knees as targets of opportunity.

A crowd this large often robbed a man of his will to fight, because the defender thought of the mob as individual men. Odds that high could sap a warrior's will and make him afraid. Mack Bolan never allowed that to happen.

Instead, he treated a mob as a single living being, an entity whose vulnerable joints were the divisions between individuals. Those individuals were, in turn, made up of similarly vulnerable connections. No matter how big the mob, no matter how large the men in the mob, Bolan had no fear. As he chopped away with his pistols, using them like axes, like irons, like brass knuckles, he worked his way always to the corners of the mass. It was here that a palpable mob was vulnerable; it was here that groups of men got in their own way. To reach him, the mobsters had to fight their way past their fellows, with the result that large portions were neutralized.

Bolan swung the empty Desert Eagle across the bridge of a man's nose. He struck outward with the Beretta and mashed another man in the throat. As the latter started to choke and gurgle, sinking to his knees, with the shadow of death spreading across his face, Bolan kicked another man, smashed yet another between his pistols and then let the weapons go.

He wrested a truncheon from first one enforcer and then another. With sticks in both hands, he became even deadlier, for now the tools he held were designed for the powerful blocks, bone-breaking strikes and crippling thrusts he was known for. Weaving the clubs before him in a figure-eight pattern, Bolan lashed out as he moved from one enforcer to the next.

He bashed one in the face and watched the man's eyes roll up in his head. He jabbed another deep in the abdomen and stepped aside as he doubled over to vomit. Then Bolan smashed the club onto the back of the man's skull.

He was working his way across the room, to the door at the far end. It was labeled simply El Presidente.

Behind him, a trail of maimed, beaten men lay dead, unmoving or moaning on the floor. Before him, the last three club-wielding thugs screamed and charged.

Bolan ducked low under the swing of the first, slashing his right club into the man's abdomen. He turned and hammered the left club across the man's right ear, allowing him to fall past and away as the Executioner moved forward. The second man was struck in the head and neck. He screamed, and Bolan drove a thrust into his groin. No sound came out of the thug after that. Bolan didn't know or care how badly hurt he was. The fourth man, seeing the carnage before him, had second thoughts. He threw down his club.

Bolan kicked him in the groin.

The thug doubled over and Bolan dropped an elbow

strike onto the nape of his neck. He hit the floor and was still.

The big American stopped and drew in a long, ragged breath. It wasn't the first time had faced a roomful of fighters like that, and it wasn't the first time he had made short work of them in this fashion. He let the truncheons fall to the floor.

The door to the president's private office was covered with a heavy iron grillework. Bolan wouldn't be kicking it in anytime soon. The lock was electronic. He reached for his secure sat phone. Stony Man Farm would be able to pop the lock for him, he had no doubt—

Then he remembered. His phone had been destroyed.

He considered the heavy metal gate, and decided he might as well do this the old-fashioned way. Using fabric tape from his bag, he secured to each corner of the door one of the grenades he had recovered from the poor, unfortunate, fingerless enforcers. He pulled the pins, watched the spoons pop free and sped from the room, ducking around the corner of the outer corridor for cover.

The explosion of the four grenades was deafening. It was followed by the loud crash of the iron bars hitting the floor. Bolan wasn't surprised to see the grillework still in one piece; obviously, the hinges holding it to the door had been the weak link.

Bolan kicked in the door.

Gaspar Castillo sat behind his desk. He rose to his feet with an automatic pistol in his hand. Bolan took a fast step forward, grabbed the man's wrist, twisted, ripped and succeeded in yanking the slide clean off the pistol as he put Castillo in a painful joint lock. Something had snapped when the slide came off; the weapon was broken now. Bolan placed the pieces on the desktop.

Castillo settled himself back behind his desk as if nothing had happened, sitting somewhat awkwardly with his arm captured in that iron grasp. Bolan let him go.

"Welcome," the dictator said easily. He massaged his wrist absently.

"Keep your hands where I can see them," Bolan warned.

"Or what?" Castillo asked. "You will shoot me? I see no guns in your hands. You've broken mine."

Bolan stepped closer to him, looming over him, watching him closely for any aggressive moves.

"You're coming with me, Castillo."

"And you are?"

"Matt Cooper," Bolan said.

"You are American?" Castillo asked. Bolan said nothing. "I see. You cannot say. No doubt your country thinks it is being very sneaky. Do you honestly think the meddling of the United States will go unnoticed on the world stage? Mexico is a sovereign nation. Your bullying us will bring you international sanction and scorn."

"I don't think so, Castillo," Bolan said. "You see, you're just going to disappear. I'm going to drop you in the deepest, darkest hole I can find. When we're done with you, you won't even remember your address, much less anything about the operation that put you there."

"Are you threatening me?" Castillo demanded. "Do you dare? I will have you know that I am Gaspar Castillo.

I am of the Race! Who are you to challenge me? Who do you think you are? I am the pinnacle of—"

Bolan slapped him hard in the mouth. The blow rocked the man as he half rose from his chair behind his desk. He hung his head, placing his palms flat on the desk blotter for support. He was silent for long moments.

When he looked up again, his bloodshot eyes were ablaze with mindless rage.

"Zeus, Apollo," Castillo said, "kill him."

CHAPTER TWENTY-THREE

The two hulking bodyguards lumbered from their alcoves, where they had been standing almost unseen. Bolan had, in fact, barely noticed them when he'd entered. Now he backed out of the office, across the anteroom littered with clubbed and broken men and corpses, and into the corridor beyond. He needed combat room. He couldn't afford to let these gorillas get their hands on him.

Castillo had called them Zeus and Apollo. In his mind, Bolan dubbed the first one out the door Zeus. He was a beefy, crag-faced, shaved-headed monster of a man, with biceps so large he couldn't even straighten his arms. Apollo, the second one, had dark brown hair close-cropped to his head, with the faintest suggestion of a beard and mustache.

The pair wore olive-drab fatigues so large they had to be custom. The sleeves had been removed, of course, for freedom of movement. Huge combat boots, worn with the laces untied, encased their feet.

Zeus smacked a fist the size of a ham into his palm. He lunged.

Bolan couldn't afford to let these backbreakers get their hands on him. They outweighed him and outclassed him in every sense for the ground-and-pound grappling game, which clearly was what they spent their time practicing. Many men would be intimidated by two such formidable opponents, the very reaction such men cultivated as they worked to expand their size and define their bodies. To allow them to intimidate him, however, was to make Bolan play their game.

The Executioner wasn't a ground fighter. He wasn't a grappler or a wrestler. He didn't go toe-to-toe with men much bigger than him and let them use their chosen tools against him. That would be both tactically unsound and physically foolish. At the moment, with his damaged ribs, even a primitive bear hug from either man would prove fatal.

In the face of overwhelming odds, outnumbered and vulnerable in hand-to-hand combat, Bolan did what any rational person did.

He used a tool.

Specifically, he used a force multiplier. He drew his big, short-sword-size Japanese blade, holding it low in front of his body. A look of disapproval crossed Zeus's catcher's-mitt face. No doubt he considered knives the weapons of weaklings who were insecure in their physical fighting skills. Bolan had seen that attitude before, primarily among those who practiced sporting martial arts.

The Executioner, however, dealt in reality. Reality was a harsh mistress who brooked no failures and accepted no excuses. She also had no feelings.

Zeus reached for him. Bolan slashed him across the hands, dealing the bodyguard a brutal cut. The big man reared back, grabbing at his palms. Then, enraged by the injury, he started for Bolan again, swinging his fists.

Bolan was normally quite fast, but in his current state

he didn't have the energy, the stamina or the agility to duck such punches forever. If just one connected, he would end up knocked into next week, and he would bet even money that he'd wake up getting stomped to death by both bodyguards. This was life-and-death.

Apollo tried to get in on the act, but the two burly men were getting in each other's way in the relatively limited space. One would grab for Bolan and then the other, but he was able to keep them at bay with the knife. Finally, Zeus threw a full-power, committed punch that Bolan couldn't dodge.

He stabbed forward with his knife.

The big blade slammed through Zeus's fist all the way to the hilt, slicing through the back of the wrist. Blood sprayed, and an inhuman wail of distress and pain spewed from the big man's mouth. Bolan pressed his advantage. He yanked his smaller knife from its sheath and began working his way down the shocked man's body, slashing his arms, working down his legs, and then up again over the chest. None of the wounds was mortal, but Zeus was streaming blood and screaming at such a high pitch he sounded like a whistle. Bolan blasted him with a front kick to the groin that would have doubled over any normal man. When that didn't work, and with Apollo struggling to get around his wounded friend and wrap his fingers around Bolan's throat, the Executioner stomped on Zeus's ankle.

The bones snapped like kindling. Bolan followed up with a front kick to the knee of the same leg. Zeus went down like a felled tree, folding on his leg and shrieking in agony. He was, in fact, crying in pain and outrage as the full extent of the damage done to him became real in his mind. He started to crawl away, taking Bolan's big knife with him. At the last minute, however, he lashed out.

Bolan saw the surprise blow coming at him. It was the sort of attack borne of pain and rage, the last desperate paw swipe of a mortally wounded bear. He stabbed his smaller knife through *that* hand. When Zeus withdrew he took that knife with him as well, collapsing in a bloody heap against the wall.

Apollo couldn't take it any longer. He shoved his fallen friend aside and threw a punch that connected with Bolan's chest. The blow sent him flying, knocking him down and pushing him several feet across the floor. To Bolan, it felt as if someone had swung a sledgehammer into his lungs. He tried to draw breath and found that he couldn't. As he lay there, choking and wheezing, Apollo advanced on him. His fingers clenched and unclenched as he reached for Bolan's throat.

"I'm going to squeeze your neck until your head pops off," the thug said in English. He had no trace of a Spanish accent; he was apparently imported talent.

Bolan struggled to get back to his feet, but could barely function. Apollo stomped over to him and reached out.

Bolan grabbed one of the big man's fingers.

He tried for the finger lock, but succeed only in snapping Apollo's digit like a twig. The sudden, sharp pain stopped the bodyguard in his tracks. He roared like a wounded lion and then reached out for Bolan again, his only thought to rend, tear and strangle with his bare hands. The Executioner snapped another finger, and then another, leaving three broken digits on Apollo's left hand.

The enraged wrestler slapped Bolan with a mighty backhand that the soldier wasn't quick enough to duck or dodge. The blow snapped his head back. He went to his knees, and Apollo grabbed him by the throat.

Bolan, dazed, could think of nothing to do.

Apollo got his thick arms around Bolan's chest. He grinned. He was going to squeeze his opponent until ribs cracked, and he could tell by Bolan's reactions that the soldier's rib cage was already hurting him badly.

As the pressure started to increase, Bolan, whose right forearm was free, brought his hand up. He stiffened his middle finger and pressed it against Apollo's eyeball.

The big man flinched. It wasn't as brutal a technique as Bolan had used in similar situations, but it was enough to gain some slack. When Apollo reared back to avoid the finger, Bolan smashed his forehead into the big man's face. His grip slackened more, but still he didn't let go. Bolan slammed a foot on his ankle, drove a knee into his groin, and when Apollo dropped him far enough, he reached out and grabbed the thug by the testicles. Grabbing, twisting and tearing as if he would rip them right off, he pulled through the motion, driving his arm forward and across his body while still holding on to the giant's scrotum.

The scream that Apollo gave rivaled that of his partner. Pain drove the bodyguard to his knees, and Bolan reached down, wrapped his arms around the thick neck, braced one arm against the other and hooked the back of the big man's head. He squeezed for all he was worth.

The bodyguard eventually went limp and Bolan dropped him. He had choked the big man out.

As Bolan passed back through the anteroom to the office, Bolan retrieving a truncheon from the floor en route. He felt every mile, every bullet, every blow and every minute of this mission. As he walked into Gaspar Castillo's office, he felt bone-weary. His limbs were leaden, his vision blurry, his breath labored.

His purpose, however, had never been more clear.

Gaspar Castillo stood once more. He stopped rubbing the wrist Bolan had captured before. From his pocket, he withdrew a knife. He snapped it open with a practiced motion, its clasp mechanism making a ratcheting noise.

"I am going to take great pleasure in this," Castillo said. "You have helped return me to my roots, American. It is not every day we remember where we came from. I had thought I was good at this, but there is nothing so humbling, so reminiscent of the past, as using a knife. Mine has ended many men, all of them either enemies or obstacles. A shame you have given up your own blades in maiming my poor boys, eh?"

"This isn't a game," Bolan said carefully. The truncheon was heavy in his right hand. He let the end drop toward the floor. "There aren't any points. There is no audience. There's nothing to prove. You don't impress me, Castillo. You won't convince me of anything. You won't leave behind a legacy."

Castillo's face twisted. His smile became a mask of rage. "You will pay for speaking to me this way! I am Gaspar Castillo!"

"I don't care," Bolan said. "You're nothing and no one to me."

Bolan raised the truncheon slightly. There would be no contest here. The Executioner had the advantage of reach and, no matter how skilled Castillo might be with his blade, Bolan also had the advantage of superior experience. It would take only seconds. He stepped forward.

Bright lights exploded in his vision. The pain of the freight-train blow to his back came only after he was already on the floor.

He struggled to get to his hands and knees. He could see, from the corner of his eye, Apollo advancing on him. How the man had recovered so quickly he didn't know. Bolan should have taken it into account, but in his weariness he hadn't. Suddenly, arms were around his throat. Apollo dragged him back and immobilized him. The truncheon fell from suddenly nerveless fingers. Blackness swirled at the edges of Bolan's vision once more.

"Hold him," Castillo said.

The Mexican president strutted back and forth in his office a few times, as if reassuring himself that he was still its owner. He tossed the knife from hand to hand. Then he closed it, tucked it away and walked up in front of Bolan, whom Apollo held completely immobile.

"You pathetic fool," Castillo said. "Do you know why it is you have lost?"

Bolan tried to say something, but Apollo had cut off his air supply so effectively he couldn't talk.

"You lost," Castillo went on, "because you are weak. You are weak because you are white. The Anglo is the inferior of the species. La Raza, the Race, is all. *We* are the chosen people. We will eventually rule. All of the lands stolen from Mexico will be returned. You, your people, *you* will be the minority, and *you* will finally know the tragic lesson of racial oppression, when the boot is on the other foot."

Apollo muttered something that Bolan couldn't hear.

"Bring him," Castillo ordered.

The giant carried Bolan, helpless, down the stairs and outside. Castillo led the way, and seemed to know just where he wanted to go. Eventually he stopped, sniffing the breeze. "It has been a very deadly day in Mexico City," he pronounced. "I smell fire and ash in the air. Well. That is enough for now, at least." He turned to Bolan. "I shall have my work cut out for me, reasserting order in the wake of your little escapade. I believe I have shall have your body sent back to your government in pieces. After it has spent some time in this hole Zapata's idiots dug. I suppose those imbeciles were good for something, after all."

He had stopped at the lip of the tiger pit. He paused when he saw Del Valle's body impaled at the bottom. "How interesting," he said. "Is *that* where he ended up? A pity. He might have been of use to me, had I been able to keep his ambitions in check. A waste of talent, that."

He turned to Apollo. "Throw him in."

Bolan, as Apollo carried him, had managed to get his hand into his pocket, and now he withdrew Tristan Zapata's folding razor. The blade flashed open, and Bolan dragged it along the inside of the giant's arm. He cut something substantial, and blood sprayed the front of his torn and dirty blacksuit. Apollo shrieked and dropped him.

Bolan fell just one foot short.

Castillo was reaching for his own knife. Bolan couldn't deal with him yet; he still had Apollo to neutralize. With no other options, he threw himself over the crouching giant's back, reached out, grabbed the man's head and drew the straight razor across his throat from ear to ear. Apollo went to his knees.

It would take him a while, but he would die, and while he was busy dying, he wouldn't be fighting anyone.

"You bastard," Castillo said. "You son of a *whore*." The knife flashed out and ratcheted open. Castillo dived in, his blade whirling in his hands, his movements practiced. This was a man who knew his way around a knife fight.

It was a pity for him that Bolan didn't knife-fight anyone. The Executioner fought with knives, yes. But he wouldn't play his adversary's dueling game.

Castillo drove a committed, brutal thrust home, one that Bolan had invited by dropping his guard. As he did so, Bolan drew the straight razor's blade across the inside and top of Castillo's extended arm, pushing the arm through the blade with his left hand. It was a *gunting,* a scissors movement, and the deep slash robbed Castillo of the ability to hold his knife.

When he dropped it, Bolan kicked it into the tiger pit.

"You Anglo piece of filth," Castillo grated. "I will tear you apart with my bare hands." He rushed forward.

Exhausted, injured and thoroughly sick of Castillo

and his racist kind, Bolan stood firm, then pushed hard against the charging Castillo.

El Presidente screamed as he toppled into the pit and became impaled on the sharpened stakes.

Bolan stood there for a long moment, after, looking down at the two dead men.

EPILOGUE

In Washington, D.C., Hal Brognola pulled up the collar of his overcoat. He enjoyed strolling by the reflecting pool, as he did now, but the weather had turned suddenly cold this morning, and it had taken most of Wonderland's residents by surprise.

His wireless phone began to vibrate in his pocket. He hated to take calls while out in public, but when he took a look at the caller ID, he snapped open the phone immediately.

"Yes, sir?" he answered.

"Hal," said the President of the United States, "I just wanted to speak with you personally. I know you've been pretty busy the last couple of days."

"Yes, sir," Brognola said. "There have been a lot of loose ends to tie up, and the diplomatic chores always fall to me. I've been running up the Justice Department's phone bill, talking to everyone and anyone in the affected nations, trying to smooth things over and coordinate with State in order to assure a satisfactory outcome."

"Well, I'd say you did that, Hal," the President told him. "Please extend my compliments to your people. I ask a lot of the Sensitive Operations Group, and you don't ever let me down."

"We never will, sir."

"Let's hope that stays that way, Hal."

"Yes, sir." Brognola closed the connection and re-placed his phone in his pocket. He had worked with a lot of presidents over the years, of nearly every political persuasion. He had his favorites, of course, but overall they knew what SOG could do and they asked him to do it. That was the agreement. That was the transaction.

Brognola sighed, continuing his slow walk around the reflecting pool, looking for his friend.

He found Mack Bolan in the crowd easily. Bolan was a tall man, but he also carried himself in a way that few people did. Something about his confidence made him stand out.

Bolan fell into step next to him as Brognola walked past, not breaking stride.

"Striker," Brognola said, "how are you feeling?"

"The Farm's medic says I'll live. I'm supposed to get plenty of bed rest until my cracked ribs heal up."

"See that you do," Brognola stated. "You might consider spending some time at the Farm. Heal, get some sleep…."

"I saw the news report today," Bolan said. "About that WKAL team being found alive when federal agents raided the building, only to discover them tied up in the basement."

"We kept the news contained for as long as we could, to help break the association with the Tucson operation," Brognola explained. "It was Field Commander Platt who suggested we raid the building. Something about the WKAL crew just didn't sit right with him. Made him suspicious. He let them leave the cordon, but phoned it in right away, and we had a team out there before they even thought to be concerned."

"Platt's a good man."

Brognola nodded. "Under interrogation, some of the men we took into custody admitted that they worked for Roderigo del Valle."

"Late of the Honduran government," Bolan recited.

"The very same," Brognola said. "It seems Del Valle was the power behind the throne. He was running Orieza. The shock troops were his, not Orieza's. The men were shock troopers who left Honduras on your heels. Apparently Del Valle was in the room when you took down Orieza."

"So he came after me for revenge, just as he said he did," Bolan said.

"Looks that way. Del Valle's men said they stayed behind at the station while a group of Tristan Zapata's La Raza terrorists took the place of the news crew. They drove the van into the Tucson government complex as part of an elaborate scheme to provide Zapata with a way out if the rest of their force met with strong resistance."

"But Zapata wasn't captured," Bolan said, "and neither was Del Valle."

"No," Brognola agreed. "We don't know how Zapata got away, not that it really matters. Del Valle escaped from the hospital. We left him in the custody of the local authorities, who got lax with him. Apparently he traded charts with some poor bastard and then smothered him with a pillow. He was officially dead in Interpol's computer several hours before you finally finished him off."

"Well," Bolan said, "I guess I won't argue the time stamps, as long as the man's off the books."

"You did a lot of good work this time out, Striker," Brognola said. "But I admit I was concerned. Barb was worried about you, too. She seems to think you went a little far off the reservation before it was all over."

"I was never on the reservation, Hal. You know I have to be able to do things my way."

"I know," Brognola said. "But that doesn't mean I don't give a damn what happens to you. Barb's the same way."

Bolan was silent for a moment. Then he said, "Hal. I don't ask for many favors."

"No, you don't."

"There's something I'd like. Can you pull some strings for me with immigration, and also with someone in one of the federal student-loan or grant programs?"

"What do you mean?" Brognola asked. "I mean, sure I can. But why?"

"There's someone I want to send to college in the United States. Her name is Maria Catlan." He recited her address. "I'd like her to have a student visa, and I'd like to see to it that her tuition gets paid. A school in California, preferably."

Brognola looked puzzled, but nodded. "I can do that. It would be a pleasure."

"Thanks, Hal. She helped me out."

"Speaking of Mexico," Brognola said, "you'll be pleased to know that things are calming down. Already, cooler heads within the government have prevailed. They're forming a moderate coalition."

"What's the word on the street about Castillo?" Bolan

said. "Are there any theories as to why he's suddenly not taking calls?"

"The conventional wisdom in the popular press is that the collapse of Castillo's hard-line government was the work of armed revolutionaries, a resistance movement that had been brewing for some time in Mexico in response to Castillo's heavy-handed tactics. Apparently one of Castillo's public statues, which he planted in one of the city's most famous plazas, was the scene of a dramatic resistance attack. For most people that's all the evidence they need."

"What's famous about that plaza?"

"Something about the concentration of cafés in the square footage," Brognola said. He waved his hand dismissively. "It was on the Travel Channel or something. My point is that the resistance targeted the one statue of Castillo that would most be noticed if it was destroyed. It was a real public-relations coup for them."

"Was it, now?"

"You don't sound like you're asking a question, Striker."

"No."

"There were some rumors of American involvement, of course," Brognola said, and this time it was his turn to remain completely deadpan, "but those didn't amount to much. Finding both Castillo and an unknown adviser thrown into a pit behind the president's residence clinched it. It looked like the sort of thing revolutionaries would do. Like trotting out the czar's family and shooting them, that type of thing. That pit made a hell of an impression."

Bolan nodded. "And Honduras?"

"The Honduran military has taken control, establishing full martial law under the regular armed forces, not Del Valle's shock troops. They say they plan to maintain control until order can be restored and a new government elected. I'm getting reports from our intelligence people that those shock troops who remain are being hunted down and killed—beaten in the street, hanged from lampposts. The military is in turn under control of certain more tractable elements of the former government, who indicate a willingness to cooperate with the West as they move toward a brighter future, or some such pabulum. No doubt they'll get around to appointing or electing a new president or maximum leader or whatever the hell it is they do."

"That's good," Bolan said. "I guess."

"Yeah," Brognola agreed. "Oh, and our friends in Guatemala extend their thanks through the State Department. If you'd like the key to the city, or country, or something, I could probably have them send one."

"I've got one already, somewhere," Bolan deadpanned.

"Yeah. Me, too," Brognola said. He produced a folded sheet of paper. "Interesting thing here. Zapata's body was recovered by Interpol at their request. So was Del Valle's, for that matter. Even though he and Castillo were found together, Del Valle wasn't deemed important to anyone. Interpol's personnel had an autopsy performed on both of them, pro forma. Guess what they found?"

"Del Valle had no heart?"

"Strangely, he did have one," Brognola said. "But that's not it. It seems Zapata had a pretty serious undiagnosed brain tumor. In your debrief you said he was acting pretty nuts at the end there. I admit I thought maybe he just cracked under the pressure of being a jet-setting racist terrorist. But it turns out he had a substantial push off the deep end. The doctors say the tumor was inoperable and it would have seriously messed with his cognitive abilities, the size it was."

"How badly?"

"'Bat-shit nuts,' I think was the technical term they were throwing around."

Bolan nodded. "I've never been one for complicated jargon."

Brognola took out a cigar and began chewing it, unlit. Around the cigar, he said, "I'm indebted to you all over again, Striker. This was difficult and you pulled it off. You did it in a way that makes the Man happy, too, and that comes from him personally."

Bolan reached into the canvas messenger bag he wore across his chest. He removed a paper-wrapped package. "I have one last favor to ask, Hal."

"Sure."

"Please see to it this makes its way back to the folks in Tucson. It's for their building, if they fix it, for whatever new government offices they put up if they can't."

"I didn't know you took such an interest in local politics, Striker," Brognola said.

"All politics is local, Hal," Bolan said, jerking his chin in the general direction of the reflecting pool. "Haven't you heard?"

"I might have at that."

Bolan reached out and shook his hand. "I'll talk to you soon, I have no doubt."

"Goodbye, Striker." Brognola watched Mack Bolan

blend with the crowd and then disappear. If he hadn't been watching closely, he'd have missed that disappearing act. He shook his head. As he walked back to his office, he opened the paper-wrapped parcel out of curiosity.

Inside was a brand-new, bright red-white-and-blue American flag.

The Executioner®
Don Pendleton's
POWDER BURN

American officials are targeted by a Colombian cartel...

When a ruthless Colombian drug lord launches a deadly campaign targeting DEA agents and U.S. diplomats, Mack Bolan is called in to infiltrate and destroy the chain of command. Bolan knows he must shut down the operation quickly but the cartel's leader has declared war on anyone who stands in his way. There's just one flaw in the plan—no one expected the Executioner!

Available February wherever books are sold.

GOLD EAGLE®

JAMES AXLER

DEATH LANDS

Playfair's Axiom

The warriors of a shattered world forge new rules for survival...

The warriors of a shattered world forge new rules for survival...

When J. B. Dix is gravely wounded in the concrete jungle of St. Louis, Ryan and his group become captive guests of a local barony. Freedom lies in the success of a deal: recapture a runaway teen, daughter of the ailing baron. But the gruesome manipulation of the holy man with the power means the group is in a life-and-death race....

Available March wherever books are sold.

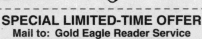

James Axler
Outlanders®

CRADLE OF DESTINY

The struggle of the Cerberus rebels stretches back to the dawn of history…

When millennia-old artifacts are discovered in the Middle East's legendary Fertile Crescent, they appear to belong to one of Cerberus's own. It's not long before Grant is plunged back through the shimmering vortex of time, forcing the rebels to lead a rescue party across a parallax to destroy a legendary god beast—before Grant is lost forever.

Available February 2011 wherever books are sold.

AleX Archer
FALSE HORIZON

The road to paradise is dark and deadly…

Archaeologist Annja Creed is in Katmandu, awash in its scents and liveliness. But this is no sightseeing trip. An old friend has a map that leads to a place that lies outside our world. But another vicious man wants the map—and he has Annja and her companions right where he wants them. Will Annja's journey end with only triumph…or tragedy?

Available March wherever books are sold.

GOLD EAGLE®

www.readgoldeagle.blogspot.com

GRA29